ALSO BY CAMILLE DeANGELIS

Mary Modern

Petty Magic

Immaculate Heart

BONES & ALL

CAMILLE DeANGELIS

ST. MARTIN'S GRIFFIN · NEW YORK

BONES & ALL. Copyright © 2015 by Camille DeAngelis. All rights reserved. Printed in the United States of America. For information, address St. Martin's Press, 175 Fifth Avenue, New York, N.Y. 10010.

www.stmartins.com

Designed by Steven Seighman

The Library of Congress has cataloged the hardcover edition as follows:

DeAngelis, Camille.
    Bones & all / Camille DeAngelis. — First edition.
        p. cm.
    ISBN 978-1-250-04650-5 (hardcover)
    ISBN 978-1-4668-4677-7 (e-book)
    I. Title.   II. Title: Bones and all.
    PS3604.E159B66 2015
    813'.6—dc23

                                        2014036349

ISBN 978-1-250-04652-9 (trade paperback)

Our books may be purchased in bulk for promotional, educational, or business use. Please contact your local bookseller or the Macmillan Corporate and Premium Sales Department at (800) 221-7945, extension 5442, or by e-mail at Macmillan SpecialMarkets@macmillan.com.

First St. Martin's Griffin Edition: March 2016

D   10   9   8   7   6   5   4   3

For Kate Garrick

Someday I'll wake up and find they've built a maze around me, and I will be relieved.

1

enny Wilson wanted a baby of her own in the worst way. That's what I figure, because she was only supposed to watch me for an hour and a half, and obviously she loved me a little too much. She must have hummed a lullaby, fondled each tiny finger and toe, kissed my cheeks and stroked the down on my head, blowing on my hair like she was making a wish on a dandelion gone to seed. I had my teeth but I was too small to swallow the bones, so when my mother came home she found them in a pile on the living room carpet.

The last time my mother had looked at Penny Wilson she'd still had a face. I know Mama screamed, because anyone would have. When I was older she told me she thought my babysitter had been the victim of a satanic cult. She'd stumbled upon stranger things in suburbia.

It wasn't a cult. If it had been, they would have snatched me away and done unspeakable things to me. There I was, asleep on the floor beside the bone pile, tears still drying on my cheeks and blood wet around my mouth. I loathed myself even then. I don't remember any of this, but I know it.

Even when my mother noticed the gore down the front of my OshKosh overalls, even when she registered the blood on my face, she didn't *see* it. When she parted my lips and put her forefinger inside—mothers are the bravest creatures, and mine is the bravest of all—she found something hard between my gums. She pulled it out and peered at it. It was the hammer of Penny Wilson's eardrum.

Penny Wilson had lived in our apartment complex, across the courtyard. She'd lived alone and worked odd jobs, so no one would miss her for days. That was the first time we had to pick up and move in a hurry, and I often wonder if my mother had an inkling then how efficient she'd become. The last time we moved she packed us up in twelve minutes flat.

Not so long ago I asked her about Penny Wilson: *What did she look like? Where was she from? How old was she? Did she read a lot of books? Was she nice?* We were in the car, but not on the way to a new city. We never talked about what I'd done right after I'd done it.

"What do you want to know all this for, Maren?" she sighed, rubbing at her eyes with her thumb and forefinger.

"I just do."

"She was blond. Long blond hair, and she always wore it loose. She was still young—younger than I was—but I don't think she had many friends. She was very quiet." Then Mama's voice snagged on a memory she hadn't wanted to find. "I remember how her face lit up when I asked if she could watch you that day." She looked angry as she brushed the tears away with the back of her hand. "See? There's no point thinking about these things when there's nothing you can do to change any of it. What's done is done."

I thought for a minute. "Mama?"

"Yeah?"

"What did you do with the bones?"

She took so long to reply that I began to be afraid of the answer. There was, after all, a suitcase that always came with us that I had never seen her open. Finally she said, "There are some things I'm never going to tell you no matter how many times you ask."

My mother was kind to me. She never said things like *what you did* or *what you are*.

Mama was gone. She'd gotten up while it was still dark, packed a few things, and left in the car. Mama didn't love me anymore. How could I blame her if she never did?

Some mornings, once we'd been in a place long enough that we could begin to forget, she'd wake me up with that song from *Singin' in the Rain*.

"Good morning, good moooooooorning! We've talked the whole night through . . ."

Except she always sounded kind of sad as she sang it.

On May 30th, the day I turned sixteen, my mother came in singing. It was a Saturday, and we had planned a full day of fun. I hugged my pillow and asked, "Why do you always sing it like that?"

She flung the curtains wide open. I watched her close her eyes and smile against the sunshine. "Like what?"

"Like you would've rather gone to bed at a reasonable hour."

She laughed, plopped herself down at the foot of my bed, and rubbed my knee through the duvet. "Happy birthday, Maren." I hadn't seen her that happy in a long time.

Over chocolate-chip pancakes I dipped my hand into a gift bag with one big book inside—*The Lord of the Rings*, three volumes in one—and a Barnes & Noble gift card. We spent most of the day at the bookstore. That night she took me out to an Italian restaurant, a *real* Italian restaurant, where the waiters and the chef all spoke to each other in the mother tongue, the walls were covered in old black-and-white family photographs, and the minestrone would keep you full for days.

It was dark in there, and I bet I'll always remember how the light from the red glass votive holder flickered on Mama's face as she raised the soupspoon to her lips. We talked about how things were going at school, how things were going at work. We talked about my going to college: what I might like to study, what I might like to be. A soft square of tiramisu arrived with a candle stuck in it, and all the waiters sang to me, but in Italian: *Buon compleanno a te.*

Afterward she took me to see *Titanic* at the last-chance cinema, and for three hours I lost myself in the story the way I could in my favorite books. I was beautiful and brave, someone destined to love and to survive, to be happy and to remember. Real life held none of those things for me, but in the pleasant darkness of that shabby old theater I forgot it never would.

I tumbled into bed, exhausted and content, because in the morning I could feast on my leftovers and read my new book. But when I woke up the apartment was too still, and I couldn't smell the coffee. Something was wrong.

I came down the hall and found a note on the kitchen table:

> *I'm your mother and I love you but I can't do this anymore.*

She couldn't be gone. She couldn't be. How could she?

I looked at my hands, palms up, palms down, like they didn't belong to me. Nothing else did: not the chair I sank into, not the table I laid my forehead on, not the window I stared through. Not even my own mother.

I didn't understand. I hadn't done the bad thing in

more than six months. Mama was all settled into her new job and we liked this apartment. None of this made sense.

I ran into her bedroom and found the sheets and comforter still on the bed. She'd left other things too. On the nightstand, paperback novels she'd already read. In the bathroom, almost-empty bottles of shampoo and hand lotion. A few blouses, the not-as-pretty ones, were still hanging in the closet on those cheap wire hangers you get at the dry cleaner's. We left stuff like this whenever we moved, but this time I was one of the things she'd left behind.

Trembling, I went back into the kitchen and read the note again. I don't know if you can read between the lines when there's only one sentence, but I could read all the things she hadn't said clearly enough:

I can't protect you anymore, Maren. Not when it's the rest of the world I should be protecting instead.

If you only knew how many times I thought about turning you in, having you locked up so you could never do it again . . .

If you only knew how I hate myself for bringing you into the world . . .

I did know. And I should have known when she took me out for my birthday, because it was too special not to have been the last thing we'd do together. That was how she'd planned it.

I'd only ever been a burden to her. A burden and a horror. All this time she'd done what she'd done because she was afraid of me.

I felt strange. There was a ringing in my ears like you get when it's too quiet, except it was like resting my head against a church bell that had just chimed.

Then I noticed something else on the table: a thick white envelope. I didn't have to open it to know there was money inside. My stomach turned over. I got up and stumbled out of the kitchen.

I went to her bed, burrowed under the comforter, and curled up as tight as I could. I didn't know what else to do. I wanted to sleep this off, to wake up and find it undone, but you know how it is when you desperately want to get back to sleep. When you desperately want *any*thing.

The rest of the day passed in a daze. I never cracked *The Lord of the Rings*. I didn't read a thing besides the words in that note. Later on I got up again and wandered around the house, too sick even to think of eating anything, and when it got dark I went to bed and lay awake for hours. I didn't want to be alive. What kind of life could I have?

I couldn't sleep in an empty apartment. I couldn't cry either, because she hadn't left me anything to cry over. If she loved it, she took it with her.

Penny Wilson was my first and last babysitter. From then on my mother kept me in daycare, where the employees were overwhelmed and underpaid and there was never any danger of anyone taking a shine to me.

Nothing happened for years. I was a model child,

quiet and sober and eager to learn, and over time my mother convinced herself I hadn't done that horrible thing. Memories distort themselves, turning over into truths that are easier to live with. It *had* been a satanic cult. They'd murdered my babysitter, bathed me in blood, and given me an eardrum to chew on. It wasn't my fault—it wasn't me. I wasn't a monster.

So when I was eight Mama sent me to summer camp. It was one of those places where the boys and the girls live in cabins on opposite sides of a lake. We sat apart in the dining hall too, and we were hardly ever allowed to play together. During arts-and-crafts hour the girls wove key chains and friendship bracelets, and later we learned how to gather kindling and build a campfire, though we never actually got to have one after dark. We slept in bunk beds, eight girls to a cabin, and every night before bed our counselor would check our heads for ticks.

We swam in the lake every morning, even on cloudy days when the water was cold and murky. The other girls only waded in up to their waists and stood listlessly in the shallows, waiting for the sound of the lunch bell.

But I was a good swimmer. I felt alive in the cold dark water. Some nights I even fell asleep in my bathing suit. One morning I decided to swim all the way across the lake to the boys' side just to say I'd done it. So I swam and swam, reveling in the feeling of my limbs cutting through the bracing water, only dimly aware of the lifeguard whistling for me to turn back.

I paused to check my progress, and that's when I saw

him. He must've had the same idea about reaching the girls' side. "Hi," he called.

"Hi," I said.

We stopped there, treading water maybe fifteen feet apart, just looking at each other. The clouds seethed overhead. The rain would start any second. On both sides the lifeguards whistled frantically. We swam a bit closer, close enough to reach out and touch fingertips. He had bright red hair and more freckles than anyone I'd ever seen, boy or girl—so freckled you could hardly see any paleness underneath. He flashed me a conspiratorial grin, as if we already knew each other and had arranged to meet here, at the dead center of a lake no one else wanted to swim in.

I glanced over my shoulder. "I think we're in trouble."

"Not if we stay here forever," he said.

I smiled. "I'm not that good a swimmer."

"I'll show you how to stay up for hours. All you have to do is rest easy and let your brain float. See?" He leaned back and let his ears sink beneath the surface. All I could see was his face in the water, turned up toward the sky where the sun should have been.

"You never get tired?" I said, louder so he could hear me.

The boy came up and shook the water out of his ears. "Nope."

So I tried it. We were close now, close enough that he reached out and touched my hand. I bobbed up again and laughed as I drummed my fingertips up and down his arm. "I know," he said. "I'm awfully frecksy."

The lifeguards on either side of the lake went on blowing—I could hear the whistles even when I let my ears go beneath the surface—but we knew they wouldn't jump in and drag us back. Not even the lifeguards wanted to swim in that water.

I have no idea how long we stayed that way, but I guess it couldn't have been as long as I remember. If this were anyone's story but mine, it would have been the first time I met my childhood sweetheart.

His name was Luke, and over the next few days he found ways of reaching me. Twice he left a note on my pillow, and one day after lunch he led me around the back of the rec hall with a shoebox under his arm. Once we'd found a sheltered place he took off the lid and showed me a collection of cicada shells. "I find them in the bushes," he said, like it was some great secret. "It's the exoskeleton. They shed 'em once in a lifetime. Isn't that cool?" He plucked one of the shells out of the box and put it in his mouth.

"They're pretty tasty," he said as he munched. "Why are you making a gross-out face?"

"I'm not."

"Yes, you are. Don't be such a girl." He took out a second shell. "Here, try one." *Crunch, crunch*. "I gotta grab a salt shaker at dinner, they'll be even tastier with some salt."

He put the shell in my palm and I looked at it. Something flickered then, in a dark corner of my mind: I knew about things that weren't meant to be eaten.

Then the whistle blew for afternoon roll call. I dropped the locust shell in the shoebox and ran away.

That night I found a third note under my pillow. He'd written the first two like he was introducing himself to a new pen pal: *My name is Luke Vanderwall, I'm from Springfield, Delaware + I have 2 little sisters, this is my 3rd summer at Camp Ameewagan + it's my favorite time of the whole year. I'm glad you're here. Now I'll have somebody to swim with even if we have to break the rules to do it. . . .*

This one was short. *Meet me outside at 11 o'clock*, it said, *+ together we will go 4th + have many adventures.*

That night I had my bathing suit on under my pajamas. I lay in bed until I heard everyone breathing evenly, and then I unlatched the screen door and slipped out of the cabin. He was already there, standing just beyond the arc of the porch light. I tiptoed down to meet him and he took my hand and tugged me into the dark. "Come on," he whispered.

"I can't." *I shouldn't.*

"'Course you can. Come on! I want to show you something." Hand in hand, we stumbled past the rec hall back to the boys' camp. After a few minutes I could see the cabins through the trees, but then he drew me away from them, deeper into the darkness.

The woods were alive in a way I'd never noticed in the daytime. The slip of an old moon hung above the trees, giving us just enough light to see by, and fireflies hovered all around, flashing their green-gold lights. I wondered what they were saying to each other. There was a night breeze, so cool and fresh that I imagined it was the pines sighing out the good clean air, and the forest hummed with an invisible orchestra of cicadas and owls and bullfrogs.

A whiff of woodsmoke tickled my nose. Outside Ameewagan, but not far off, someone was having a campfire. "I could sure go for a hot dog," Luke said wistfully. A moment later I saw a glimmer of something ahead, but as we came closer I could see it wasn't a fire.

There was a red tent in the woods, all lit up from within. It wasn't a real tent—the kind with retractable metal rods and a zipper that you could buy in a store—which made it seem all the more mysterious. He'd found a red tarpaulin and cast it over a length of clothesline strung between two trees. For a moment or two I stood there admiring it. From here I could pretend it was a magic tent that I could step inside and find myself in the thick of a Moroccan bazaar.

"You made this?"

"Yeah," he said. "For you."

This is the first time I can remember feeling it. Standing next to Luke in the darkness, I breathed in the warm night air and found I could smell him down to the lint between his toes. He still had the stink of the lake on him, dank and rotten-eggy. He hadn't brushed his teeth after dinner, and I could smell the chili powder from the sloppy joes every time he breathed.

It trickled over me then, making me shudder: the hunger, and the certainty. I didn't know anything about Penny Wilson. I just had a feeling I had done something horrible when I was little and that I was on the verge of repeating it. The tent wasn't magic, but I knew one of us wasn't coming out again.

"I have to go back," I said.

"Don't be a wimp! Nobody's going to find us. Everyone's asleep. Don't you want to play with me?"

"I do," I whispered. "But . . ."

He took my hand and led me under the flap.

For a makeshift hideaway, it was pretty well stocked: two cans of Sprite, a package of Fig Newtons and a bag of Doritos, a blue sleeping bag, his shoebox of locust shells, an electric lantern, a Choose Your Own Adventure novel, and a deck of cards. Luke sat cross-legged and pulled a pillow out of his sleeping bag. "I thought we could spend the night here. I cleared out all the sticks. The ground's still hard, but I figure it's good wilderness survival training. When I grow up I'm going to be a forest ranger. You know what a forest ranger is?" I shook my head. "They patrol the forests and make sure no one's cutting down trees or shooting animals or doing other bad stuff. So that's what I'm gonna do."

I picked up the Choose Your Own Adventure: *Escape from Utopia.* On the cover were two kids lost in a jungle, the ground crumbling into an abyss beneath their feet. *Choose from 13 different endings! Your choice may lead to success or disaster!*

Disaster. I had a feeling.

"Sprite?" He popped open a can and handed it to me. "Here, have a Fig Newton." He took one for himself and nibbled around the edges. "But before I become a forest ranger I'm gonna do triathlons."

"What's triathlons?"

"That's when you run a hundred miles, bike a hundred miles, and swim a hundred miles, all in one day."

"That's crazy," I said. "Nobody can swim a hundred miles."

"How do you know? Did you ever try?"

I laughed. "Of course not."

"Well, now you know how to float forever. That's a good start. I can float forever but I've got to be able to swim forever too. So I'm going to train and train, for as long as it takes, until I can. And then I'm gonna ride my horse across the Rockies and fight forest fires and live in a tree house I built myself. It's going to have two stories, like a real house, except you'll climb up to it with a rope ladder and come down again on a sliding pole." He frowned as something occurred to him. "The sliding pole will have to be made of metal though, so I don't get splinters."

"How are you going to eat? You have to have a kitchen, but then you might burn your house down."

"Oh, I'll have a wife to cook for me. I just don't know yet if the kitchen will be on the ground or up in the tree."

"Will your wife have her own tree house?"

"I don't think she'll need her own house, but she can

have her own room on another branch if she wants it. Maybe she'll be an artist or something."

"That sounds nice," I said sadly.

"What is it? I thought you liked being outside."

"I do."

"I thought this would make you happy."

"It does. But you're going to get in trouble if you don't go back to your cabin."

"Oh, I don't mind wiping tables in the mess hall to-morrow," he said with a careless wave of his hand. "This is worth it."

Tomorrow. The word sounded strange, like it didn't mean anything anymore. "That's not what I meant."

"You can worry about it in the morning. Sit down next to me and we'll play some old maid before we go to sleep."

I sat down beside him and he picked up the deck of cards. We began to play. He held up his cards, and I picked one (the old maid, sure enough). I stuck it into my hand and offered it to him, and he shook his head and told me to shuffle. I couldn't think about the game. I just kept smelling the chili powder and the rotten eggs and the cotton lint. His eagerness, his spirit, his thirst for the outdoors: all that had a smell too, like wet leaves, and salty skin, and hot cocoa in a tin cup that knew the shape of his hands.

"I don't want to play anymore," I whispered. *He won't grow up. He'll never be a forest ranger. He'll never ride an-other horse. He won't fight forest fires. He'll never live in a tree house.*

Luke dropped his cards and took both my hands. "Don't go, Maren. I want you to stay."

I didn't want to. I really, really wanted to. I leaned in and sniffed him. Chili powder—rotten eggs—cotton lint. I pressed my lips to his throat and felt him stiffen with anticipation. He put a hand to my ponytail and stroked it, like he was petting a horse. He breathed on me, I smelled the chili, and just like that there was no going back.

I stumbled out of the red tent toward the lake, out to the edge of the dock, and flung the grocery bag into the water. Then I pulled off my pajamas and threw them out as far as I could. I watched my *Little Mermaid* T-shirt sink below the surface of the lake, heard the plastic bag gurgling as it filled.

I fell onto the dock, rocking back and forth with my hands clamped over my mouth to keep the scream in, but it pounded against my face until I felt like my eyeballs were going to pop out. Finally I couldn't hold it in anymore, so I lay down on the boards, dunked my head, and let it out until the water came up and burned my nose.

It was only as I walked back up the path through the pine trees—wet, cold, and shivering on the outside, horribly warm and full underneath—that I thought of my mother. *Oh, Mama. You won't love me anymore once you hear what I've done.*

I crept back into my cabin as quietly as I could and put my spare pajamas on over my bathing suit. If anyone asked I'd say I'd only gone to the bathroom. I lay in bed shivering, curled up tight as if I could keep the world out. I wanted to be a cicada. I wanted to pull my skin off and leave it in the bushes and nobody would recognize me, not even my own mother. I would be a completely different person and I wouldn't remember a thing.

In the morning it was raining, and my fingernails were rimmed in red. I put on my poncho, hid my hands, and ran to the bathroom. I scrubbed and scrubbed under the faucet, and even then I could still see it. Somebody came out of the stalls to wash her hands and gave me a funny look. My nails were as clean as they were going to get.

I followed the other girls to the mess hall, so numb I couldn't feel the ground beneath my feet. I stood in line at the buffet counter. I took a waffle, but I couldn't taste it. The camp director stood up in front of us and switched on his microphone. "We are very sorry to have to tell you that one of your campmates is missing. For your safety we have notified your parents, and all of you will be picked up this afternoon. In the meantime you will finish breakfast and return to your cabins. No one will be allowed anywhere else on the campsite until their parents arrive."

We filed out of the mess hall and found vans from the

local news stations in the parking lot. The camp director wouldn't speak to the reporters.

The girls in my cabin huddled around the picnic table at the center of the room. "I heard the director talking outside the bathroom," somebody whispered. "They think Luke was murdered."

The others gasped. "Why would they think that? Who did it?"

"Girls," our counselor cut in from across the room. She was standing with her arms folded at the screen door, watching the rain turn to mud in the walkway between the trees. "I don't want to hear any more of that talk. That's enough, now." She'd been fun before, always willing to braid our hair or go in on a game of go fish. It was my fault she wasn't smiling anymore—my fault Luke was gone—my fault everyone had to go home. I lay on my bed facing the window, pretending to read.

The storm rages on, the water rising to your waist in a river of mud. You wander through the jungle for days, unable to find a dry place to sleep. Exhausted, you close your eyes and slip beneath the surface, and the current washes you away.
THE END.

I closed the book with a heavy sigh. *I wish.*

"He said Luke was out in the woods by himself last night," the first girl continued, quieter this time. "They found his sleeping bag and it had blood all over it."

"I said *that's enough.*"

No one spoke again. The others started new friendship bracelets while I lay in the corner wishing I could disappear. After an hour the first parents came, and the girls went out with their duffel bags one by one.

My mother arrived, pale and silent, and led me out to the parking lot. Other parents stood in groups, arms crossed or nervously jingling their key chains. They whispered among themselves, but I could hear some of what they said.

"... ran wild ... had no business being out in the woods ... no discipline in this camp whatsoever ... That director's got his thumb up his ass all right. ... I'm just thankful my Betsy is better behaved. ... They say it definitely wasn't a bear. ... The sleeping bag was positively drenched in blood; they say there's no way he's alive. ... Suppose they'll be dredging the lake. ... I hear they're interviewing everybody within a ten-mile radius—they think it must be someone who lives nearby. ..."

Where were *his* parents? If they showed up before Mama could take me away, would they look at me and know I'd done it? I dropped her hand and ran back to the cabin.

Everyone had gone, and all the bedsheets lay in a pile on the floorboards. I stumbled to my bunk in the corner and fell onto the bare mattress, burying my face in the lumpy old pillow. My mother came in and sat down on the edge of the bed. "Maren," she murmured. "Maren, look at me."

I lifted my face from the pillow, but I couldn't bring myself to look her in the eye.

"Look at me."

I looked at her. She was eerily calm for a person who knew her daughter had eaten somebody. "Tell me it isn't true," she said.

Again I hid my face. "I can't."

She had to carry me out to the car. *Poor girl,* the parents said. *She's taking it awfully hard.*

Mama wanted to leave right away. Camp Ameewagan was a three-hour drive, but the director had our address on file, and if they found out I'd been with Luke that night they could trace us back. Calmly she explained all this to me and said I'd have to gather my things as quickly as I was able.

"We're just going to leave?"

Pulling some slack on the seatbelt, I leaned forward and rested my chin on the front seat. I watched the wipers squeak across the windshield and the asphalt vanish in a blur under the hood of the car until my eyes milked over. I felt strange. Going to third grade at a different school?

"I don't know what else to do."

"You said I should always tell the truth."

She sighed. "I did, and you should. But I've thought about this, Maren. We can't tell anybody. No one will believe it."

"But if I tell them about Luke, and you tell them about Penny . . ."

"It isn't that simple. Sometimes people confess to a murder they didn't commit."

"Why would they do that?"

"For the attention, I guess."

We drove on in silence, but Mama's words hung in the air: a murder, and I had committed it. That made me a murderer. I thought of Luke and his horse and his tree house and his hundred-mile swim. I tried not to think of his fingers or the sloppy joe or how his blood was warm and tasted like old pennies.

There was a cicada in my ear. It wriggled out of its shell and sat humming behind my right eye. I slumped in the seat and leaned my forehead against the window, but that only made the humming worse.

I'm frecksy. Don't be such a girl. I gotta learn how to swim forever.

My ear began to hurt, but I told myself it was nothing compared to what he felt. "But you said nobody ever really gets away with anything," I mumbled.

For a minute or two she didn't reply, and I thought maybe she wasn't going to. "Someday you'll have to answer for this," she said, her eyes on the road. "Someday someone will believe you."

I'd much rather answer for it now, I thought. I rubbed at my ear. *Take me away, piece by piece. My life for his.*

Mama looked at me through the rearview mirror. "What's wrong?"

"My ear hurts."

By the time we pulled into the driveway the ache had

all but eclipsed the horror of the night before. I could hear her muttering as she pulled me out of the car— "I *knew* that lake was polluted. . . . I don't suppose they ever gave you ear drops after swimming. . . . I never should have let you go to that stupid camp. . . ."—but she sounded strange, like she was miles underwater. She put me to bed and shook a couple of Tylenol out of a bottle.

That night a man knelt by my bed and jabbed me through the eardrum with a knife so sharp it was invisible. Of course, I couldn't see the man either, but I knew he was there, sticking me in time to the beating of my heart. *Knife, twist, knife, twist.* I dreamed he showed me my eardrum, stuck on the tip of his blade, and pressed it to my lips. His fingers were long and bony, and his breath was cold. Mama had left the light on in the hallway, but I couldn't see his face. Maybe he didn't have one.

I turned over, and a shadow fell across the doorway. "Maren?" My mother darted to the bed and put her finger in my mouth, just like when I was a baby. "What is it? What are you chewing?"

My eardrum.

She dropped to her knees, laid her cheek on the bed, and began to cry. *She sees him,* I thought. *She knows who it is, but she can't make him go away.*

In the morning I heard her phone the temp agency and tell them she wouldn't be able to finish her assignment. Then she came in with a glass of ginger ale, stirring out the bubbles with a tablespoon. "I know he's punishing me," I said.

She looked at me curiously. "Who is?"

"God."

"Maren . . ." Mama sat on the edge of my bed, closed her eyes, and rubbed the bridge of her nose. "There isn't any God."

"How do you know?"

"Nobody knows. But I think it's pretty safe to say God is something people invented to make sense of their lives. So there's somebody to blame when terrible things happen."

The words she stopped short of saying hung in the air once she'd left me alone. *If there is no God, our lives make sense.*

I didn't eat for days. I didn't drink the ginger ale, and I pressed my lips tight when she tried to give me an anti-biotic. Spots swam across my vision, my lips shriveled and cracked, and there was a desert in my mouth, but I didn't care. The pain in my ear had eased into a dull throb. I could hardly hear my mother when she begged me to drink.

"You're so dehydrated." She took me by the shoulders and tried to make me sit up, but I was a lead weight. "If you keep this up, I'll have to take you to the hospital."

I didn't listen. I didn't move. Soon enough I closed my eyes and everything fell away.

When I woke up I was in the pediatric ward. Mama was sitting in a chair beside my bed, nibbling on her thumb-nail and staring at nothing, a dog-eared paperback splayed across her knee. A nurse hovered at my other side, smiling vaguely as she fiddled with the needle stuck into the inside of my elbow. "It's all right," the woman murmured, smoothing my hair back from my face as if she knew me. "You're going to be all right now."

Mama put the paperback on the windowsill and leaned in as the nurse moved to the far side of the room to fill a little paper cup from the faucet. She took my hand, but she didn't say anything. Mama wouldn't try to comfort me with things that weren't true.

"Why did you bring me here?" Even after what I'd done, she wanted me to live.

"I'm your mother," she said. "I had to."

"Because you love me?"

She hesitated so briefly that no one else would have noticed it. "Of course," she said, and let go of my hand as the nurse came back with the cup of water.

"You must be awfully thirsty," chirped the nurse.

Later that day a woman who was not a nurse appeared in the doorway and asked to speak with my mother. They went down the hall together and were gone for a long time.

The nurse came in again with a new IV bag. "Well! I'm glad to see you've got some color back in your cheeks. Now that you're awake, we can give you some real food. How about a hamburger for dinner? Jell-O or ice cream for dessert?" She hit the foot pedal on the medical waste bin and tossed the empty IV bag. "Or maybe Jell-O *and* ice cream?" She flashed me another smile, *our little secret*. "Tomorrow, as long as you start eating and drinking again, we'll take you off the IV. You're a lucky girl, Maren."

There was nothing lucky about it. A strange woman called me by name in a place full of odd smells, brisk voices, and mechanical ticks and beeps. My name in her mouth made me cringe. "I want my mother," I said. "Who was that woman who went with my mother?"

"She's a social worker. She wants to work together with your mom so that you can get well."

A lie, of course. I just looked at her until she averted her eyes and hurried out of the room.

After maybe an hour Mama came back. She looked really, really tired. "What did she want?" I asked.

"She thought I wasn't feeding you."

"What did you tell her?"

"The truth—the better part of it, anyway. I said you were upset because you had a friend at summer camp who'd been . . ." She sighed. "I had to give her the details, otherwise she wouldn't have believed me." She pressed her thumb and forefinger together. "You came *this close* to going into foster care."

I stared at her, amazed. I could have been somebody else's problem.

"Please, just eat and drink everything they bring you so we can get out of here, all right?"

Early the next day, before Mama arrived, the social worker came back with her clipboard. She shook my hand, told me her name was Donna, and asked me questions about Mama and what our life was like. I told her Mama had always taken good care of me, that I always had plenty to eat, and Donna watched me as I prodded my scrambled eggs with a plastic fork. Finally she ran out of

questions and left me alone. She'd never asked about
summer camp.

I was discharged the next day. Mama put her arm
around me as we walked out to the car, and when we got
there I saw one side of the backseat filled to the ceiling
with garbage bags and cardboard boxes. There were
more bags in the front passenger's seat and, no doubt,
plenty more in the trunk. While I was eating Jell-O out
of a plastic cup, she'd been stuffing our car with as much
of our lives as would fit.

**T**he morning after Mama left I went into the kitchen and threw a dish on the floor just to see what it felt like. Stepping over the pieces, I picked up the fat white envelope, but I found more than money inside. She'd left me my birth certificate. It was blue and crinkly, and I took my time unfolding it. A birth certificate is sort of a sacred document for the person in question, even a monster like me.

I only remember asking about my father one time. "He's gone," she said.

"But what was his name?"

"What does it matter?"

"I just want to know."

"He didn't have one."

"Everybody has a name!"

She didn't answer, and I let it go. A few weeks later I heard the kids in my class whispering about another girl, Tina, whose mother had been with so many men that Tina would never know who her father was. I didn't see how they could have known this, but they pointed their fingers like they had it on good authority.

At first I thought maybe Tina and I were in the same boat, but my mother wasn't like the other single moms. She still wore a ring on her left hand, she never had boyfriends, and we had the same last name. So my parents must have been married. Maybe they had been living in that apartment in Pennsylvania when my mom came home to Penny Wilson's bones on the carpet, and that's when he went away. As for why she never dated—well, that was easy enough. I was a particularly heavy piece of baggage.

I opened the birth certificate and smoothed out the creases before I let myself read it. *General Hospital of Friendship, Wisconsin.* There was my name, my birthday—female, 20½ inches long, 7 pounds 12½ ounces—my mother's maiden name, Janelle Shields, in the space marked *Mother* (*Place of birth: Edgartown, Pennsylvania*), and in the space marked *Father* there was a name I'd never seen before: *Francis Yearly.* I had a father! A real father! I'd known I had one, of course, but it made all the difference to see his name there in faded type on the dotted line.

It settled over me slowly, like a cracked egg trickling down around my ears: *Sandhorn, Minnesota.* That's where she expected me to go with the money she'd given me.

Mama wanted me to hop on a bus, find my father, and forget all about her.

And what if I *found* my dad—what then? Something in me lurched. I couldn't, I just couldn't. I had to figure out a way to make things right with Mama.

I'd pasted the Christmas card envelope with my grandparents' address onto the inside cover of my notebook, even though I'd learned it by heart as soon as I'd fished it out of the trashcan. I hadn't seen my grandparents since before Penny Wilson—and I knew better than to ask, I knew my mother would never take me to see them—but that was where she'd gone, so that was where I was going. I didn't know what I would say to her; I only knew that a hundred dollars was more than enough to get me there.

I ate what was left in the fridge, took a shower, and packed. Whenever we moved I stuffed most of my things into an old army rucksack labeled SHIELDS and U.S. ARMY in big black letters. It was my grandfather's, but I wasn't supposed to know that. This time it had to fit everything.

I had to be picky about the books I brought with me because I knew the pack would feel heavier and heavier the longer I carried it. I packed my birthday book and my two-volume set of *Alice's Adventures in Wonderland* and *Through the Looking-Glass, and What Alice Found There*. I packed the other books, *their* books, along with the other things I'd taken—a glow-in-the-dark compass, a pair of tortoiseshell eyeglasses.

I left the house key on the table, went out to the end of the street, and got on the local bus. A man tried to smile at me, but he wound up looking like he was in pain. He hadn't shaved in at least a week. "Goin' some-place?"

I glared at him. "Aren't we all?"

He turned back in his seat, chuckling, and I clasped my hands over the rucksack and looked out the window. It felt strange to be leaving a place when I hadn't done the bad thing. We passed by my school. I was supposed to have a geometry test today.

I got off at the Greyhound station and spent too much of the money Mama left me on a one-way ticket to Edgartown. All through the trip I ate out of pit-stop vending machines: untoasted Pop-Tarts for breakfast, Snyder's pretzels for lunch, Fritos for dinner. I had to switch buses three times, and every time I got on the driver raised his eyebrows as if to say, *Aren't you supposed to be in school?*

The closer we got, the more I felt my guts twisting up. I was nervous about seeing my own mother.

I used to have two kinds of dreams about Luke, and I could never decide which was worse. In the first kind I didn't see him, I only heard his voice in my ear. *My tree house will have three stories and only a ladder on the way up the trunk, and there'll be real staircases inside it— spiral staircases and lots of windows on every side so you can watch the birds and the sunset and the sunrise too, if you get up early enough. I'll have a wife, and she'll be pretty like you, and we'll sleep in bunk beds on the third floor. I like the top bunk best but if she'd rather have the top then I'll give it to her because that's what men do, it's*

called shill-vurry. And I'll have a horse too, for when I go
out on my forest rangering, but I guess we'll have to build
the stable on the ground. . . .

In the other kind we were back in the tent. The camping lantern had run out of battery and I couldn't make
out the shape of Luke's face, but he looked at me with
red, glowing eyes. I would cringe against his breath,
hot and foul as mine must have been, and then he bared
a mouthful of gleaming fangs and tore my face off. You'd
think that one would be worse, but even though it's
happening to me it's just like in the horror movies. It
isn't that scary when people are getting what they deserve.

"Do you think anyone else does it too? The bad thing?"
I asked my mother once.

She hesitated. "If there were others, would it make
you feel better or worse?"

"I want to say better, but I know I shouldn't. It's the
same as wishing even more people . . ." I trailed off. "But
I wouldn't be alone."

I wanted her to say, *You aren't alone, honey. You've got*
me. But Mama never said things just to make me feel
better. She never called me *honey,* and she wouldn't say
anything unless it was true.

I only found people like me in storybooks I read in the
library. Giants. Trolls. Witches. Ghouls. The Minotaur.
If this were a Greek epic, I would be the hero's narrow
escape. Chronos, the god of time, was convinced that one
of his children would overthrow him, so every time his
wife gave birth he gobbled up the baby.

Gobble. That word was the reason I dreaded Thanks-giving. One time my fourth-grade teacher told Mama I was a voracious reader, and Mama got really upset and pretended she was feeling sick so she could get out of the parent-teacher conference. But maybe she wasn't pretending. Mama never read me fairy tales, and I knew why.

Wherever I was going to school, I spent all my free time in the library. My mother wouldn't buy me *The BFG,* so I read it during lunch period, but Roald Dahl disap-pointed me. The heroine never ate anybody, and the nasty man-eating giants all got their comeuppance.

What was I expecting? Somebody like me could never be the good one.

I collected all the monster stories I could find and put them in a notebook. Sometimes I copied out whole pas-sages, and I always photocopied the pictures. *Saturn Devouring His Son.* Goya. Painted around 1820. Sawney Beane, head of a clan of cannibals living in a cave along the Scottish coast. I used to hide myself away in the qui-etest corner to avoid the librarians coming up to ask what I was working on. *Be he alive or be he dead, I'll grind his bones to make my bread.*

I got to Edgartown and asked for directions from a man behind the counter at McDonald's. It was almost dark by the time I got to my grandparents' neighborhood, if I could call them that.

They lived in one of those split-levels built in the '50s,

in a neighborhood where every house and yard is bounded on three sides by others just like it. It made my heart hurt to see our car in the driveway, behind a dark blue Cadillac that had to be my grandfather's. I waited until dark, walked around the block, and hopped the back neighbor's fence. Better to be caught by someone who didn't know me.

I figured out the kitchen was at the back of the house, so I crouched by the neighbor's fence looking in. They shouldn't call picture windows that because you have a pretty view looking out. They're picture windows because everything inside is all lit up, and in the darkness you can see people sitting down to dinner like you're watching them on a movie screen.

Mama brought the salad bowl to the table, they took their seats, and her father poured her a glass of wine. I couldn't get a good view of either of my grandparents because my grandfather's back was turned to the window and my grandmother was seated directly opposite. I could see my mother clearly though. I saw her pushing her food around her plate exactly the way she'd told me not to, I saw her lips form one-word answers, and I saw when she dropped her fork and hid her face in her hands. My grandmother got up from the table and put her arms around my mother, and Mama clung to her and cried. She'd probably told them everything.

I thought I'd understood how hard it was for my mother. I was sorry and I wished I could be different, but that wasn't the same as understanding. I didn't understand when she locked herself in the bathroom, didn't understand when I saw the empty wine bottles lined up along the kitchen counter, didn't understand when I heard her crying through the wall. Now I was beginning to.

She wore herself out, and her mother handed her a tissue. My grandfather lit a cigarette. He offered Mama the pack, and she reached out and took one. This really shocked me, because Mama *never* smoked.

My grandmother cleared the table and washed the dishes, while my mother and her father sat and smoked in silence. Then the woman put her arm around Mama's shoulders and led her from the room. Her father turned out the kitchen light, and I went over the fence again and out of the neighborhood.

I walked along a busy road lined with shops already closed for the night. There wasn't even a place where I could order a slice of pizza.

I walked around to the back of the strip mall, thinking maybe there'd be some food that was still clean enough to eat, even though the thought of eating out of a garbage bin grossed me out. There wasn't anything edible in there, but I did find a car parked behind the Dumpster. I tried the handle and found it unlocked. It was a Cadillac, like my grandfather's, but there were newspapers and empty soda cans all over the seats and gaping holes in the upholstery, as though the car had been left there and forgotten months ago. I cleaned off the backseat as best I could, climbed inside, and locked the doors behind me. The car smelled like mold and cigarettes and the unwashed body of whoever had driven it last, but it was better than wandering up and down the highway all night.

I laid my head on my pack and eventually fell asleep, and when I woke up my head was in a woman's lap and she was stroking my hair. My grandmother looked down at me, and her face was earnest and concerned. I asked her questions as she conjured a plaid car blanket out of the darkness and draped it over me—*Where's Mama? Does she know you've come?*—but she only smiled and tucked a lock of hair behind my ear, just like Mama used to.

In the driver's seat, my grandfather was smoking a cigarette. He raised his eyes to the rearview mirror and we looked at each other, but he didn't greet me. He sighed out a stream of smoke, flicked the cigarette into the street, and rolled up the window.

We drove in silence through the empty town, the street lamps washing the darkened Caddy with hazy orange light at steady intervals. I slid sideways and laid my head on the cold leather seat, and when I woke up I was back in the empty car, damp and shivering.

Sometimes out of the blue I'd have that taste in my mouth—the taste of things no honest person knows the taste of—and I would stumble into the bathroom for the Listerine. I'd gargle and gargle some more, letting it linger in my mouth until it stung, but as soon as I'd spat I could taste it again, the bad taste after the bad thing. At school other girls would come into the bathroom and catch me in the middle of rinsing. Through the mirror they would stare at me as I spit, screwed the cap back on a bottle of Listerine, and stuffed it in my backpack. Maybe that was why I never made friends with girls.

In sixth grade we had to do our first research papers, with footnotes and a bibliography and everything. I was used to looking things up in books, so I would have enjoyed choosing my own topic, but everyone had to write their papers on termites. Our English class went to the library every day for a week.

On Thursday morning somebody wandered over to my table, and I looked up. It was Stuart, the smart kid. I felt him leaning over my shoulder to see what I was reading, I felt his nearness and smelled the tuna fish on his breath, but he didn't make me feel funny. He was one of those boys who never thought of girls in that way, or at least he wouldn't for a long time yet. Finally I asked, "Do you need this book or something?"

"No. I finished my report at home last night. What are you looking at?"

"Nothing."

"We're supposed to be looking up termites," he said.

"Who's going to tell?"

I felt him shrug behind me. "Anyway, you're right. Australian redback spiders are much more interesting." He kept reading over my shoulder. "This entry is incomplete. The entomological encyclopedia I have at home is better. Do you know why they're called black widows?"

"Why?"

"Because their mates all die. Because she eats him."

Stuart sat down across from me as he spoke. "She eats him right after they copulate, sometimes even while they're still doing it. He lets her eat him because she needs the protein for her young, and anyway, his reproductive destiny has been fulfilled."

His reproductive destiny has been fulfilled? I would have laughed at him for memorizing whole lines from the encyclopedia, but all of a sudden I was too nervous to say anything. My heart was thumping like it was trying to get out.

"It's called sexual cannibalism," he was saying. "It's the most important thing to know about the Australian redback spider, and it's not in there at all."

"It's a kids' encyclopedia," I said. "They can't put the word 'sex' in it." I paused. "Stuart?"

"Yeah?"

"Do other species do that?"

"Do what? Eat each other?"

I nodded.

"The black widows, like I said. And there are a couple more kinds of spiders that would die after copulation anyway—the males, I mean—so even though the female doesn't attack during copulation"—he was using the word 'copulation' too often and too loudly; other kids were looking up from their notebooks—"she might as well eat him afterward, you know?"

"For the protein," I said, careful to keep my voice low.

"Right, for the protein."

"But are there species besides insects that do it? Like mammals?"

Stuart gave me a funny look and didn't answer. I was very aware that we had been having a conversation, and now we were not, and I could have kicked myself.

"Why do you wear black all the time?" he asked.

Just in case.

So the mess wouldn't show.

What I said was, "So I never have to match."

"You should wear colors. Then maybe people wouldn't talk so much about how weird you are." We locked eyes, but only for a second. "Sorry. But it's the truth."

We outcasts had a way of organizing ourselves into concentric circles, so kids like Stuart could feel bad for someone like me on the very outer fringe and feel relieved that they weren't on it. I said, "They'll think I'm weird no matter what I wear."

He looked at me. "Yeah." He got up from the table and hugged his Trapper Keeper to his chest. "You're probably right." Then he went back to sit at a table by himself.

The boys who wanted to be my friends, they were like me—well, "like me" in that there was something odd about them no one could put their finger on—and so, like me, they were pushed to the margins of the gym and lunchroom. They were boys who moved too often, boys with an ever-present inhaler or a stutter or a lazy eye, boys who were too smart not to be resented for it.

So after I'd been at a new school for a month or two, one of those boys might find an excuse to talk to me. He'd ask for the math assignment as if he didn't always write it down. He'd slide into the chair opposite me in the lunchroom and tell me about his plans for his science fair project or Halloween costume. And one day, months down the road, he'd invite me over after school—to study for a history test, or to try out the mechanism on the science project. At some point I learned the word for this: a pretext, a reason that's really an excuse. The boy's parents were still at work. We went up to his room. It almost always happened that way.

I should have said no. Every time, I wanted to say no. I knew it was the right thing to tell him to leave me alone, but he'd already been snubbed by our classmates a hundred times over. How could I say no?

So that's what happened with Dmitri and Joe and Kevin and Noble and Marcus and C. J. Every time I went over to his house thinking this time I could avoid it, this time he wouldn't be too nice or come too close. This time I wouldn't be tempted.

Eventually I realized something. Whenever you tell yourself, *This time it will be different*, it's as good as a promise that it'll turn out the same as it always has.

After C. J. we moved to Cincinnati, Ohio. We were in the car one morning and I said, "Maybe I shouldn't go to school anymore." She didn't answer. "Mama?"

"I'll think about it." But by that point I guess she'd already decided to leave.

The highway seemed just as desolate as it had the night before, nothing but gas stations and empty strip malls. I brightened at the sight of an awning proclaiming FRESH

HOT BAGELS before I noticed FOR RENT in the window. I'd almost reached the Greyhound station when I saw a sign marked EDGARTOWN, HISTORIC TOWN CENTER. Maybe I could stop at a real restaurant, warm up and get a good breakfast before I bought my ticket to Sandhorn.

After a few blocks the road turned into a good old-fashioned Main Street. It was still early, and most of the shops weren't open yet: an ice cream parlor, a second-hand bookshop, an Italian restaurant. A church, a real estate agent, an art gallery with pictures of sailboats in the front window, another church, a florist, a drugstore, another church: it seemed to go on and on before I found the coffee shop, where a handwritten sign in the window offered 2 EGGS, HASH BROWNS & TOAST, $1.99. Just what I needed.

As dead as it was on the street, the bustle in the little one-room diner more than made up for it. I smelled coffee and felt a pang of longing for Mama. A waitress eyed my rucksack and told me I could sit at the counter. All the people in the booths along the wall looked up from their plates as I passed, bumping my rucksack into the other waitress as I went, and I mumbled an apology.

I got to the counter and one or two of the men glanced up from their newspapers. There wasn't a single stool.

After Luke we moved to Baltimore. My mom got a job in a law office—it was always accounting or law; her typing speed was the one thing she could take anywhere—and for a while we pretended everything was normal.

Then, just before Christmas, Mama brought me to a party at her boss's house. Like I said, after what happened with Luke and Penny Wilson she could never trust me with a babysitter.

Before we left she sat me down on the sofa. "This is the first really good job I've ever had, Maren. I have friends—people I can talk to, people I can have a laugh with at lunch. And there's something else: I might be up for a promotion soon."

"That's great, Mama." But I couldn't be happy for her, not when she was only telling me this out of fear that I'd ruin it for her, that I'd slip up again and we'd have to move away.

"It could be great for both of us, if you could only . . ." She sighed. "Please, please, *please* be good. Promise me you'll be good this time."

I nodded, but it was never a matter of trying hard enough to be good. It was like leading me to a banquet and telling me not to eat.

It was a proper grown-up cocktail party, with shrimp arranged around bowls of bloodred dipping sauce and women with perfect manicures sipping from long-stemmed martini glasses, laughing a little too loudly as they popped their olives. There was a cathedral ceiling in the living room, and the Christmas tree went up all the way to the top.

There was a spare room near the front door, and Mrs. Gash told us we could go in and put our coats on the bed. No one came in behind us, so my mother closed the door and said, "Don't talk to anyone. If anyone says hello or asks your name you can tell them, but that's it—I don't want anybody thinking you're rude. Just read your book."

"Where?"

She pointed to an armchair in the corner of the room, and I went over and dropped into it with a sigh. "I'll bring you a plate and something to drink. *Please*, Maren—please stay here and be good." In a few minutes she returned with the promised plate of shrimp and crackers, asked me one more time not to leave the room, and left again. I ate the shrimp and watched as three women came in, shrugging off their coats and shaking the cold out. No one noticed me sitting in the corner.

The pile of coats grew and grew, and after a while people stopped coming in. I could see a fur coat peeking out at the bottom of the pile and I got up, reached in, and petted the sleeve. I thought I might like to burrow into the coat pile and take a nap so that when I woke up it would be time to go home, so that's what I did.

Under the coat pile it was warm and safe and cozy, and in every breath I smelled perfume and cigar smoke. I fell asleep. The shrimp hadn't satisfied me, though, and my stomach rumbled as I dozed.

Some time later I felt something brush my cheek, and in a second I was fully awake, my heart pounding. In the darkness I sensed a hand reach into a pocket by my shoulder, fumble around, and pull something out—I heard the soft rattle of a box of matches. Then I felt the pause, because whoever it was had realized I was inside. I felt a sharp poke from above.

"Hey!" I said, swimming out of the pile of tweed and

Gore-Tex and boiled wool. A boy stood beside the bed.
He had a pointy, turned-up nose that made him look like
some friendly rodent in a storybook, and tortoiseshell
glasses that were too big for his face. On the carpet at his
feet was a small pile of things from other people's coat
pockets. "Who are you?" I asked.

"I live here. Who are you?"

"I belong to one of the secretaries." He had his left
hand in a fist still held out in front of him, as if I wouldn't
notice unless he made a move to conceal it. "You were
going through the pockets, weren't you? I saw you. You
took out a matchbox."

"I wasn't going to steal anything. I was only going to
look."

"Yeah, right." I wriggled out of the coat pile and stood
in front of him. "What's your name?"

"Jamie. What's yours?"

"Maren."

"That's a funny name."

I rolled my eyes. "Like I've never heard that before."

He looked at the floor. "Sorry."

"Find anything good?"

Jamie opened his hand, and an accordion of condom
packets spilled out. Of course, I didn't know what they
were then. Maybe he didn't either, and that's why neither
of us asked.

I pointed to the pile on the floor. "You said you were
going to put this stuff back, didn't you?" He nodded.
"But how can you keep track of which pockets you found
them in?"

"Oh. I hadn't thought about that."

"Maybe put them back in the pockets, any pockets if you can't remember, and then they can figure it out at work on Monday."

"All right." He plucked a pack of Marlboros out of the pile and tucked it in the pocket of a navy blue peacoat. I helped him put everything back, and when the floor was clear he just stood there and looked at me for a minute.

"What?" I said.

"You like stars?"

"The kind in the sky?"

He nodded. "I've got a telescope. Want to see it?"

"Sure." I followed him out of the guest room and up the stairs.

"I got it for Christmas last year," Jamie said over his shoulder. "My dad studied astronomy in college, so he knows a lot." His bedroom was at the end of the hall and by the time we got there I could hardly hear the noise of the party.

I'd never been in a boy's room before. There were Star Wars things everywhere—the sheets and the comforter and a poster of Han Solo and Princess Leia on the wall above the bed. There was a full-size cardboard cutout of Darth Vader in the corner by the closet door and a coin bank shaped like R2-D2 on the night table. It was very tidy, and I could picture Mrs. Gash reminding him to clean it even though no guests would be coming upstairs. Mrs. Gash was a just-so kind of mother.

Jamie had a bookcase above his dresser, and I cocked

my head and scanned the spines—*The War of the Worlds*, Isaac Asimov, and a row of Choose Your Own Adventures that turned my stomach at the thought of Luke— as he went to the big black telescope on a tripod by the window and made some adjustments. Then he opened the window and a cold gust shot through the room, sending the pieces of a solar system mobile clattering above the bed. "Now turn off the light," he said.

I flipped the switch by the door and came over to stand beside him, shivering in the draft. "Obviously it's better when we take it up to the roof, but I'm not allowed up there without my dad." He stepped away from the telescope and gestured that it was my turn. "Here, I'll show you the Pleiades. You can see them without the telescope, but it's much cooler with it." I bent forward and put my eye to the lens. A perfect cluster of stars shone brightly at the end of a dark tunnel. "See them?"

"Yeah," I whispered. He was standing close to me, so close I could smell him. Irish Spring. His mother had made him bathe before the party.

"You know the myth about the Pleiades?"

"No."

"They were the daughters of Atlas. You know, the guy who had to hold up the world?"

"Yeah?"

"So after the Titans lost to the Olympians and Atlas was punished, the sisters were so upset that they all killed themselves, and then Zeus felt sorry for them and made them into stars so they could keep their father company for the rest of time. That's just one version, but it's the one I like the best. My dad tells me how all the constellations got their names."

I stepped away from the telescope. "Now I'll show you the Milky Way," he said.

I could hear footsteps on the stairs, and a moment later Mrs. Gash turned the light back on. "Jamie? What are you doing up here?" It hadn't felt like we were doing anything wrong—I'd completely forgotten Mama's warning—but there was something funny in his mother's voice.

"Jamie was just showing me his telescope," I said. "We're looking at the Pleiades." The boy still had his face pressed to the eyepiece.

Mrs. Gash nodded to me. "Jamie, listen to me. I don't want you and Maren up here by yourselves."

He turned around only to say, "All right." Then he went back to the telescope, and his mother folded her arms, watching us.

"I mean *now,* Jamie. Why don't you bring our guest downstairs and get her something to eat? Do you like shrimp, Maren?"

"Yes, Mrs. Gash."

"Try the sugar cookies too. Jamie and I made them from scratch."

Jamie sighed as he followed us out of the bedroom and down the stairs. We wandered over to the beverage table set up near the Christmas tree, where he poured two cups of punch out of a cut-crystal bowl and handed one to me. "Sorry about that."

I shrugged. "Thanks for showing me the Pleiades."

Mrs. Gash had gone back to her hostess duties, and no one else seemed to notice us. I saw Mama talking to two women over by the fireplace. She was telling a joke, and when she got to the punch line they threw back their heads and laughed.

"C'mon!" Jamie grabbed my free hand and pulled me down the hall, away from the noise of the party, and I hastily sipped my punch so I wouldn't spill any on the carpet.

"Where are we going?"

"There's something else I want to show you downstairs."

The basement door was next to the spare room. It was cold down there, and it smelled like paint and mold and mothballs, and the only light came from a naked bulb in a ceiling crisscrossed with unfinished beams. There was a washer and dryer at the foot of the steps, and the rest of the space was full of old furniture and stacks of cardboard boxes. The concrete floor was bare apart from a gray length of carpet in front of the laundry machines. "Why did you bring me down here?" I asked. "It's nicer upstairs."

He laid his punch glass on top of the dryer. "Let me see it."

"See what?"

He tugged at a belt loop on his jeans, his eyes on the carpet between our feet. "You know."

There's something I want to show you downstairs. My mistake. "No," I said. "You first."

He unzipped his fly and let his jeans fall to his ankles.

There were comets and rockets on his underpants. Then he tucked his thumbs inside the waistband and pulled them down and back up again so fast that I hardly got a look at it. "Now you."

I shook my head.

"You said you would."

"No, I didn't."

I could see him thinking back over the past minute and a half. He frowned when he realized I was right. "Well, now I feel stupid."

"Don't," I said.

"This was a bad idea. I never should have brought you down here."

I took a step toward the stairs. "It's okay. Let's go up now."

"Can you let me do just one thing?"

"What?"

He mumbled something.

"Huh?"

"Let me . . . kiss you?"

I knew I shouldn't, but I'd already hurt his feelings once. *Hurt them one more time, and you'll be doing him a favor. Leave. Now. Go.*

But he took a step closer, and I didn't turn and run. Something in me was seizing up. I felt a rumble of panic down deep in my guts. *Go, go, go now—if he comes any closer you won't be able to stop it.*

The naked lightbulb buzzed overhead, the chain swaying gently in a cold draft. For a second it was like I was an ordinary girl about to get her first kiss.

Go—leave—NOW . . .

I put my lips to his neck, pressed them there, and drank him in. I could smell the cocktail sauce on his breath, the little pieces of shellfish rotting in the dark corners of his mouth. I stepped back and looked at him. His eyes were closed and he was smiling like I could do anything I wanted to him and he'd be over the moon about it. *This won't be what you have in mind,* I thought. *But it's too late now.*

When I was finished I fell onto the scrap of carpet in front of the dryer, shivering so badly I made the machine rumble like it was working. No one upstairs could have heard any of it. Through the speakers in the living room some sister act was crooning, *"Take good care of yourself, you belooooong to me . . ."*

I sat there awhile longer, thinking about his telescope and his Chewbacca pillowcase and the Rubik's Cube on his dresser. Would they keep everything in the room the way it was? Why couldn't he have left me alone?

I found a crumpled plastic bag on the floor by the washing machine and I stuffed everything into it, his jeans and his red button-down shirt and his boy-who-fell-to-Earth underpants and the bits I couldn't eat—everything but the tortoiseshell glasses—and then I reached a hand into the cobwebs behind the dryer, searching out the gap where the hose met the drywall so I could cram the bag into the wall. I dragged the stained carpet scrap into the darkest corner of the basement. Someone would find it all eventually. *I'm sorry. I'm so sorry.*

I washed my face, pulled off my pants and turtleneck,

and squeezed out the mess under the faucet in the util-
ity tub. There was blood on my undershirt too, but no one
would see it. I could wash it at home.

No, not home. There wouldn't be time for that.

I rinsed out my mouth and sat on the concrete floor
with my back to the dryer, waiting for my clothes to dry.
I jumped at every sound from the floor above, terrified
that someone would come downstairs and find me.

Mama. I had to tell Mama.

I put on my shirt and pants and started up the basement stairs like I'd never arrive at the top. She was
coming out of the spare room, our coats slung over her
arm. Quickly I closed the door behind me and took a step
away from it.

"Maren! We're leaving, okay? I've got your coat." She
handed me my jacket, and I put it on. "Where have you
been?" she hissed.

"In the bathroom."

"You know better than to lie to me. Why were you in
the basement?"

I stood there in miserable silence as we heard Mrs.
Gash in another room calling Jamie's name. I felt Mama
stiffen beside me. Jamie's mother came into the front
hall a moment later. "Where has that boy gone off to
now?"

"He's not in his room?" Mr. Gash asked. He was standing by the front door, shaking people's hands before they
went back into the cold. His white teeth shone beneath
his shiny black mustache.

"Of *course* he's not in his room."

"Check the roof," Mr. Gash said, laughing over his shoulder as he reached for my mother's hand. "I'm so glad you could make it, Janelle." He nodded to me. "Nice meeting you, Maren." Then, turning back to my mother, he said in a low voice, "We'll talk first thing Monday morning, all right? Looking forward to it."

Mrs. Gash went to the foot of the stairs. "Jamie! Jamie, where are you?"

"Me too," Mama said faintly. She glanced down at me, and I could see how hard she was straining not to show her panic, her horror. Every time this happened she got a little better at hiding it. *You didn't. Please say you didn't.*

Mrs. Gash turned back to us. "You were playing with Jamie earlier, weren't you, Maren?"

I shrugged, keeping my eyes on her shoes. How could I look her in the face? I was very close to tears again, and Mrs. Gash made the assumption that saved me.

"You poor thing! I just know he said something to upset her. He's a good boy, but he does have a tendency to alienate other children. A little too smart for his own good, if you know what I mean, Janelle. No harm done, I'm sure."

Mama wasn't listening to a word Mrs. Gash was saying, and Mr. Gash was saying his goodbyes to someone else now. She clutched my hand so hard I gasped, and she took a step backward toward the front door, the wheels turning in her head all the while. She was calculating how long it would take us to pack and leave, tallying up a new list of disappointments. Come Monday there'd be no talk of a promotion—she'd never see any of these people again—and I felt her anger coursing down her arm, through her hand and into mine.

Mrs. Gash folded her arms tight across her chest and looked over her shoulder. "He's probably out back with his telescope. I'd better go and look for him."

"Thank you for a lovely party," my mother murmured.

Jamie's mother was already heading down the hallway toward the back door. "Thank you for coming, and drive safely," she called as my mother turned the knob and pulled me out of the house. I wished so hard that I could undo it, that Mrs. Gash would find her son on the tire swing in the backyard, sulking because I wouldn't pull down my underpants.

We drove home in silence, ten miles above the speed limit the whole way. Mama glanced over when I took Jamie's eyeglasses out of my pocket and turned them over in my hands. She never said a word. I'd finished my homework before the party, but I never turned it in.

That night I learned there are two kinds of hunger. The first I can satisfy with cheeseburgers and chocolate milk, but there's a second part of me, biding its time. It can go on like that for months, maybe even years, but sooner or later I'll give in to it. It's like there's a great big hole inside me, and once it takes his shape he's the only thing that can fill it.

3

couldn't face standing in that coffee shop waiting like an idiot for someone to leave me his seat. With burning cheeks I hurried out of the diner and kept walking.

A few blocks later I came to an Acme. I felt a little funny with my rucksack on my back but I went in anyway. I walked through the produce section, picked up an apple, circled around, and put it back. I turned the corner into the canned goods aisle and saw an elderly lady hurrying after a can rolling away along the shiny white linoleum. I picked it up and handed it to her.

The old lady beamed at me through pearly-pink cat-eye reading glasses. She was dressed in a pale green jacket with a red silk rose pinned to the lapel, a gray tweed skirt, and leather oxford shoes, as if going to the grocery store were a proper outing. "Thank you ever so much." She handed the tin back to me. "Can you read that for me, dear? These eyeglasses are useless, I really must get myself a new pair."

"Fresh Pear Halves in White Grape Juice," I told her.

"Oh good, that's the kind I want." She placed the tin in her cart. "Thank you."

I was about to wish her a nice day when she asked, "Are you on your own, dear?"

I nodded.

"Doing the food shopping for your mother? How nice." I didn't know how to answer that, and I guess that's when she decided to adopt me. "I could use some help bringing my groceries home. I take the bus, you see, because I never learned how to drive. Have you gotten your license yet?"

I shook my head.

"My husband always drove me wherever I needed to go." As she spoke I looked over the contents of her cart: two red onions, kidney beans, a carton of eggs, orange juice, buttermilk, a package of bacon, four tins of cat food, and the pears. "Would you like some extra pocket money?" she asked. "Only if you don't have too many of your own bags to carry and you aren't too busy."

I would have helped her for nothing. "I'd be glad to."

"That's splendid. What's your name, dear?"

"Maren."

Her hand was cold, but her grip was firm. "Maren! What a lovely name. Mine is Lydia Harmon."

After she paid for her groceries we went outside and

waited at the bus stop. It occurred to me that she might live near my grandparents, and I hoped she didn't. Mrs. Harmon sat on the bench beside a mother with too many kids to keep track of. The children laughed and hit each other, kicking at stones, while the woman just sat smoking a cigarette and staring through the pavement. Mrs. Harmon, oblivious, smiled up at me and asked if I was hungry.

When the bus came Mrs. Harmon paid my fare. As we pulled away from the curb I caught sight of an old brick building with EDGARTOWN PUBLIC LIBRARY etched in stone above the doorway. I watched a boy, nine or ten, hold the front door open for an old woman as she went in.

To my relief, we seemed to be going in the opposite direction of my grandparents' house. A block or two later I caught sight of someone else on the sidewalk—an older man, though not as old as Mrs. Harmon, in a red plaid shirt with rolled-up sleeves who didn't seem to be going anywhere or looking at anything. As the bus began to pass he gazed up at the windows, scanning the passengers' faces as if he were looking for someone. When he saw me, he smiled as if I were the person he'd been searching for. In that instant I noticed that the top half of one ear was gone, slashed on a diagonal. It made him look like an alley cat. I turned in my seat as we passed. He was still looking at me, smiling faintly, and he lifted his hand as the bus turned a corner.

"See someone you know, dear?" asked Mrs. Harmon.

"No. Just somebody who seemed to know me."

"Oh," she replied. "Isn't it funny when that happens?"

Ten years ago Mrs. Harmon's house would have been beautifully kept, but now the paint on the shutters was peeling slightly and the grass had grown high between the slats of the white picket fence. Still, it was a nice little house, white with cornflower-blue trim and a cheerful red door. The living room was bright and cozy—there were rows of records and hardback books in glass-fronted cases, and pictures of far-off places, the Grand Canyon and the Taj Mahal, and real sunflowers in a glass vase on an end table. I heard the clock on the mantelpiece before I saw it.

A cat with a mane, like a tiny white lion, jumped off a cushioned stool in front of the fireplace and marched across the carpet toward the kitchen. Mrs. Harmon laid her grocery bags on a chair by the door and bent down to pet him as he passed. "How's my Puss, eh?" Then she picked up the bags again and followed the cat into the kitchen. "He knows it's time to eat. He can hear the clinking of the tins in the bag." She laughed. "And what would *you* like for breakfast, dear? I have eggs, and bacon, and maybe even a hash brown or two. . . ."

Perfect. This was so perfect. "That would be wonderful, thank you, Mrs. Harmon." I stashed my rucksack behind an armchair and followed her into the kitchen with the rest of the groceries. Everything was just what I pictured a real home to have: photos of laughing children on the refrigerator, quilted calico place mats around the table, stained-glass suncatchers in the windows—a frog, a sailboat, a four-leaf clover. Above the light switch a painted angel carried a banner that read BLESS THIS HOUSE AND EVERYONE IN IT. We'd never had things like this anyplace we'd lived. The room smelled like cinnamon.

After opening a few cabinets I figured out where the groceries should go. The fridge was pretty well stocked for one person, and I could see by the big glass jars of flour and sugar on the counter that Mrs. Harmon loved to bake. There was a cake, I couldn't tell what kind, in a clear Tupperware box next to a bowl of apples and bananas.

She shrugged out of her jacket and traded it for a red gingham apron hanging on a hook beside the refrigerator. "The electric can opener is the greatest invention of the twentieth century," she said as she used it to open a tin of cat food. "When you get to be as old as I am you'll see why."

Puss (was that really his name? It was like calling myself "Girl") waited by a stainless steel bowl on the floor by the window, swishing his tail, as Mrs. Harmon came over and dished out the cat food with a fork. "Now for *our* breakfast." She took out a frying pan and pointed to the sofa in the living room. "Make yourself at home, Maren. Can I get you something to drink? Orange juice?"

"Orange juice would be great, thanks." I sat down and ran my hand over a blue and red zigzag afghan draped over the back of the sofa. We'd never had throw blankets at home—if we got cold we'd just take the comforters off our beds. Throw blankets, like place mats or window ornaments, were not necessary.

I turned to look at the pictures on the end table as Mrs. Harmon shook her new carton of orange juice, opened it, and filled a pair of glasses. Her wedding portrait was watercolored, so that her cheeks were pink like cotton candy and the garden around her and her husband glowed like the Emerald City. Sometimes people change so much you can't see them in their younger selves, but Mrs. Harmon wasn't that different. They looked like they could've been movie stars. The photograph had brown matting, and in gold script at the bottom I read:

MR. AND MRS. DOUGLAS HARMON
JUNE 2, 1933

"Your husband was very handsome," I said as she handed me the glass.

"Thank you, dear. We were married fifty-two years." She sighed. "Dear Dougie. I'll be joining him soon enough."

"Oh, don't say that," I said automatically.

She shrugged and went back to the kitchen, lighting the burner and dropping a big dollop of butter into the frying pan. "Can you guess how old I am, Maren?"

"I'm no good at guessing people's ages."

"You'll get better at it as you get older. I'm eighty-eight and a half."

She was older than she looked. "I hope I'm like you when I'm eighty-eight and a half."

"Why, thank you, dear! If there's a nicer compliment I can't think of it." I looked around the room as Mrs.

Harmon let the frozen hash browns cook with the bacon. We lapsed into an easy silence. I found it comforting, the ticking of the clock on the mantelpiece. "It doesn't bother you, does it?" she asked.

"What?"

"The clock. My niece says it ticks so loudly she can't hear herself think." She put her hand on her hip as she transferred the hash browns and bacon to a spare plate and started on the eggs. "I find it reassuring, myself. After all, the passage of time is the only thing we can be sure of in this world." Mrs. Harmon dropped two slices of bread in the toaster, took the eggs off the stove, and arranged our plates.

It was the best breakfast I'd ever tasted. You can't feel entirely hopeless with a warm meal in your belly—a warm, *honest* meal—and being with Mrs. Harmon was even better. She made me forget, for a little while at least, that I didn't have a place to go home to anymore. Mrs. Harmon smiled at me as she sipped her orange juice, and it hit me then: She trusted me.

I took our plates to the sink and washed them along with the frying pan, and with a murmur of thanks she laid herself down on the sofa and pulled the red and blue afghan over her. The white cat hopped up and settled itself on her tummy. "Ah, Puss," she said, and rubbed him behind the ears.

I sat in the armchair by the door and noticed on the table beside it a white wicker basket brimming with balls of yarn in sherbet colors, raspberry and peach and baby blue. "Do you knit?" Mrs. Harmon asked, and I shook my head. "I have bags and bags of wool, but I'll never be able to use it all. I can't do much needlework these days—my arthritis prevents it."

"Maybe you could teach me. I mean, if it wouldn't hurt your hands too much." I'd never thought of learning how to knit before, but now out of nowhere I wanted to very much. I wanted to knit myself a sweater I could hide inside.

"I'd love to, dear. I'll just have a little rest first." In my mind I was already knitting a hood like the Grim Reaper's. I would wear it up so no one could see my face.

"You look tired yourself, Maren. Why don't you take a nap in the spare room?" Every time I hear the words "spare room" I think of Narnia. *Daughter of Eve from the far land of Spare Oom, where eternal summer reigns around the bright city of War Drobe . . .*

"No one has come to stay with me for ages," Mrs. Harmon was saying. "I think spare rooms ought to be used as much as possible, don't you? It's the first door on the right past the kitchen. Then when you wake up, we'll have tea and cake. I baked a carrot cake yesterday. And I'll teach you how to knit, and when you go home I'll give you a bag of yarn to take with you. Won't that be nice?"

After a night in an abandoned Cadillac, it sounded like a dream.

I watched her eyelids grow heavy. "Have a nice rest, Maren."

"You too, Mrs. Harmon."

Then she startled herself awake with a thought. "Oh! Perhaps you should call your mother?"

I shook my head. "She's not expecting me back until later." I didn't like lying to her, but maybe it wasn't as much of a lie if you wished it were true.

"Ah. Good." Mrs. Harmon closed her eyes, and I went down the hall and opened the door on the right. It was the fanciest bed I'd ever seen, with a dark mahogany headboard carved with laughing cherubs—too old, too strange, and much too marvelous for an ordinary house like this—and a pinwheel quilt in yellow and blue. A big chest of drawers with a mirror on top stood at the far wall, and there was a chair in the corner with a red velvet cushion. It was the nicest Spare Oom there ever was.

On the night table I found an antique sculpture, a sphinx cast in bronze with wings outspread. I picked it up—it was much heavier than I expected, and covered in soft emerald-green felt on the bottom—and when I read the inscription I realized it was a trophy:

THE LUCRETIAN CUP IS HEREBY PRESENTED
TO DOUGLAS HARMON, WITH GREAT ESTEEM
AND ADMIRATION FOR HIS OUTSTANDING ESSAY ON
THE NATURE OF HUMAN CONSCIOUSNESS.
THE CLASSICAL SOCIETY OF THE
UNIVERSITY OF PENNSYLVANIA, JUNE 1930

It was a proper prize, not one of those cheap-looking knickknacks my classmates would get for winning a softball championship. I ran my fingers over the sphinx, over her paws and her wings and her face, proud and remote. She made me want to strive for something, to earn something beautiful I could hold on to for the rest of my life.

I put the trophy back on the table and turned down the bedclothes, peeled off my dirty socks, and slid between the snowy covers. The pillow was cool on my cheek. I understood now why the smell of laundry soap was so comforting: Things couldn't be too hopeless if somebody was still bothering to wash the sheets.

I slept, and when I woke up I stretched like a cat. The house was still. I went into the living room and knelt beside the sofa. "Mrs. Harmon?" I don't know why I kept calling her name. As soon as I touched her hand I knew she was dead.

I'd never seen a dead person before—well, you know what I mean. A funny feeling went through the fingers I'd touched her with and spread up my arm and all through the rest of me, and even though I was kneeling by the sofa the floor seemed to fall away beneath my feet.

I shook myself and stood up. The white cat was curled up on his cushioned stool by the fireplace as if nothing had changed. He lifted his head and looked at me, then closed his eyes and rubbed the side of his face against his paw—as if to say, *So what?*

No more Fancy Feast for you, *that's* what. I went back to the sofa and tugged the afghan up to Mrs. Harmon's chin, as if I could warm her up. Again I caught sight of the knitting basket, and I took a couple of balls and a set of wooden needles and slipped them into my rucksack. "Thanks, Mrs. Harmon," I whispered.

Then I wandered through the rooms of the tidy little house, looking at old pictures and fingering all her handi-work—the doilies along the center of the dining-room table; the pearl-buttoned cardigan draped over the back of a chair, as if it were resting on somebody's shoulders; the embroidered proverb, A MERRY HEART DOETH GOOD LIKE A MEDICINE, above the light switch in her bedroom—without really seeing any of it. I went back into the Spare Oom and got into bed, only because I didn't know what else to do. I couldn't leave her like that, but I didn't know who to call, and even if I did I wouldn't have known how to explain my being here. Someone was bound to think I'd done something wrong.

I decided to go back to sleep and pretend for a while like none of it had happened. I didn't know what else to do.

No cake—no knitting lesson—and no one left to trust me.

There was a noise in another part of the house, and that's what woke me the second time. It must have been early evening. I sat still in the bed, straining my ears, and in a few seconds I heard it again. There was somebody here—somebody still living.

I opened the door and it drifted down the hallway, the sourness of a meal that should have only been tasted once. I smelled blood too, but it wasn't quite the odor I knew. Maybe a dead person's blood doesn't smell or taste the same.

There was a figure framed in the darkened hallway, kneeling over the sofa. It was the old man I'd spotted from the bus. I could see his missing ear. His head was burrowed deep into Mrs. Harmon's belly—there were shreds of her blouse on the carpet—and her arm fell across his back, stiff as a plank, as he plunged into her nose-first. Mrs. Harmon's head was gone, but there were thick locks of silver hair across the arm of the sofa.

I opened my mouth, but no sound came out. How could I scream, when it was all so familiar to me?

If he knew I was there he gave no sign of it, nor did he seem the slightest bit agitated. I couldn't see his face, but I knew he wasn't sorry. He chomped and chewed and swallowed calmly, methodically even. *Is that what I look like when I do it? Do I make those horrible noises?*

When he was done with her belly he reached back and grabbed her long purple fingers, and the crunching started. He inched down the sofa, still sitting on his heels, as he munched on her legs. I wanted to look away, but I never did.

When he was finished he rocked back on his heels and let out a belch that would have registered on the Richter scale. "Pardon me," he muttered as he drew a grubby yellow handkerchief out of his back pocket and wiped his mouth. "You got nothin' to worry about," he said as he stuffed the kerchief back in his pocket. "I never eat 'em live." At no point had he turned to look at me. Somehow he just knew I was there.

He reached around him, gathering the scraps of her clothing and stuffing them into one of the bags we'd brought the groceries home in. Her brown leather shoes stood neatly where her feet had been, awaiting their next outing like it would ever happen. The man glanced at me, then reached over and slid them behind the floral dust-flap.

When I finally spoke my voice sounded like I'd borrowed it. "I thought I was the only one."

He shrugged. "Everybody does." He pulled something out of the crumpled afghan on the sofa and jingled it in his hand. It was a tangle of Mrs. Harmon's jewelry, the rings that had been on her fingers and the locket of cream and pink enamel around her neck. Cupping the jewelry in a dirty hand, he got up to the sound of creaking bones and settled himself in the armchair beside the sofa. He made as if to dip his hand into his shirt pocket, then decided against it.

"Here," he said. The stranger leaned forward, and I held out my hand to accept the little pile of jewelry. Then he drew a tarnished silver flask out of his shirt pocket and tipped it. I watched his Adam's apple bob as he gulped. *Washing her down.* I'd only known Mrs. Harmon for an hour, but in that moment I missed her like I'd known her all my life.

I went to the mantelpiece and untangled the rings from the chain, laying the jewelry out piece by piece in front of the old pictures Mrs. Harmon had remembered her husband by. A dashing Douglas Harmon in soft focus regarded me with a benevolence I didn't deserve.

"Listen here. High time we introduced ourselves. Name's Sullivan." The man got to his feet and held out his hand. His eyes were pale blue under his shaggy gray eyebrows. "Sully, for short."

Before I had a chance to refuse him he glanced down at his fingers—stained red, especially around the cuticles—and thought better of offering his hand. He went into the kitchen and ran his hands under the faucet, glancing over his shoulder at me. "Well? Don't you got a name, girl?"

I'd never met anyone who talked like him before. He must have been from somewhere south, someplace rural, like West Virginia. "Maren," I said.

"Nice name. Never heard it before," Sullivan said as he dried his hands on Mrs. Harmon's dish towel. His fingers still weren't what I would have called clean. For all I knew, though, whiskey might have been way more effective than Listerine.

"How did you know?" I asked.

He lifted a hoary eyebrow. "You mean how did I know about you?" I nodded, and Sully paused, as if he were deciding how to answer. "I just know," he said.

"You saw me . . . this morning, on the bus . . . and you knew? Just like that?"

"I knew it was you," he said.

"You said, 'Everybody does,'" I said. "Like there are others."

"What, like we stick together or somethin'?" Sully laughed as he pulled out a chair and sat down at the kitchen table, where Mrs. Harmon had savored her eggs and bacon a few hours before. "Get together for poker on Thursday nights?" He laughed again, a big jolly laugh, like I could close my eyes and picture a gin-swilling, chain-smoking Santa Claus—except he was so lean I could see his bones poking through his shirt. "You're on your own, and you always will be. That's the way it's gotta be, get it?"

I leaned in the doorway and folded my arms. "That sounds like a self-fulfilling prophecy."

"Missy, you got a lot to learn. You may be dangerous to a whole lot of people out there, but that don't mean there ain't a whole lot of people who can hurt you just as bad. Can't come near your own kind, not if you wanna keep your face."

"What about you?"

"What about me?"

"You just said I should stay away from you."

"Ah, but I ain't like you, and you ain't like me. You got a pulse, and I ain't been a teenager since the nineteenth century. That's how we can sit down for a meal together, see?"

I felt my belly rumble at the mention of dinner, but something he had said made me stop short. "How did you know?" I asked. "That I . . . that I eat . . . ?"

"Who else you gonna eat, at your age?" He chuckled, and I smiled.

"Are you really that old?"

The old man clucked his tongue. "I seen it all, but I ain't anywhere near a hundred."

"Have you met a lot of us?"

"Here and there," he said with a shrug. "But like I said, it's best not to make friends."

It wasn't just Sully's ear—he was missing most of his left index finger too. He saw me looking at it and held out his hand to me, waggling his digits as if he were a young girl expecting me to admire her engagement ring. "Lost it in a bar fight," he said. "Bit it clean off, the bastard. Swallowed it before I could get it back." He got up from the table and started opening cabinets. He took out a skillet. "You hungry? I'm gonna make us some dinner."

"You're still hungry?"

"I'm always hungry." Sully grabbed a bunch of onions and potatoes from a bowl on the counter and dropped them on a chopping board. "Git over here and make yourself useful. I'm gonna show you how to make a hobo casserole."

I picked up a knife and chopped an onion in half. "What's in a hobo casserole?" I couldn't resist. "Hoboes?"

When he laughed he threw back his head and actually slapped his knee. "Nah, nah. Just whatever you got to hand." He opened the refrigerator and poked through one of the produce drawers. "Let's see if she got some ground beef in here . . . ha! Got some carrots too." Sully turned on the oven—"Four hundred," he said over his shoulder—and pulled the meat out of the wrapper with his bare hands. I could still see the blood around his cuticles. I'd have to try not to think about it.

I watched him find his way around the kitchen, pulling down two tins of baked beans and fiddling with the electric can opener. Leaving the meat and vegetables to cook, Sully homed in on the Tupperware cake box, pulled off the lid, and leaned in for a sniff. "Mmm, what's this?"

"I think it's carrot cake."

"Made her own frosting too. Cream cheese. Looks mighty tasty." He replaced the lid and looked at me. "What were you doin' with her, anyway?"

"Nothing," I said. "She asked me to help her with her groceries, and then she invited me in for breakfast."

"Then she got tired and told you to make yourself at home, is that it?"

I didn't know why I felt so guilty all of a sudden, especially after what I'd just seen *him* do. "She was nice to me," I said. "I didn't do anything wrong."

The man gave me a look I couldn't read. "Never said you did." He mixed the ingredients together in a casserole dish, sprinkled the top with shredded cheddar, and slid it into the oven.

The clock on the mantel chimed six as Sully brought his pack in from the living room, propped it against the refrigerator, and drew a long ropelike object out of the opening. At first I did think it was a rope, but then he pulled out the thick, silvery knot of Mrs. Harmon's chignon and laid it out on the calico place mat with a sort of reverence, and I realized what the ropelike thing was made of. There were all sorts of hair woven into it, red and brown and black and silver, curly and kinky and slippery-straight. I never knew something could be so grotesque and so beautiful at the same time.

Sully laid the end of the rope across his knee, gently

pulling a lock of Mrs. Harmon's hair out of the chignon and into two, then four, even pieces. "Been workin' on it for years," he said, glancing up as he began to weave in the first piece. "That brimstone look of yours ain't so pretty. Here's the first thing you need to know about old Sully: I ain't gonna change my ways to suit ya." He shrugged. "Anyhow, it's kinda poetical, when you think about it."

"What do you mean?"

"Makin' somethin' useful, somethin' lovely, out of somethin' that's done and gone. A hundred years ago they used to make bracelets outta corpses' hair, d'you ever hear that?"

I shook my head.

"A widow wore her husband's hair all the rest of her days." The coil twitched as Sully began to weave in the pieces. "Somethin' lovely," he said again, softly, as if to himself. "Somethin' to remember him by." His hands were rough and gnarled, but when he worked in the locks he did it deftly. "Gotta keep my hands busy," he said. "'Idle hands do the devil's work,' that's what the preacher used to tell us in Sunday school when I was a boy. And anyhow, it's better than whittlin' out the same damn chess pieces over and over like some folks do."

"It would be all right," I ventured, "if you played chess."

He scoffed. "What am I gonna do, play against myself?"

For a minute or two I watched him weave the silver pieces into the strands that were already there. "What are you going to do with it when it's finished?"

He shrugged. "Who says it'll ever be finished?"

"But I don't see what the point of it is, if you're not going to finish it."

"Can't you say the same for livin'? Just goes on and on, and no reason for it."

I couldn't argue with that. Suddenly the days and weeks and months stretching out before me looked even bleaker than they had yesterday or the day before.

"Here," Sully said, pulling another few feet of rope out of his sack and offering it to me. "Give it a good tug. Plenty strong enough to hang a man."

I hesitated, partly because I didn't really want to touch it but also because I was afraid I'd tear it in half and he'd be angry with me. "Go on," he said. "It won't break."

So I grabbed it with both fists and pulled, but it was as he'd said. I bet I could have climbed it to the ceiling like that rope we had in elementary school gym class. "How did you learn to do that?"

"My daddy was a rope-maker." He paused, then added quietly, "Among other things." He flicked his wrist, and the rope of hair leapt and twitched like a snake. I jumped, and he laughed at me. "Now," he said. "Tell me about your first one."

I traced my finger along the quilting of Mrs. Harmon's calico place mat. "It was my babysitter."

"You remember?"

I shook my head.

He pulled out his flask and took another gulp. "Your mama found you?"

I nodded. "What about you?"

Sully chuckled to himself. "Ate my own granddad while they were waitin' on the undertaker." He licked his lips and tossed me a look as he screwed the cap back on the flask. "Saved my daddy near three hundred dollars." After a moment he asked, "Why you on your own? Your mama left you?"

"How did you know?"

He shrugged. "That's why you're here?"

I nodded.

"Let me guess," he sighed. "You went over there thinkin' you were gonna make some kind of a bargain. Then you got there and saw there was no way in hell you were gonna ring that doorbell."

I hated that this man, a complete stranger, had me all figured out. It had been easier to leave my grandparents' yard thinking I might go back, but he was right. I *couldn't* go back. There could be no asking forgiveness for what I'd done.

"Listen here," Sully went on. "You ain't never gonna feel nothin' other people ain't been through a million times before." He frowned, remembering something. "I wanted to say goodbye to my mama. Slept in the woods for weeks, waitin' for my chance."

I drew a deep breath and tried to push all thoughts of Mama out of my head. "Wasn't it hard? Sleeping outdoors and finding all your own food and stuff?"

"Nah. It ain't hard once somebody shows you how to shoot, and how to forage, and how to start a fire. I had a bow and arrow, and I used it to catch my supper. Rabbits, squirrels. My granddaddy, he taught me all that."

"But wasn't it hard to fall asleep outside?"

"Your mama never took you campin', I can see that."
He laughed. "Why sleep under a ceiling when you got a
sky full of stars out there?" He gave a backward nod toward the kitchen window.

"Do you always sleep outside?"

"Not in a built-up place like this. You're liable to get
taken in by the cops and charged with vagrancy. It don't
matter if you ain't stole nothin', or camped on public land.
If we were in the woods, I'd have cooked up that casserole on an open fire." He sighed. "Ain't nothin' better in
all the world than the smell of woodsmoke. If we was out
in the woods, I'd find us a clearing and show you how to
see the pictures between the stars."

I thought of Jamie Gash, and winced.

"But you set me off on a tangent, Missy. Like I was
sayin': I'd come back and watch my mama through the
kitchen window. Tryin' to get up the courage. I was gonna
do it while my daddy was away."

"Did you?"

He shook his head. "I had my chances, and I let every
one of 'em pass. I knew she would've jumped like a rab-
bit at the sight of me, and the more time that went by,
the more scared she'd have been." His eyes were on his
place mat, but I could tell he was seeing his mother's face,
framed in the kitchen window. "That's the worst part,"
he said finally. "When your own kin are afraid of ya." He
cocked his head and eyed me for a moment or two. "How
old are you, Missy—sixteen, seventeen?"

"Sixteen."

"That's young," he said. "But then, you're never too young to be on your own. I left home when I was fourteen."

"Fourteen!"

Sully shrugged. "What else was I gonna do? My daddy didn't want me home no more."

"Was it because of . . ."

"Nah. My daddy always used to say I wasn't right, but he never knew why. Aside from my granddad, I never did it in the house."

"And they never knew it was you?"

He shook his head. "I was keepin' watch over the body—that's how they used to do it back in the old country, you'd never leave the corpse alone in the room—but I told them that I'd had to take a leak and when I came back the body was gone. Everybody was terrible upset, but nobody blamed me. I was only ten, they said, I didn't know no better. My aunt took it into her head that he got up and wandered out of the house." He began to laugh, a low, rumbling chuckle at first, then a full-on howl. "She went knockin' on doors all up and down the road for miles, askin' had anybody seen her dead daddy." His laughter lifted me up somehow, and it made me forget who we were even as we were laughing about it. I laughed too. He laughed until he cried, and then we sat there for a few minutes in a comfortable silence, Sully dabbing at his eyes with his knuckles.

I thought of something. "Did you ever meet another girl who . . . ?"

There was a soft, rasping sound, like sandpaper on

wood, when the old man ran his hand over his stubbly cheeks. "Knew a couple of women," he said. "Long time ago now."

"How did you meet them?"

He shrugged. "Same way I met you."

"What sort of people did they eat?"

Sully cocked his head and squinted at me. "Eh?"

"I mean, did they eat people who were kind to them, or people who were mean to them, or . . . ?"

"Mix of both, I reckon."

I made one more attempt: "Do you know what happened to them?"

He shrugged again. "Like I said, Missy: I went my way, they went theirs."

The white cat ambled into the kitchen. I'd forgotten all about him, and I hoped he hadn't been in the room while Mrs. Harmon was getting eaten. Catching sight of the rope of hair, the cat sat on his haunches and began to bat at it. "Shoo!" Sully waved his hand. "Git! Go on!" Puss wasn't deterred until the man put out his boot and nudged him in the side. "You ever have a cat?"

"My mom said we couldn't have a pet. We moved a lot."

"Never liked cats." He sniffed. "Cats are only out for themselves."

I smiled. "Like most people, I guess."

Sully didn't answer. Puss had lost interest in the hair rope, but he had no intention of leaving us alone. He sat there on the linoleum, swishing his tail and looking from me to Sully, like he was part of the conversation.

"Dumb cat," Sully muttered. "Shoo!"

"I think he's hungry." I got up and opened a tin of cat food, and Puss rubbed against my legs as I spooned it into the bowl on the floor.

"That's it, y'see. Cats are only out for themselves."

Satisfied, Puss wandered out again, and for a few minutes I watched Sully weave. Mrs. Harmon had a lot of hair for an eighty-eight-year-old. "You really only eat people who're already dead?"

He nodded. "After a while I could kind of sniff it on somebody, if they was gonna die soon, or see it in their faces. Don't ask me how—it ain't a smell or a look I could describe to nobody. I just know." He dropped the hair rope in his lap, plucked an apple out of Mrs. Harmon's fruit bowl, pulled an army knife out of the chest pocket of his red flannel shirt, flicked it open, and began to peel off the skin in one long, twirling piece. "Used to feel like a vulture, parkin' myself outside somebody's house, but I don't think like that no more." He jabbed his knife in the air at me, making his point. "Can't help what you are, Missy. That's rule number one."

Sully cut a wedge out of the peeled apple and offered it to me on the tip of his knife. I was still a little grossed out at the thought of Mrs. Harmon on his hands—not to mention the hair of God only knew how many dead people—but I didn't want to offend him, so I took it.

"You heard of them islands in the South Pacific?" I nodded. "Some of them island tribes eat their dead, and it's a sacred thing. They make a feast of it." He cut another slice and popped it in his mouth, talking as he chewed.

"The dead man would've eaten his granddad's liver right off the spit, his daddy's pickled tongue, and his mama's heart in a stew, and now it's his turn, and if what's left of him could sit up off of that table and talk he'd tell you he'd want it no other way. He learned a lot of things over a long life, and his children think they can know them things too if they take him apart and eat him."

"That doesn't make sense," I said. "Why doesn't he just teach his kids what he knows while he's still alive?"

Sully laughed. "Wisdom can't be taught, girl."

"Is that what you do? Eat people and hope you learn something?"

"Nah," he said with a sniff. "I just eat 'em."

When the oven timer went off he got up, arranged the rope in a neat little coil on the yellow linoleum, and took the casserole out of the oven while I set the table. Sully laid the steaming dish at the center of the table and began spooning it out. The cheese was perfect, crusty on top and gooey underneath. He dug into the casserole like he hadn't eaten a morsel all day. I took seconds, then thirds. It was like a bunch of melted vegetables mixed into a mashed-up cheeseburger.

"Ah," he said. "That's mighty tasty. Never tastes the same way twice."

Contentedly full, I leaned back in my chair.

"You had your fill?" I nodded, and he kept eating until he was just scraping out the crusty cheddar along the lip of the dish. I'd never seen anyone show such a bottomless appetite, but there were hollows under his cheeks like he'd had nothing all his life but bread and water.

Sully got up and took our dishes to the sink. I looked over at him as he began to wash them. "Don't look so surprised, Missy. I always leave everything just like I found it, even if she don't know the difference."

When he was through with the dishes he took the tin of pear halves in white grape juice out of the cabinet and managed to open it after a moment or two struggling with the electric can opener. With his stained and gnarly fingers he pulled the pale, tender pieces out of the juice one at a time, laying them on a small baking sheet.

"What are you making now?" I asked as he turned on the broiler at the bottom of the oven.

"Car'melized pears." He slipped a chunk of butter into the frying pan and dropped in heaping spoonfuls of brown sugar as it melted. "Why have one sweet when you can have two?"

Once the sugar mixture had melted to his liking, he drizzled it onto the pears, sprinkled them with cinnamon and cloves, and tucked them in the broiler. Then he brought the carrot cake over to the table and cut himself a wedge as big as his head. "Want some?"

I shook my head. I did, but it wouldn't have felt right when Mrs. Harmon and I were meant to have it together. Sully gobbled up the cake, drank Mrs. Harmon's buttermilk straight from the carton, and went back to his weaving while the pears sizzled in the oven.

I took Mrs. Harmon's yarn and needles out of my bag and found a little pattern pamphlet for a baby cardigan at the bottom of her basket. There were cast-on instructions on the back, which I frowned over before giving up to watch Sully loop and tuck and wind the silver locks.

"Do you remember who all the different kinds of hair belonged to?"

He held up a section of the rope and pointed to it with a crooked pinky finger. "See this thick fuzzied-up bit here? That's what kids today call a dreadlock. Had a mighty tricky time weavin' them in, but I did it." He shook his head. "Found that boy drowned in his own spew." I cringed. "Had a lot of cleanin' up to do before I could eat that one. Still, a stomach tastes better when there ain't nothin' in it."

I wouldn't know. My eye caught on a length of red-gold hair a few inches down from the dreadlocks. It was the loveliest color I'd ever seen. "What about that one?"

"That one . . ." He paused. "She *meant* it."

It hit me then, the difference between us. I had victims. He did not.

I carried my dish to the sink and rinsed it out. "You said you were ten when your grandfather died?"

He nodded. "Why?"

"It just seems kind of old for your first one."

"Corpses ain't so easy to come by," he pointed out. "My daddy wasn't the undertaker."

"But you said he told you that you were different."

"I used to eat things," he said. "Gobbled up the fleece in my mama's basket faster than she could spin it. She knew my daddy would try roughin' it out of me if he found out, so she hid it from him. Went on for years. I'd tear up an old shoe and keep on chewin' 'til I could swallow.

Only the soft things. One time I ate a whole quilt my grandmother sewed in nineteen oh-two. Wouldn't eat nothin' that would give me away to the old man." He kept weaving as he talked, but he had this remote look in his eyes again, like he could see the past in a swirl of mist hovering over my right shoulder. "When my mama cut my sister's hair I swallowed the clippings straight off the floor like they were oysters. Gobbled up her rag doll, and she cried and cried. Too scared of me to say nothin' to my daddy." He paused. "I sure am sorry for that." Sully looked at me. "You ever eat somethin' you wasn't supposed to?"

I gave him a look. "Apart from that," he added, and I shook my head. "They got a name for it now," he went on. "A fancy word for when you can't help gobblin' up things that ain't meant to be eaten. Newspapers, dirt, glass. Hell, even poo. Makes you wonder if they don't got a name for this." He leaned back in his chair and rested his hands on his belly.

That gave me a thought. "Have you ever been to a doctor?"

Sully raised an eyebrow. "You ever been to the moon?"

I smiled as I rolled my eyes. "What I mean is . . . do you think it's hereditary?" His lips curled slowly into a cat-and-canary smile. It made me shiver. "What?" I said.

He leaned back in his chair and scratched the side of his neck, the smile fading. "I can't say for sure my grand-daddy was an eater, but I got my reasons for thinkin' he might have been."

I felt curiosity prickling beneath my skin. "What kind of reasons?"

"Thinkin' back over all the time we passed in the woods together . . . huntin', fishin', learnin' to get by in the wild . . . some memories are clear, and others are hazy. And I think maybe the hazy ones are hazy for a reason."

I thought I understood. It was kind of like how I knew that Penny Wilson had hair so blond it was almost white, and a long, sharp nose in a long face, and blue eyes a little too prominent to be pretty. "Like you might actually remember, or you might just be making it up?"

"Nah," he said. "I ain't makin' it up."

"What about your dad?"

Sully shot me a hard look. "What about him?"

I shrugged. "If your granddad was an eater, maybe . . ."

"Maybe nothin'," Sully retorted. "I never had nothin' in common with my daddy, and that's a fact." He rose and took the pears out of the broiler, spooned them into dessert dishes, and poured out the extra caramel sauce straight off the pan.

After he set the dish in front of me I thanked him, took a bite of pear, and sighed. The taste of the cloves and caramel mingled with the pears so perfectly. I decided I was done talking about dead people. "This is really good."

"Sure it's good," he said between bites. He wolfed his down in two or three seconds. "I never have just one sweet. Life's too short."

When we were finished Sully said, "I feel like a bit of music." He went into the living room, bent low on his heels, and began to browse the record collection in the glass-fronted cabinet under the front window.

"You got better taste than I'd have given you credit for," Sully said to Douglas Harmon's portrait on the mantelpiece. "He's got Bobby Johnson. One of the best guitar players of all time." He slid the record out of its sleeve and laid it on the turntable. "They say Bobby Johnson met the devil on the road one night, somewhere in Alabama, and the devil said, 'I'll teach you to play the blues better than anybody, and all it'll cost is your soul.' And Bobby Johnson made the bargain."

I sat down in the armchair by the fireplace as the music came on. It was a scratchy recording, the singer humming as he picked at the strings of his guitar, and when he began to sing I heard something untempered, something rich and unrestrained. "*Ah, the woman I love, took from my best friend, some joker got lucky, stole her back again . . .*"

Sully pulled a pipe and a pouch of tobacco out of his pack, stuffed a pinch of it into the bowl, and struck a match. He took a puff on his pipe.

"*When a woman gets in trouble, everybody throws her down. Lookin' for a good friend, none can be found . . .*"

The record ended, and I said, "There isn't any devil, you know."

"Why, you think he's only a story?" Sully threw back his head and laughed. "I'll tell you somethin'. Sometime I make a little game of going into bars, orderin' a round of drinks, and tellin' 'em all about me"—he cupped his hand to the side of his mouth, as if whispering on a stage—"only they don't know it's me. And all the boys say I got a mighty fine imagination. I tell 'em to watch behind 'em as they're walkin' home, lock the door, and look under the bed, and they just go on laughin'." He took the skipping needle off the record and turned it to the B side. "That's how stories start. We tell 'em about ourselves like they ain't true, 'cause that's the only way anybody's gonna believe us."

A memory of my own drifted up, of the time somebody stole the radio out of our station wagon and Mama made me go with her into the police station to report it. I must have been about twelve—the list of names on my heart wasn't that long yet—but I was terrified the cops would take one look at me and know what I'd done. There was a framed needlepoint above the door that said THE TRUTH WILL SET YOU FREE, and I remembered the man behind the counter noticing me looking at it and laughing at how ironic it was.

I was still thinking of that needlepoint when the phone rang. Sully didn't react, and the answering machine on the kitchen counter clicked on. He puffed on his pipe as we listened to the message. "Hi, Aunt Liddy, it's Carol. Just calling for a chat. I was thinking about driving down to Edgartown tomorrow for some shopping, and I thought I could take you out to lunch. Give me a call when you get this, okay? Lots of love, talk to you soon, bye."

Sully grunted and took the pipe from his mouth as the machine clicked off. "Where you headed after this?"

"Minnesota."

The man lifted a caterpillar eyebrow. "What you goin' to Minnesota for?"

"That's where my dad's from. And I don't know . . . maybe he's still there."

"Ain't you been listenin', Missy? I told ya, go pokin' through the past and you'll only come to grief."

"Isn't it better to know?" I pulled a ball of yarn out of the wicker knitting basket and ran my fingers over the soft wool. "You said you thought your grandfather was an eater. I think my dad is too." It was the first time I'd consciously thought it, let alone said it out loud, and I made myself shiver. "I want to know where he came from, and why he left us."

Sully shook his head. "It don't matter why your daddy left you, he left and that's that."

I teared up. I couldn't help it. "I don't have anywhere else to go."

"Ah, now," he said kindly. "I'm always movin' from place to place, but as long as I'm kickin', you got a home with me."

"I thought you said it was better not to make friends."

"I been known to change my mind." Sully blew a plume of smoke and paused to admire it as it dissipated. "What do you say?"

"Thanks." I plucked a tissue from a box on the side table and pressed it to my eyes. "I'll think about it."

The ticking clock reinserted itself into the silence, and Sully picked up the newspaper. Finally he said, "You better git to bed. We gotta be up early so her niece don't find us here."

I stood, lobbed the ball of yarn back into the basket, and picked up my rucksack. "Well," I said. "Goodnight, Sully."

He kept puffing on the pipe as he turned the page and scanned the headlines. "Sleep tight, Missy."

I changed into my pajamas, brushed my teeth, and went into the Spare Oom. As I was closing the door the white cat bounded out of Mrs. Harmon's room down the hallway and stuck his paw between the door and jamb, mewing like he wanted to be let in. "Sorry, Puss." I kneeled and gently pushed him back into the hallway. I'd never slept with an animal before, and I was afraid he'd keep me awake.

Something made me turn the key in the lock. If he was honest, he'd never know.

I flipped off the light and got into bed. The moonlight glinted off the sphinx on the night table and the faces of the cherubs carved along the headboard, casting lights in their little wooden eyes as if they were watching me. Watching *over* me. I missed Mrs. Harmon and wondered how long it would be before somebody slept in this spare bed again. Probably never.

Of course, I'd napped far too long that afternoon. Sleep wouldn't come. The dark was oppressive, and the silence covered me like a blanket I didn't need. When I finally drifted off I dreamed of the invisible man and his invisible knife, and through the fog I felt the pain wending its way back into my ear. *Knife, twist. Knife, twist.* He pressed the knife to my mouth.

In the morning I found another note on the kitchen table, but this one made me smile.

MISSY:

I got a feeling you won't take my advice to heart about not looking for your daddy. But if you change your mind, just come back to town and wait somewhere for me and I'll find you. Life with ole Sully is never dully.

SULLIVAN

P.S. Picked this up in my travels, thought you might like to have it.

Beside the note was a paperback book, the size of my palm and at least fifty years old. The crimson cover was stamped in silver: *RINGLING BROS. KEEPSAKE BOOK.* I opened it at random and found no words, only a red-and-black illustration of three tiny acrobats in midair. Two had big, curling mustaches, and the other wore red slippers that laced up to her knees. I turned the page, and another. *Aha,* I thought. *A flip book!* So I flipped, and the gentlemen on their trapezes flung the lady acrobat from one page to the next and back again. Maybe it's not so bad if a stranger knows you better than you think.

After a quick breakfast I said goodbye to the friends I'd made over the past twenty-four hours, the brass sphinx and the white cat and Mrs. Harmon at her Emerald City wedding. At the mantel my fingers hovered over the row of lovely old jewelry, and I picked up the cream and pink enamel locket. When I pressed the button, the lid popped open and there he was again, Mr. Harmon, smiling to the side. I closed the locket, unfastened the clasp, and put it around my neck. I knew I shouldn't take it—the jewelry, all of it, rightfully belonged to her niece—but I needed something to remember her by.

A few minutes later I boarded the local bus, and this time I knew I was going in the opposite direction of the Shieldses' house. I would never see my mother again, not even through a picture window.

There was nothing of interest in Edgartown now, so instead of looking out the bus window I played with the circus flip book. I closed my eyes and imagined what it must be like to sail through the air, pretending you could fly while you waited for someone to grab you by the ankles.

It was just before ten o'clock when I got to the Greyhound station. I went up to the counter, where a woman wearing too much lipstick sat filing her nails. "When's the next bus to Minnesota?" I asked. "I need to go to Sandhorn."

"That near St. Paul?"

"I don't think so."

"If you don't know where you're going, then how d'you expect me to help you?"

I wanted to grab that nail file and shove it up her nose. "I thought you'd be able to tell me where the nearest station is," I said.

"Look, kid. You can get yourself a map, or you can get on that bus to St. Louis that's pulling out of gate one in about a minute and a half. That's what I'd do, if I were you. Won't be another westbound bus 'til eight o'clock tonight."

The clerk was rude but sensible. I bought the ticket to St. Louis.

4

ore highways, more snoring strangers and queasy attempts at losing myself in a book, more meals out of vending machines. It took two days to get to St. Louis, so I had plenty of time to mull over all the strange and wonderful things Sully had talked about: sleeping rough and killing your own supper, getting thoroughly comfortable living out of a rucksack, devil's bargains, and telling the truth like it's only a story—that part I thought about for a long while, because you can accept it even if nobody else can.

Then I thought of how life might be once I found my dad, and it felt like unwrapping a peppermint candy I'd been saving for ages. I knew there had to be a good reason why he'd left us, because even though Mama never talked about him I knew she still loved him. Why else would she go on wearing his ring?

Hour after hour I stared out the bus window, imagining his face and his voice and his hands. He was half a head taller than Mama, and he still wore his wedding ring too, and he wouldn't wait 'til he was dead to tell me everything he knew. I even pictured how he would sign *Francis Yearly* on the credit card slip when he took me out to an Italian restaurant. My dad would teach me how to get on in the world, so it wouldn't matter that no one knew the truth about me. We would find friends like Sully, and that would be enough. My dad and I would live in a house with place mats and picture frames, and we would volunteer at a soup kitchen on Sunday mornings when everyone else was at church.

I was in a weird mood when I finally got off the bus—exhausted and elated at the same time, as if I knew exactly how to get to that castle I'd built in the sky. I only realized when I got in line to buy my next ticket that I had fifteen dollars left in my wallet.

How could I? How could I be so stupid?

It made sense, of course, from Mama's point of view. I wouldn't have needed more than a hundred dollars to get me from Cincinnati to Sandhorn. I'd wasted most of it going in the opposite direction.

I lugged my rucksack into a filthy restroom, locked myself in the last stall, and cried. I was nearly penniless and definitely homeless. Why hadn't I taken Sully up on his offer? Why hadn't I listened?

I wore myself out, then emerged from the restroom

with stinging eyes but a fresh sense of purpose. I'd get to Sandhorn the way any broke person would: by sticking out my thumb.

Out on the street, I asked the nicest-looking taxi driver I could find how best to hitch a ride to Minnesota. "I'd go up the street to the college," he said, pointing the way. "Good time to find a lift, with all the students going home for the summer."

After twenty minutes I came to the edge of the college campus, with tidy brick sidewalks and a bright green lawn beyond the open gate. There were students all over the place: walking from one hall to another, reading on park benches, and playing Frisbee. I fished a piece of cardboard out of a trash bin and wrote NEED A RIDE TO MINNESOTA. Then I sat down to wait. I tried to read, but the words danced, rearranging themselves on the page. Eventually I closed my book and thought of my dad and how we'd spend our first weekend together painting the walls in my new bedroom. Lavender or teal?

An hour later a shadow fell across my lap. "I'm driving home to Minneapolis," the girl said. "Can you help pay for gas?" She was tall and tanned and wearing a T-shirt that said MISSOURI STATE VOLLEYBALL.

I nodded, uncrossed my legs, and, wobbling a little, got to my feet.

"Cool," she said. "You're lucky, I was on my way out."

Her name was Samantha, and she wasn't interested in getting chummy, which was just as well. Like I said, I'd never had a girl friend.

We stopped for gas somewhere in Iowa, and when Samantha got back in the car she said, "It was twenty bucks. Can you give me ten?"

"I've only got fifteen dollars left."

"I hate to break it to you, but fifteen bucks isn't going to get you very far anyway. What are you going to do once you get to Minneapolis?"

"I'll just find another ride to Sandhorn."

Samantha gave me a funny look, then she started the engine and we got back onto the highway. I took out a five-dollar bill and tucked it in the ashtray, where she kept the spare change, but she didn't say anything. I'd told her I would help pay for gas, and it would have been mean of me to go back on it, even if she could have been nicer.

An hour later I told her I had to go to the bathroom, and she seemed annoyed. "You couldn't have gone when we stopped for gas?"

"I didn't have to go then."

We drove on in silence for a couple more miles, but when we passed a sign for Walmart she took the exit and pulled into the parking lot.

"Thanks," I said, and ran inside.

When I came out again I found my rucksack in an empty parking space. I couldn't believe it. I just stood there awhile staring at where her car had been. What was the point of giving her gas money if she was only going to leave me in the middle of nowhere?

I took out my wallet and counted my money again. Ten bucks and a smattering of dimes and quarters. The thought of hitching another ride made me want to lock myself back in the restroom and never come out.

Wait a minute, I thought. This wasn't my fault. What she'd done made no sense. Why offer me a ride and then turn me out?

Maybe she'd smelled it on me. None of the girls at school had ever liked me either.

I tried to take a deep breath and think of what I should do next. But I didn't want to do anything next. I didn't want to be here—I didn't want to be anywhere.

I pressed my fists to my eyes, and for a few minutes I forgot the world. I couldn't even think clearly enough to wish again that I'd gone with Sully. I didn't have any tissues so I wiped my cheeks and nose with the sleeve of my T-shirt, and all the while people were walking past me into the store. Some tried not to look at me, and others stared at me like I had three heads. I looked up at one man in a Cubs jersey. He turned as red as the logo on his shirt and hurried through the automatic doors.

Suddenly I thought of my mother, crying her heart out over the salad bowl in a kitchen I'd never see the inside of. I got up, dusted the grit off the backside of my jeans, and picked up my rucksack.

The gust of refrigerated air as I walked through the automatic doors almost dried my cheeks. A Walmart is a city unto itself, every department its own neighborhood, blue shopping carts gliding between them like cars. You could go for miles under those cold fluorescent lights, past the lawnmowers and paint chips and crib sets and lipstick displays. You could even sleep here, in theory anyway, on beds heaped with too many throw pillows.

In the cafeteria I stood at the long glass counter and surveyed my options: shrink-wrapped tuna fish on Wonder Bread; a sausage patty on an English muffin; and under a heating lamp, a red and white paper boat of macaroni and cheese dried to an orange crust on top. If I was going to spend half my remaining cash on food tonight, I wouldn't drop it here.

Candy. If I could only have a Snickers bar, I could forget all this. For a minute and a half I could pretend I was normal.

I rounded the corner of the candy section and stopped short. There was a man in his underwear teetering up the aisle. I've seen all kinds of weirdos at Walmart, and in the summer there are always men heading for the refrigerated section in their swimming trunks and flip-flops, but this guy was a whole new species.

Swimming trunks and cowboy boots would have been ridiculous enough, but he was wearing cowboy boots, a Stetson, a wifebeater, and a pair of tatty old boxer shorts you could kind of see through. There were long brown stains beneath the arms of his undershirt, like he'd drunk so much beer he'd begun to sweat it.

Maybe if he'd been old and drunk off his rocker the sight of him would've just been sad, but he was too young and too sober not to be totally creepy. He swung his basket as he walked—if *walked* was the word—and muttered to himself. "I don't gotta take this shit. I'm sick an' tired a' you blamin' me for *everything*, woman.

I'm gonna show you, oh boy, am I gonna *show* you, woman."

A recorded message came on the loudspeaker as the drunk man ranted to himself. *"Walmart Value of the Day! Family-size bottles of Tide detergent are buy one, get one free, for a limited time only!"*

He should take advantage of that one. Behind me a woman with a shopping cart turned into the aisle, and as she passed me I saw her catch sight of the drunken cowboy and freeze. *No,* I could almost hear her thinking. *It's too late to turn around.* He'd already seen her. So she moved down the aisle, cautiously, glancing up only to make sure she wasn't going to run into him with her cart.

But that was enough. "What'choo lookin' at?" he called to her. Well, she certainly wasn't going to say *A drunken moron,* so she didn't say anything. He swung his head around and stared at her with glassy eyes. "I *saaaaaaaid,* what'choo *lookin'* at, bitch?"

She froze, clenching the handlebar of her shopping cart with pale knuckles. She looked back at me, and I tried to smile sympathetically. We both glanced up and down the aisle, but no one in a blue polo shirt was coming to escort him out. It was too quiet beneath the elevator music on the loudspeaker, as if all the Walmart employees had gone on their dinner break at the same time.

"What, you deaf, bitch?" the drunk guy was shouting. "Hear *this,* you dumb ho?"

"Hey!" Now someone else was striding down the aisle

behind me. He passed me and stood in front of the woman's shopping cart. He had tousled dirty blond hair and was wearing a green baseball jersey, jeans, and work boots. "You can't talk to a lady like that. You're out of control, pal."

"Pal!" the cowboy scoffed. "I ain't your *pal*." There was spittle in the corners of his mouth. Yup. Rabid.

From the back I could tell the guy in the green jersey was older than I was—eighteen, maybe twenty. He gave the woman a look over his shoulder. Mouthing "Thanks," she turned and wheeled her cart out of the aisle. I should have left too, but you know how it is when somebody's behaving badly in public. You're riveted to the spot just waiting to see what will happen next.

The drunken cowboy reached for the boy in green, but he neatly ducked out of the way. "Now you listen here, you dumb-ass pretty-boy son of a bitch," the cowboy yelled, making another grab for the boy's shirt, "you ain't got no right to tell me what to do."

The boy turned his head and looked at me then, and a funny feeling ran clear through me. If he felt it too, he didn't let on. He turned back to the drunk guy and said, so calmly it gave me goose bumps, "You're right. But either way, I think we should take it outside." Without another glance at me he walked toward the back of the store, which struck me as odd, but the cowboy probably couldn't think that clearly even when he was sober. He stumbled after the boy in green, dropping his basket on the floor, but then he doubled back and picked up a six-pack of beer before staggering out of the aisle. I peeked in the overturned basket: beef jerky and a jumbo bag of Milky Way bars. A can of baked beans rolled out onto the white linoleum.

For a while I wandered through the aisles—garden tools, pet food, cosmetics—trying to calm down after what I'd seen, not just the crazy drunken cowboy but the boy in the green jersey too. I still felt weird, like when I found Mrs. Harmon and the floor fell away from my feet.

A mother and daughter were poring over the Maybelline display. "Here, how about this one," the woman said, handing her daughter a compact of pale blue eye shadow. "That'll go good with your eyes." The girl didn't look old enough to be wearing makeup. At least, Mama wouldn't have thought so.

I went back to the canned goods aisle, picked up a can of chickpeas, and put it down again. What was wrong with me? I needed to eat, and making a decision shouldn't require a spreadsheet. It wasn't like having ten bucks left would actually do me any good if I held on to it, like it could keep me fed beyond a couple of highway diner meals.

I didn't *have* to spend it. I'd never shoplifted before, and as I weighed the prospect I temporarily lost my appetite. I didn't want to be that kind of person, and anyway I wasn't hungry enough to shoplift.

That's true, I thought. *But I will be eventually.*

A can of chickpeas, such a stupid thing to steal—it only cost fifty-nine cents—but I figured taking something cheaper wasn't quite as wrong. There was no one else in the aisle. I stuffed the can into my rucksack and walked out of the canned goods section as casually as I could.

It would have been a mistake to leave the store right away, so I forced myself to keep wandering. I turned the corner into the stationery aisle, looked over a shelf of three-subject notebooks, and noticed something out of place: a shrink-wrapped sandwich. White bread, tuna salad, a colorless leaf of iceberg lettuce peeking out. It was like it had *Take me, you might as well* written on it in big red letters. I picked it up and stuffed it in with the chickpeas. I didn't even want the stupid sandwich, but it would fill me up and no one else would have bought it anyway.

And then, before I realized it, I was back in the candy aisle. There was nobody here now, and the drunken cowboy's shopping basket was still tipped over on the floor. I jumped when the next Walmart special came chirping out of nowhere: *"Get ready for the best Memorial Day ever with a brand-new Weber grill, fifty dollars off for a limited time only! Grill those burgers in style!"*

I headed back to the front of the store, past the cafeteria and the checkout aisles and the lawnmower and patio furniture displays. I thought about the drunken cowboy and the boy in green. I've been to a hundred Walmarts, and there's never an exit in the back.

I passed through the automatic doors and sighed. No alarm went off and nobody came running after me. I sat down on the curb past the shopping carts, but I didn't take out the sandwich. I wasn't all that hungry now that I actually had something to eat.

A fluorescent bulb flickered in the twilight. I heard the automatic doors open and close, and a shadow fell across my lap for the second time that day. I glanced up and saw a skinny boy in a blue polo shirt standing at the curb a few feet away from me. He worked here. "Hey," he said.

"Hey." *Man, I thought, his acne is really bad.* I turned back to my sneakers. I hate it when there's something wrong with somebody and you end up thinking of them as the girl or boy with the problem, as if the hundred extra pounds or the lazy eye is the only important thing there is to know about them.

The boy pulled out a pack of cigarettes and stuck one between his lips. "You got a can opener in your purse?"

My heart began to thud. "What?"

"That tin of beans." He struck a match and lit the cigarette, and for a second it made him seem older. He couldn't have been more than eighteen. He had the biggest Adam's apple I'd ever seen. I didn't say anything. "It's a strange thing to steal," he went on. "Usually girls take lipstick or nail polish."

"You were watching me?"

"I didn't see you do it. I just noticed the can peeking out of your bag as you were walking out."

"I'm sorry," I said. "If you have to tell your boss, I understand. I wouldn't want you to lose your job."

The boy shrugged. "My boss steals shit all the time. Especially stuff from the electronics department. We're supposed to send the floor models back after a while, but sometimes he'll tell the home office they're damaged so he can keep them. He must have a TV in every room in his house by now. Bathrooms too."

"That's crazy," I said.

"Lots of people steal and never get caught." He looked me in the eye as he took a drag on the cigarette. "I don't see why you should."

I might as well tell him about the tuna. "I took this too." I drew the sandwich out of my bag.

"Probably past its sell-by date." He shrugged again. "Doesn't count as stealing if it was going in the Dumpster."

"Oh." I pulled off the cellophane and offered him half, then felt stupid for doing it.

"Nah," he said. "Thanks though. My name's Andy. What's yours?"

"Maren."

"That's a nice name. I've never heard it before."

"Yeah," I said between bites of tuna fish. "Usually it's Karen."

"It's nicer than Karen."

"Thanks." I watched Andy take a puff on the cigarette and exhale through his nose. "You shouldn't smoke." Then I laughed. Me, calling out somebody else's vice!

He gave me a funny look. "Are you still hungry?"

I shook my head.

"Yeah, you are. You look like you haven't had much to eat lately."

"It lasts longer if you don't eat as much."

"Money, you mean?"

I nodded, and he paused. "Listen—I get off in an hour. Do you want to stick around?"

I nodded again. Andy was nice, and it wasn't like I had anyplace else to go. Maybe he had a couch I could sleep on. In my head a little voice said, *Watch it.*

He stamped out his cigarette, and I followed him back into the store. The can of chickpeas was burning a hole in my bag. I was amazed nobody took any notice of me.

Andy pulled out a pack of cinnamon gum and offered me a stick. "No, thanks," I said. Mama had never let me chew gum.

"I'm in receiving," he said, "so I'm usually in the back. I'll meet you by the TVs at nine, okay?" I nodded, and he disappeared through the swinging doors into the storage room.

I went to the home furnishings department and hid my bag under the dust ruffle on one of the show beds, and then walked to the canned goods aisle to return the chickpeas. I went through all the aisles of toys, watching kids beg for Pokémon cards or Spice Girls dolls from their parents. I passed by the little girls saying "Pleeeeeeeeeeeeeeeease," and everybody looked straight through me. It felt good to pretend I was invisible.

I wandered back to the electronics section. It was time for the nightly news, and President Clinton's face was on every television on the wall. Someday all these TVs would belong to Andy's boss. There was still half an hour left before Andy got off work, but I kept watching because I was tired of going up and down the aisles looking at all the things I couldn't buy.

They showed a piece of old footage, from the whole

impeachment thing earlier that year. "I did not have sexual relations with that woman," said the president.

"It's one thing to tell lies," I heard someone beside me say. "It's something else to do it on national television." It was the other guy from the candy aisle—the boy in green.

"Yeah." (Why couldn't I think of a better reply?)

"You from around here?"

"No. You?"

"No." He didn't say any more after that, so we just stood there for a while, in silence, watching the wall of TVs. Monica Lewinsky had hired new lawyers.

Someone tapped me on the shoulder, and I turned around. Andy was carrying a plastic bag. "Ready?"

"See you later," I said to the boy in green. I just wanted him to turn around and look at me, but he didn't take his eyes off the TV screen as I went by behind him. It seemed like he was trying to act like he didn't care. "See ya," he said.

Something nagged at me as I turned the corner out of the electronics section. That hat . . . He hadn't had a hat on before. And now he was wearing a Stetson.

Before we left I went back to the bedding department for my rucksack. I walked a few steps behind Andy to the far end of the parking lot, to a gold Chevy Nova loaded with bumper stickers. MEAN PEOPLE SUCK. FOREVER GRATEFUL, FOREVER DEAD. WHEN I GET MY POWERS BACK, YOU WILL ALL GROVEL BEFORE ME.

He unlocked the passenger's-side door first and handed me the bag. "I'm not going to take you anywhere," he said.

"Not unless you want me to. I just thought we could sit for a while and you could eat and we could talk."

I stashed my rucksack in the backseat, sat in the front, and opened the grocery bag in my lap. He'd gotten me a snack-size package of Oreos, a banana, a carton of cherry yogurt (spoon included), and a shrink-wrapped corn muffin. Andy slid into the driver's seat and closed the door. I thanked him, and he watched me eat. I offered him an Oreo, and for the second time that night I felt like an idiot for asking him if he wanted food that didn't belong to me.

As I was eating the banana, I nudged a book on the floor with my foot. I picked it up: *The Master and Margarita*. On the cover was a grinning cat holding a pistol. I opened the book, flipped to a random page, and read:

Everything will turn out right, the world is built on that.

For other people, maybe. Definitely not for me.

"I'm reading that for Russian lit," Andy was saying. "It's really good. Do you like to read?" I nodded. "What's your favorite book?"

"I have a lot of favorites. I like *The Phantom Tollbooth*, and *A Wrinkle in Time*, and the Narnia books." *Spare Oom.* I shivered.

"Are you cold? I can turn on the heater."

"No, thanks. I'm all right."

"Well, if you like those books then you'd probably like *The Master and Margarita*. Have you read Gormenghast?" I shook my head. "That's one of my favorites. It's a trilogy. If I see you again, I'll give you my copy."

"You're being too nice," I said as I polished off the yogurt and tied up the plastic bag with my trash inside. I looked at him and waited.

He reached over and took my hand, lacing his fingers through mine and letting them rest on the console between our seats. "Can I do this? Is this all right?"

"That's all?" I asked. His breath smelled like Fritos and Pepsi and cigarettes.

He nodded. His hand was warm and sweaty, but it felt nice. For a moment—just the one moment—I felt safe.

"No." I took my hand away and tucked it in the crook of my knee. "You shouldn't."

"It's okay." He ran his fingers along the bumps on the steering wheel. "You don't have to do anything."

"I don't *want* to do anything."

"That's okay. I just want to sit here and hold your hand."

"You want more than that though."

He shrugged. "Every guy wants more than that." He hesitated. "But it's not only that."

"No?"

"Listen, I know what it's like. I'm on my own too. Left home last year—I had to. My dad is horrible when he's drunk. I moved out after he put me in the hospital."

"What did he do?" Andy lifted his shirt, and I gasped at the sight of a wobbly pink gash across his ribs. "Broken beer bottle." He paused. "I keep trying to get her to leave him, but she won't go."

"I'm sorry."

"Not your fault the man who spawned me is a jerk." If a laugh could slice an eardrum, this one came close. I knew my father would never do something like that. Mama had married a good-hearted man.

Andy sighed. "Anyway, I've got an extra futon in my apartment, in case she ever changes her mind. You know what they say—*Better the devil you know?* It's the thought of being on her own that terrifies her. Like life could actually be worse than it is now."

"She wouldn't be on her own," I said. "She'd have you."

Andy gave me a look then—kind, and grateful for my kindness, but making it clear I was missing the point. "Do you ever stop what you're doing and go, *This is my life?*" He was staring at me. He could see I was ready to cry, and that was answer enough.

"I go to this shitty little community college in Williston, and then I go to work in *this* hellhole"—he jerked his thumb at the blue Walmart sign lit up over his left shoulder—"and *then* I go home to a shitty little apartment over an all-night laundromat in Plainsburg. It sucks, you know? It really sucks. And then you show up and I think, *Yeah. She could understand me.*"

I folded my arms tightly over my chest. "You don't know me."

"It doesn't really take that long to learn everything you need to know about a person."

"I stole a can of chickpeas, Andy. That makes me a thief."

"That's just it. You're even more desperate than I am." He was still staring at me. "You're beautiful," he said.

"No, I'm not."

"No, you really are. Girls think because they don't look like models on magazine covers they aren't beautiful. They airbrush everything, you know. It's all bullshit."

"I know," I said. "It's not that."

"What is it, then? You've listened to me. Now let me listen to you."

"Please." I shook my head. "Please don't be so nice to me."

He lifted a hand to my cheek and stroked it. "Why shouldn't I?"

I smelled him—the corn chips and cinnamon gum and cigarette smoke—and it was making me twitch. I had to get out of there. I reached for the handle and heard the click as he pressed a button and locked all four doors.

"If you really want to go, then fine, I won't keep you," he said. "But I know you don't *have* anyplace to go. So why won't you let me help you?"

"You don't understand, Andy. I've done horrible things, and if you don't let me leave I'll end up doing it to you too." I put my hand on the lock, but he grabbed my shoulder and pulled me toward him.

"Please," he whispered. "Just let me hold you." As he kissed my neck, he ran his fingers down my leg to my knees and gently pried them apart.

Your mother.

I'm sorry.

She'll never leave him now.

He could have guilt-tripped me. He could have made

me do things for him, but he didn't. He was alone, and he knew I didn't have anybody either, so to him it made merciful good sense that we should sit in his car and eat Oreos and hold each other's hands. But as I ate, a little voice inside me whispered, *Everyone is lonely, you can't do something just because you're lonely.*

I tripped on the pavement coming out of the car and skinned my knee. I had no idea how many people might have seen me—I'd never done it out of doors before apart from Luke, never in such a public place—and I ran out of the parking lot into the night like there was someone right behind me. I was so out of my head that I couldn't have heard them even if they *had* been there.

The Walmart had gone up in the middle of the cornfields, so there was nowhere to run except back to the highway. It had to be ten o'clock, but there was still a lot of traffic. A hot gust of air blew the hair off my forehead as a Mack truck hurtled past.

All thoughts of finding my dad drifted out of my head like the smoke from Andy's cigarette. It would be so easy, wouldn't it—to take one step into the road and let the next truck rid the world of me? The driver wouldn't be hurt, and no one would blame him. They'd be able to tell I wasn't hit from behind.

It was a beautiful plan. It was simple. It made sense.

I didn't have long to wait. I stepped into the road and let the headlights flood my vision. The driver came down heavy on the brakes and the horn. I was dazzled by the lights but forced myself not to raise my hands to my eyes, and in another second or two I felt the red heat of the grille on my face—

Getting hit by a truck didn't feel like I thought it would. I felt myself yanked sideways, as if gravity were giving out. I came down hard on the pavement as the truck tore by, the driver still pounding his fist on the horn and shouting obscenities out the open window.

"Are you insane?" I heard someone say, and for one wild second I thought the voice belonged to Andy. He was all right. I hadn't done it.

I felt a hand under my arm, and gasped. "Sorry," he said as he grabbed me gently by the inner elbow and drew me up. "There wasn't time to organize a smoother landing." Not Andy. It was the boy in green. He brushed some grit from my shoulder. "You're gonna hurt tomorrow, but not as bad as if that truck had gotten you."

I wouldn't have to wait until tomorrow. I hurt *every-where*. I put my hand to my lips and remembered what I must look like. I covered my mouth and turned away, but he laid a gentle hand on my shoulder. "You're all right."

"I'm not," I mumbled through my fingers. "I'm really not."

The boy put an arm around my waist and helped me over the metal barrier and back down the embankment. "You did something to that man." My side hurt when I talked, but I had to ask. "That horrible drunk guy who came into the store in his boxer shorts."

"Yeah," he said.

"Where did you get that hat?" But I knew where he'd gotten that hat.

With his free hand he took something jingly out of his back pocket and dangled it where I could see it. "Same place I got these keys."

"It was *his* hat."

He put the keys back in his pocket and laid his hand on the Stetson as if to reassure himself it was still on his head. "He won't be needing it anymore."

We reached the bottom of the embankment and walked across the empty parking lot. I had so many thoughts, but none of them would connect. What had he done to that man?

"Don't worry," he said. "The only person who saw what you did is me, and believe me, I'm not telling anyone. Nobody's noticed his car yet. We're all right."

We're all right.

"You . . ."

We stopped walking then, and for what felt like ages we stood there looking at each other. "Yeah," he said finally. "Me too."

I was just waiting for him to come out and say it before I let the relief of not being alone anymore take me over. It felt so strange to have this second chance at friendship when every other good thing in the world had fallen away from me. "How did you . . . ?"

"The men's room. Followed him in and locked the door."

"I *knew* there was something weird going on. You were leading him away from the exit." He gave me a half smile.

"Are you sure no one else saw?" I asked.

"I'm sure. But we'd better get out of here."

So I hurried, hobbling a little, back to Andy's car. The boy followed me, and when I opened the back door to get my rucksack he opened the driver's-side door, pulled a crumpled shopping bag from under the seat, and began gathering Andy's clothes, and the other bits. On the floor was the book about the pistol-wielding cat he'd been reading for his Russian lit class, bookmarked midway through with a receipt for a sixteen-ounce Pepsi and a chicken sandwich. *He'll never know how it ends.*

I tucked the book in my bag as the boy pushed down the mess—*my* mess—with his bare hand before double knotting the bag handles. "That your book?" I shook my head. "You take things too, then."

"Yeah," I mumbled. "Thanks for doing that."

"Someday you can return the favor." When he smiled there was a twist in it. "We'll toss it someplace else." He hooked the bulging plastic bag with his index finger, slammed the door, and strode away from the store, toward the drunken cowboy's black pickup truck parked out of the radius of the floodlight. To no one's surprise, the cab reeked of beer and cigarettes. We climbed into the front seat, and he turned the key in the ignition. He knew how to drive a stick.

"Where are we going?"

He plucked an envelope from a stack of papers on the dashboard and tossed it in my lap. It looked like an electric bill. *BARRY COOK*, it said. *5278 Route 13, Pittston, IA.*

We drove in silence for a few minutes, taking the exit for Route 13, before the boy said, "Hey, what's your name?"

"Maren. What's yours?"

"Lee."

"Where are you from, Lee?"

He shot me a wary look. "Does it matter?"

I shrugged. "I was just making conversation."

"Sorry. Haven't had one of those in a while, unless you count that drunken cowboy toad. Guess I'm a bit rusty."

"Well, can I ask how you got to that Walmart? I mean, didn't you leave your car?"

"Nope. Clutch blew out on my last ride five miles up the highway. I was just as stuck as you were."

"How do you know *I* was stuck?"

Lee smiled. "'Cause we'd have taken your car instead."

I rolled down the window and let the cool night air hit me full in the face. I thought of Sully. "Why now?" I asked, half to myself.

"What do you mean?"

"All my life I thought I was the only one," I said, "and then I meet two other people like me in less than a week."

"Hold up a second. Who's the *other* one?"

"I can't tell you the whole story now," I murmured. "My head hurts."

I felt him shrug. "You can tell me when you feel better."

"It's just so weird," I went on. "None, and then two."

"And who knows how many more."

"Really? You think there are lots of us?"

He shrugged again. "It's like anything else, I guess. You've never heard of it, and then once you have you see it everywhere you look."

I gave him a doubtful look.

"You find what you expect. That's what I'm getting at."

"Maybe." I was thinking of a history teacher I'd had three schools ago, when we lived in Maine. Miss Anderson was young and pretty and nice enough, but she wasn't anybody's favorite. One day, after the last bell rang, she was going over my chapter test at her desk. I was looking over her shoulder, and when she turned and smiled up at me I could've sworn I smelled it on her breath, the rotten old-penny smell hiding under the mouthwash. I snatched up my test paper and ran out of the room, and the next day she acted like nothing had happened.

I convinced myself I'd imagined it. People didn't *like* her, but they didn't avoid her the way they avoided me, and she didn't wear black. We're all different, I knew that now.

gain, no surprise: the drunken cowboy had lived alone. It was a tiny house, just a den with a kitchen beyond it, and a bathroom and bedroom off to the left. The whole place smelled like he'd done nothing but smoke and drink in it every day for a hundred years.

I dropped onto the sofa and looked around. The den was done in fiberboard paneling, and behind the TV there was a floor-to-ceiling KISS poster in a dented metal frame. There were empty beer cans and Marlboro packs strewn across the coffee table along with a stack of grease-stained pizza boxes. I found a magazine opened to a spread of naked women, peroxide blondes who might have been made of plastic, each of the pictures captioned with a 900 number. I closed the magazine and threw it behind a La-Z-Boy in the corner.

Lee was in the kitchen, flipping through a pile of mail on the table, parting the curtains and looking out the side window. Even from where I sat I could see the dishes in the sink were covered in mold. He opened the freezer. "There's a box of Ellio's in here," he said. "But you're not hungry, are you?"

I shook my head.

"Yeah," he said. "Me neither."

I took my toiletries and pajamas out of my rucksack and pointed to the bathroom door. "Do you mind if I . . . ?"

"Nope. Go right ahead." He grinned at the idea of telling me I could do this or that, like this was his house, and I smiled a little as I closed the door behind me.

Sure enough, there was a red stain around my mouth, down my chin, and between all my teeth. It didn't matter that he did it too, I hated that he'd seen me like this. I brushed my teeth four times and gargled with Listerine again and again, but I could still taste Andy under the mint.

There were several pairs of boxer shorts crumpled on the tiled floor, right where Barry Cook had stepped out of them, and the bath mat looked like it had never seen the inside of a washing machine. Two little turds and a half dozen cigarette butts floated in the toilet bowl. I took off my T-shirt and shorts and rubbed at them with a nub of soap under the faucet, and then I hung them over the towel rack to dry.

I looked over my body in the mirror. There was a bruise forming along the bottom of my rib cage, another on my shoulder, and a cut on my forehead. I looked like I'd been in a street fight. I stepped into the bathtub and turned on the showerhead. The hot water felt good, and I turned it hotter and hotter, as though I could get it hot enough to wash away the things I'd done. My knee stung as I soaped out the grit.

I patted myself off with the cleanest-looking towel I could find on the door hooks, and I looked at myself in the mirror again. Could I be pretty to anyone besides Andy? Now there was a laugh. What difference did it make?

When I came out of the bathroom Lee was sitting at the kitchen table, chewing on a stick of beef jerky and reading Barry Cook's mail. "I thought you weren't hungry."

"Habit." He shrugged, his eyes still on the letter. "He's from Kentucky," he said as he chewed. "That explains the accent. Hasn't been back to see his parents in ten years." Lee shook his head. "This is from his mom. She says his dad's got cancer. Postmarked four months ago. He never opened it." He took another bite of jerky.

I found the remote, plopped down on the sofa, and turned on the television. I watched two men pace off amid the tumbleweeds, turn to face each other, and fire their pistols. Lee sat down in the La-Z-Boy, noticed the porn magazine splayed on the carpet, picked it up, flipped through it for a second or two, and tossed it back on the floor.

One man was lying in the dirt, and a woman of ill repute was weeping over his corpse. "Are you watching this?" I asked.

"You're the one who turned it on."

I flipped it off again and dropped the remote into the mess on the coffee table. "Why are we here, anyway?"

"Did you have someplace else to be?"

I wrinkled my nose. "Please tell me we're not staying here tonight."

"Nobody's making you," he said. "You can do whatever you want." He slumped back in the chair. "Look, I know we've only known each other for an hour, but I hope you know I have no intention of staying here longer than one night."

I looked at him.

"Sheesh, I know I'm never gonna win Citizen of the Month, but would you give me *some* credit? It's late and we need a place to stay."

"You've done this before," I said.

"So have you."

"How do you know?"

"I don't. But I don't see how you can be on your own and not do it."

"You're right," I sighed. "But it wasn't like this before. I was invited."

He cocked an eyebrow.

"It's true." I picked at my fingernail. "I'll tell you about it some other time."

"We've got time now."

"Is this . . . how you live?"

"Not every night. But yeah, sometimes."

He wasn't looking at me, but I felt like he was looking

me over. "Well, I don't know about you," I said, "but I need this day to be over already."

I sat on the edge of the waterbed, took out my journal, and added Andy's name to my list. Lee appeared in the doorway, and when he made a running leap onto the mattress it rolled and sloshed beneath him. "A waterbed!" He turned onto his back, folded his arms behind his head, and smiled at me. "Now all we need is a mirror on the ceiling."

I felt the warmth creeping into my cheeks, because if we had been different people—*normal* people—what he'd just said would have meant something. I lay down on the bed beside him, not too close but not at the very edge either. Being that near to him made me feel good. We were safe with each other, safe from each other. My ribs ached, but that sort of pain was easy to live with.

I must have been staring at him because he inched toward the far side of the bed and said, "What?"

I yawned. "I'm wondering if I made you up."

He didn't answer, just rolled over onto his back to stare at the ceiling, and the waterbed rippled beneath us. I closed my eyes and pretended we were drifting at sea. A ship rocking gently as a cradle on still water. The far-off horizon, blue on blue. A mermaid on a rock, running a comb made of shell through her silvery hair.

A little while later I opened my eyes. "Do you remember your first time?"

"Yeah. You?"

"I was too little. I think I can remember it sometimes, but I don't think it's real."

"Why, did somebody tell you about it? Your mom?"

I nodded. "When I got older I asked why she never went anyplace like the other mothers. She said she couldn't ever leave me with anybody—not after what happened."

"Yeah," he said. "Mine was the babysitter too."

Lee wasn't beside me when I woke up. I found him on the sofa in the den, snoring softly with his mouth wide open, and felt a pang of what felt suspiciously like disappointment.

I went into the kitchen and opened the fridge, but all I found was beer and ketchup. I took the box of Ellio's out of the freezer, turned on the toaster oven, and laid four squares of pizza on the rack.

A moment later someone pounded on the door. I dropped to a crouch on the grimy linoleum, my heart in my throat. This was it.

"Barry!" a woman shouted. "Where's the check, Barry? Do you even care if your daughter has enough to eat?"

I sighed. No reckoning for us today—nor for Barry, come to think of it. Maybe Lee had done him a favor. I could see her, whoever she was, squinting through the ruffled red curtain across the front window. She couldn't see Lee on the sofa, or at least she couldn't tell he wasn't Barry. I caught a glimpse of disheveled dark hair and darting eyes.

"I know you're home, you asshole!"

Lee opened his eyes, looked at me, dropped quietly off the sofa onto the carpet, and came over to join me.

The screen door hinges screeched in protest as she pounded on the front door. "Open up, you useless piece of shit!" She jiggled the knob, and I was really glad I'd locked it the night before.

"Look." He pulled back the curtain on the side window and pointed to the Subaru hatchback in the driveway. "She's got her kid in the car. Jesus."

I thought back over the rest of the house. There were no toys, no board books, no tiny T-shirts or Velcro shoes. His child had never stayed there.

"What should we do?" I whispered. There was another door at the back of the kitchen, but a chain-link fence ran around the backyard and I knew we couldn't get away without her seeing us.

"You stupid, lazy-ass son of a bitch!" She kicked the door and gave the screen door one last slam. "You're not gonna get away with it this time, Barry. I'm coming back with the cops!"

We heard her get into her car and drive off. Then we gathered our things and went outside. "Shit," Lee said. She'd slashed one of the front tires.

"What are we going to do?"

He hopped up onto the truck bed, bent over, and picked up a spare tire. "Had it together enough to have a spare. Which is kind of surprising, knowing Barry as we do." Lee smirked to himself. "Good thing she was too pissed off to notice it was back here. Gimme a hand?"

He passed me the tire and opened the cargo box to look for the tools he'd need. He found the jack and lug wrench and hopped down off the flatbed.

"What if she comes back while you're working on it?"

He laid the tools on the asphalt and pried off the hubcap. "Around here it takes at least twenty minutes to get anyplace. I can change this in seven minutes flat."

"Can you really?"

I watched his jaw clench as he pumped up the jack. "Go ahead and time me."

"I believe you," I said. I didn't time him, but seven minutes seemed about right. He worked quickly, with confidence in every movement. I wondered if his dad was a mechanic.

"We'll have to get a new tire, but I think we should drive a ways first. Can't have anybody recognizing this truck."

He left the slashed tire in the driveway. We got inside and Lee turned the key in the ignition. "I need to go home," he said.

"Where's home?"

"A place called Tingley, in Virginia. Just over the Kentucky border. Where did you say you were headed?"

"Minnesota."

"You in a hurry?"

I shrugged. I thought I did a pretty good job of keeping my hope under wraps.

"I really do need to get back, even if just for a few hours," he went on. "Then I can take you where you need to go. It's a lot of driving, but I'm up for it if you are."

I thrilled to the ends of my fingertips. I couldn't help it. "You mean . . . you want me to come with you? Back to Virginia?"

"Unless you got something better to do," he said dryly.

I wiped away my smile with the back of my hand.

"I'm not saying we're friends or anything. I just think it's good to have someone to look out for you."

"Isn't that what a friend is?"

"Wouldn't know," he said. "Never had one."

"Sure you have."

"Why? How many friends have *you* had?"

I looked out the window. "I make friends," I said. "I just can't keep them."

I felt him flick me a look. *That's what I thought.*

"Shoot," I said. "I left the pizza in the toaster oven."

For several miles we drove in silence. A flock of birds came whirling up out of a meadow ringed in fir trees. Lee glanced over. "You said the last time you'd stayed in some-body's house you were invited."

"You want to hear the whole story?"

"We got plenty of time." When he yawned, a long, ex-travagant yawn, it made him look for a second like he was six years old. "But you should start at the beginning. If you start telling me a bunch of stories all out of order I'm gonna get confused." He shot me a sideways glance. "Where you from?"

"I was born in Wisconsin, but we moved all over."

"Oh," he said. "I get it."

"I went to Pennsylvania after my mom left. I figured she'd gone to her parents' house." I paused. "I never met my grandparents. But they sent her birthday and Christmas cards, and one time I saved the envelope."

"Was she there?"

I nodded.

"Did you talk to her?"

"No."

He gave me a sympathetic look. "Prob'ly best."

We stopped for breakfast at a diner along the highway and ordered eggs, bacon, and home fries from a waitress with a smoker's rasp who kept calling us both "hon." She was probably half as old as she looked. Lee ordered a coffee so I did too, even though I'd never really liked the taste when Mama let me try it.

Once the waitress had brought our mugs I began to tell him about Mrs. Harmon, how I'd met her at the supermarket and helped her with her groceries and how she'd fed me and promised to teach me how to knit. The coffee tasted bitter even with one of those tiny white cups of half and half, so I dumped in a second and gave it a stir. I told him about going for a nap, getting up again and finding her, *you know*, and then getting up again and seeing Sully bent over her. I was very careful with the words I used. I never forgot we were in public. Lee didn't comment, but I could tell he was listening to me— really listening. No matter what he called himself, I knew he was my friend.

Our breakfast came. "Never expected to meet somebody like me," Lee said as he munched on a slice of bacon.
"Can you imagine how surprised I was when I walked out
into the parking lot and saw you in that guy's car?"

I dropped my eyes and wrung my paper napkin. "Please
don't remind me."

"You never did it in a car before?" He reached for another slice. "Don't be embarrassed. After a minute nobody
can see what you're doing with all the windows fogged up.
I just happened to catch you at the start."

I felt myself getting hot in the cheeks again. We'd
only met yesterday and I knew hardly anything about
him, but we understood each other as we talked around
the bad thing we both did. Somebody eavesdropping
from the next booth over would have thought I was the
kind of girl to do things with boys in the backseat of a
car, and for a second I wished I *was* that kind of girl.
Better a slut than a monster.

I cleared my throat. "You've really never met anybody
else who . . . ?"

"Nope," he said. "You're the first."

"You would be too, except for Sully."

"What was he like, anyway? Did you get along?"

"Yup, pretty well." I mopped up an egg yolk with a
slice of toast. "He's all right. Weird, but all right."

"Guess it's easy to get weird when you're traveling on
your own. What sort of eater is he?"

"That's just it," I said slowly. "He isn't like us. He says
he can smell it on somebody, when they're about to die,
and *then* he . . . you know."

Lee raised an eyebrow. "And you believe him?"

"He didn't give me any reason not to." I frowned. "That's how it happened with Mrs. Harmon. That morning he saw us on the bus, and he just knew."

He sipped pensively at his coffee. "There are all kinds, I guess. It's funny how I never thought to wonder about any of it before." Lee set down his mug and ran a finger along his plate to catch a few stray bits of bacon. "How come you and he parted ways?"

"He said I could go along with him, but I wanted to find my dad first."

"Your dad's the reason you're going to Minnesota?"

I nodded.

"You think your father was one of us, and that's why he had to leave you?"

I nodded again, but when he put it that way I felt a little foolish, like it was much too tidy an explanation.

"How do you know he's in Minnesota?"

"I don't. I just know it's where he's from."

"Might take you a while to find him, then. *If* you find him."

It hadn't occurred to me that I wouldn't find my dad. I couldn't afford to think like that, so I thought of how he would play Beatles records for me on weekend mornings as he cooked us a breakfast like the one I'd just had, only better. Absently, under my breath, I hummed the chorus of "Eleanor Rigby." The waitress came by, and Lee smiled up at her as she refilled his coffee. She walked away and he took a swig, his eyes on the Formica.

"So why are you going home?" I asked. "Just visiting your family?"

"Sort of. I've promised to give my sister some driving lessons before she takes her test."

"Do you get home often?"

"Not often, no."

"How long have you been on your own?"

"Left when I was seventeen."

"How old are you now?"

"Nineteen." He paused and looked me over like he was seeing me for the first time. "What are you—fifteen? Sixteen?"

"Sixteen," I replied stiffly. Looking younger couldn't be a good thing when you were out on your own. "What's your sister's name?"

"Kayla. She's a good girl." I could almost see him weighing the facts in his head and separating them into piles—what to tell me, what not to. "We got different fathers," he said finally. "My mom, well . . . she's like that."

"Why did you leave?"

"Why d'you think?"

I leaned forward and lowered my voice. "I can't see how you were a danger to them."

"Doesn't matter. I know what I am." He downed his coffee, raised his eyebrows, and tilted his head toward the door.

We paid our bill and climbed back into the truck. Lee switched on the radio and fiddled with the dial until he found a song he could drive to. "You like Shania Twain?"

"Sure." It was a bright sunny morning now. We passed

field after field of freshly turned soil, the air filled with the peaceful drone of a tractor. The world felt new again. I thought of Barry Cook's baby daughter and hoped her mother wasn't always that angry. I hoped she'd find another man, a nice man, somebody who didn't drink too much and curse at strangers in the candy aisle.

We were into Illinois when Lee decided it was safe to stop for a new tire. We parked at a service station, and he went inside.

I kicked at an empty pack of Marlboros and looked around the inside of the truck. Disgusting, of course. Not only had Barry Cook been King of the Fast-Food Drive-In, he apparently couldn't tell the difference between his truck and a garbage can. Every time he finished a meal he tossed the take-out bag on the passenger's-side floor. The only nasty thing I couldn't blame on Barry Cook was the white and blue Walmart bag stuffed under the driver's seat.

It looked like we'd be spending the better part of our days in here, so I figured I might as well tidy it up. I scrounged up a plastic bag and started collecting the cigarette packs, McDonald's burger wrappers, and empty soda cups. I'd gathered three bulging bags' worth by the time I got out of the truck to toss them in the Dumpster along with the remnants of Andy's clothes.

Lee came out and suggested we go for some necessaries while we were waiting on the mechanic. From a hardware store across the road he bought a ten-gallon water canister, and the owner let him fill it at a pump out back. There was also a Dumpster brimming with wood scraps, and while the canister was filling up, Lee peered inside and fished out a big piece of plywood.

"What's that for?"

"Truck bed."

"Huh?"

"You'll see."

When the mechanic was finished, Lee took out Barry's wallet to pay the bill and we went back out to the truck.

"Wait a minute," I said. "Did you change the license plates?"

"Got them changed, for an additional fee." He laughed a little. "Otherwise we can't keep driving it."

I raised an eyebrow. Lee looked at me and laughed again. "And just who crowned *you* queen of all that's good and proper?"

By nightfall we were two hours into Kentucky. "How do you feel about sleeping out of doors? There's a state park entrance not too far from here. It's safe. I've slept there before."

"What do you do when it's cold out?"

He smiled. "Head south."

We took the turnoff for the state park, but I didn't see any signs for campsites. Lee pulled into a small lay-by in front of a signboard of the local flora and fauna, with blue arrows along the various walking routes you could take to appreciate them. "Do you have a tent?" I asked.

"Don't need one. We can sleep in the back."

When he'd said *truck bed* I hadn't realized he meant it literally. "What if somebody finds us?"

"They won't. We'll be gone first thing in the morning."

"Why plywood though?"

"Even in the summer the metal can get pretty cold at night. No sense buying a piece of foam—it'll fall to pieces in no time and it's not that much more comfortable anyway."

"You think of everything," I said, and he shrugged.

"Once you find yourself out and alone without the things you need, you get practical pretty fast." I watched him draw all sorts of useful things out of his rucksack: a sleeping bag and a spare blanket, a flashlight, a tin pot, a fistful of Bic lighters ("Mementos," he said with that twist in his lip), and a tiny propane camp stove. "How's bean soup sound for dinner?"

"Perfect," I said. Like magic, two tin cups, two spoons, and a packet of soup mix appeared out of the rucksack, which was still quite full. Lee laid everything out on an old picnic table scarred with the initials of people who were, most likely, no longer in love. The forest was alive with the hum of the cicadas. In the gathering darkness my new friend cooked our meal while I grabbed his flashlight so I could write in my journal.

"Lee?"

"Yeah?"

"What were you doing in Iowa?"

"Do you always ask this many questions?"

"Pretty much." I paused. "If you ever feel like ditching me, will you please just say so?"

Lee cocked his head. "What kind of a question is that?"

I told him about Samantha, hoping he'd say he'd never feel like ditching me. He only said, "I don't like people who go back on their word," but that seemed as good as a promise.

Once it was good and dark we settled onto the flatbed—Lee gave me his sleeping bag, folding the spare blanket into a pallet for himself—and for a little while we talked about things that had nothing to do with a lost father, or the hazards of hitchhiking, or things that weren't meant to be eaten. He held up a finger to trace constellations he made up as he went along—a giraffe, a blimp, a chocolate-chip cookie—which reminded me of Jamie Gash, and it was my fault our conversation petered out into awkward silence. Again I was the first to fall asleep, not that I slept well, and again Lee wasn't beside me when I woke up. My brain jangled inside my head from lying on the plywood all night.

Lee was sitting on the picnic table, boiling water for coffee on the camp stove. He handed me a steaming tin cup and we drank quickly, in silence, before we got back in the truck and hit the road. I looked up at the brightening sky and thought of my dad. Francis Yearly was out there someplace—somewhere behind us, but not for long. In that moment I knew for sure he'd only left because he believed I'd be safer that way. "Did you ever go looking for your father?" I asked.

"Nope. No way to find him even if I wanted to."

"Don't you ever think about it though? Like if there was some way to find him—would you do it?"

"Nah. If we ever met he'd only end up dead."

I laughed, and so did he, but his laughter fell away into a pensive silence. "Do you think your mom was afraid of you?"

My stomach turned over. I stared at him.

"Sorry," Lee said. "Maybe I shouldn't have asked that."

The next time we stopped for gas I locked myself in the mini-mart restroom. The floor was filthy and I couldn't bring myself to sit down, so I squatted on my heels, wedged my face between my knees, and cried.

The truth is like the waiting jaws of a monster, a more menacing monster than I'll ever be. It yawns beneath your feet, and you can't escape it, and as soon as you drop, it chews you to pieces. Of course it had sort of half occurred to me that my mother had been afraid of me, but it felt way more likely to be true now that someone else had put the words around it. She'd never loved me, had she? She'd felt responsible for me, like everything I'd ever done was her fault for having brought me into the world. Every kindness she'd ever shown me had come out of guilt, not love. All that time she was only waiting until I was old enough to get by on my own.

I jumped at a knock on the door. "Maren? Are you all right?"

"Yeah." I grabbed a wad of toilet paper. "I'll be out in a minute." I blew my nose a few times and looked at it. No matter what happened, no matter how things fell apart, I always felt better looking at my own snot.

When I opened the door Lee was standing right out-side. "You have to go?" I asked.

"Nah." He was still looking at me, arms folded, brow furrowed. For a second I thought he was going to give me a hug, but then he turned around and strode back to the truck. When I opened the passenger door I found a can of Coke and something wrapped in aluminum foil waiting for me on the seat. "Figured you'd be hungry," he said as he bit into his sandwich. Roast beef.

"Thanks," I said. I couldn't even taste it. Mama had kept me fed, but all along she'd been wishing she could lock me in a cage. It wasn't dinner she made me each night—it was a sacrifice.

"Look, I'm sorry if I upset you," Lee said. "But I'm not gonna tiptoe around your feelings."

I shrugged and looked out the window.

We got to Tingley late that night. Lee pulled to the curb in a neighborhood of narrow two-story houses that seemed to be clinging to the memory of middle-class re-spectability. The windows and doors in one or two of the houses were boarded up, and it was so quiet I could hear the hum of the fluorescent bulbs in the street lamps. We got out of the truck and I followed him down the side-walk, passing a few houses before Lee turned up a drive-way. It was a sad-looking house, with weeds growing tall in the flower beds along the front walk.

"Whose house is this?" I whispered.

"Nobody's anymore." He glanced up at me as he bent to retrieve a key from under a weather-beaten welcome mat. "Oh, relax. It used to be my great-aunt's. She died two months ago, and nobody wants to buy it."

"I'm sorry for your loss." I felt stupid for saying it, but I couldn't say nothing.

"Yeah, well." He shrugged as he turned the key in the lock. "We can stay here tonight. Then I have to find my sister in the morning, and after that we'll head back to Minnesota."

Lee's aunt hadn't kept her house as well as Mrs. Harmon had. The air was stale. It smelled of sickness and disuse. I reached for the light switch, and Lee put up a hand to stop me. "Nobody can know we're here. Just try not to bump into anything."

"But I can't see!"

"You'll get used to it."

We were in a tiny kitchen. From the streetlights I could make out a glass lamp hung over a round table to our right, an L-shaped counter along the wall to the left, and a refrigerator. Suddenly I thought of food. Lee must have had the same idea, because he opened a cabinet over the stove and peered inside. "Oh, good. There's still some soup and beans in here."

He laid the tins on the counter, opened another drawer, and took out a can opener. We had microwaved soup, and afterward I took out my journal and the flashlight. "You're always writing in that book."

I shrugged.

"Can I look at the pictures?"

I handed it to him. "Don't read the writing, okay?"

"Sure."

All the Scotch tape around the pictures made a crinkling sound as he turned the pages. He stared at the etching I'd found in a library book called *Weird and Wonderful Legends of Scotland*. The caption read: *The constabulary discover the lair of Sawney Beane and his cannibal clan*. There were piles of bones in the corners, limbs hanging from the ceiling, dozens of faces leering out of the darkness, and a bubbling cauldron attended to by an old hag who could only be Sawney's wife, her fangs bared in the firelight. At the mouth of the cave was a row of men in uniform, gaping in horror at the evidence of decades' worth of carnage. Sawney himself was lifting an ax against the intruders.

Before today I couldn't have pictured myself in that cave. Now it looked almost cozy.

"Sick," Lee said finally, then turned the page to the photocopy of *Saturn Devouring His Son*. He laid his finger on the space where the baby's head should have been. "I saw this painting in a book once. Made me wonder if he was one of us."

"Who, Goya?"

"Is that his name?" He closed the notebook and slid it across the table. "It's like a book of monsters," he said.

I ran my fingers over the marbled black-and-white cover. "It makes me feel less alone."

He got up and rinsed out the dishes. "I'm gonna sleep on the couch in the living room. You can take the bedroom up those stairs and to the right. It has the best bed. Just don't turn on any lights or open the windows. The neighbors notice everything."

It felt a little like being back in Mrs. Harmon's house, except not as comfortable because I hadn't been invited. On my way up I pointed the flashlight at the framed family pictures on every wall and dresser, but I didn't see any pictures of Lee.

The mattress was old, and the bedsprings dug into my ribs. For a long time I lay awake, the air in the room weighing on my chest like a gremlin, and when I finally fell under I dreamed I was racing down long, dark corridors that zigged and zagged. There were words on the walls in big, dripping letters. I knew my dad had painted the words, but I didn't know how to read them. You can't smell anything in dreams, but I could tell they were luring me with the scent of dinner.

6

I came down in the morning and found a note on the table: *Driving lesson, be back soon.* I was afraid to leave the house in case anybody saw me, but I felt almost as uneasy staying inside. What if a real estate agent showed up?

Nothing I could do about it, really. So I took out Mrs. Harmon's yarn and needles and tried to cast on again. Knitting, or trying to, made me feel normal. I turned on the TV and watched *The Price Is Right.* When I heard the door slam I switched it off and tiptoed into the kitchen.

Still wearing his cowboy hat, Lee was moving all the canned goods from the cabinets into a plastic dairy crate on the counter. He pointed to a McDonald's bag on the table. "Got you something for breakfast."

I thanked him, and as I wolfed down my Egg McMuffin

I watched a girl ride a bike up the street and turn into the driveway. She hopped off and nudged down the kickstand with the tip of her sandal. "Who's that?"

Lee glanced out the window and sighed. "My sister. I'll just go and talk to her." He paused. "It'd be better if you stayed inside."

"Why?"

"No offense, all right?"

"But . . ."

He went out, letting the screen door slam behind him, and his sister leapt into his arms. She was really pretty, tanned and green-eyed like him, but she would've been even prettier without so much makeup on. I crept to the door to see her better. So much for hiding from the neighbors.

"What are you doing here?" I heard him say. "You've already missed enough school for one day."

Kayla grinned. "Your fault, for not coming on the weekend."

"You're right. I should've planned it better. Now go back to school."

"We're basically done for the year anyway." Jagged shapes on her fingernails caught the light, electric blue. It had been a few weeks since she'd painted her nails. "I had such a good time this morning, Lee. It was so easy to pretend you'd never left."

"I had a good time too."

"Don't you miss me when you're gone?"

"You know you're the only person in the world I ever miss."

Kayla gave him a doubtful look.

"Don't go there," he said. "There's no point."

"And what about Mom?"

"What about her?"

"She's really worried about you."

Lee thrust his hands in his pockets and kicked at a stone in the driveway. "Who're you kidding?"

"All right. *I'm* worried."

"I'm sorry, Kay. I wish I didn't have to."

"You *don't* have to!"

"Yeah, I do. You know I do."

"I don't know why, Lee. You never tell me anything. I might not see you again for months!"

"I promise it won't be that long this time."

"Who am I going to celebrate with when I pass the test?"

He grinned. "*If* you pass the test."

"If I don't pass, it'll be your fault for not giving me enough lessons." Kayla glanced over his shoulder and saw me standing behind the screen door. "Who's that?"

Lee turned around and shot me a cold look. I knew I shouldn't eavesdrop, but I'd rather have him be annoyed with me than let him shrug off my questions later on. I smiled at Kayla and gave her a little wave. She smiled back, but only with her lips. *She doesn't like me*, I thought. *She doesn't like me because I'm with her brother and she's not.*

"Is she your girlfriend? Can I meet her?"

"She's just a friend. Maybe you can meet her some other time."

He hugged her again and held on. "We can't stay. I just needed to see you. To make sure you're all right."

"I'd be a whole lot better if you'd come home."

He backed away from her, holding up his hand for goodbye. "I'm sorry, Kay. I really am."

She folded her arms and furrowed her brow. "I hate this, Lee. I *hate* that you do this."

"I'll see you soon, all right? I'll come by the house and we'll celebrate your new license with a movie or something."

"And I *really* hate that hat," she called after him.

"I know," he said. "I heard you the first three times."

I stepped aside to let him back in. Kayla stood in the driveway, head bowed, working her knuckles against her eyes. I drew back from the door screen.

Lee was cramming a few last things into his rucksack. "You got your stuff together?"

He guessed it would take us three days to drive to Minnesota, taking a more northerly route than we had taken to get to Tingley: through the Appalachian Mountains of West Virginia into Ohio, then Indiana, up past Chicago, and across Wisconsin. The longer we drove, the more I felt the hum of excitement creeping out of the pit of my stomach and wending its way down my limbs and around my heart. Every mile on the odometer brought me closer to my dad.

Toward the end of the day's driving I figured I'd waited

long enough to broach the subject of Kayla. "So how'd she do?" I asked.

"Hmm?"

"The driving lesson. How'd it go?"

"Oh," he said. "All right. I think she'll pass."

"Did you teach her with the truck?"

"Yup. I figured if she could handle this thing she'd have no trouble with my mom's sedan."

"Is she going to get her own car once she passes?"

Lee paused before answering, and I started to feel like I was asking too many questions again. "I don't think so," he said finally. "She's got a job at an ice cream parlor, but I still can't see how she'll be able to afford it. I wish I could get her a car of her own."

A thought formed in my head and presented itself before I could push it away. *You could get her a car of her own, and you wouldn't have to pay a dime for it.*

"I just want her to be able to leave if she has to, you know? All you need is a car that runs, and you have that freedom. Hell, you don't even need a license." He sighed. "I really hate that she's trapped in that house with my mom."

I rolled the window all the way down and stuck my head out. *You* deserve *to be broke and alone, thinking things like that.* "Did you ever think about taking her with you?" I asked.

"No. She deserves better than this." As he spoke he leaned forward in the driver's seat, clenching the wheel with both hands. "I want her to go to college. I want her to have a normal life. A *good* life."

"I'm sure she will."

He flicked me a skeptical look.

"Do you think, maybe . . . if we have time, and there's a good place for it . . . maybe you could teach me how to drive too?"

Lee rolled his eyes, but at least he was smiling. "Good grief," he said. "Next you'll be asking me to be your date to the prom."

Again I turned to the window, so he wouldn't see how red my face was. "Then you won't teach me?"

"Yeah, I'll teach you. When it gets dark, we'll find a big parking lot someplace, after all the stores have closed."

"As long as it's not a Walmart," I said, and he grinned.

My first driving lesson took place in a Home Depot parking lot somewhere in Ohio, and it was not a success. I had a hard time remembering to press the clutch when I needed to shift gears, and I cringed every time I heard the crunching sound of metal on unhappy metal.

Lee was a good teacher though. "It's fine," he said. "Just go slow. Stay in first gear. For now just get used to being behind the wheel."

After an hour we switched places and picked up a pizza with extra cheese and pepperoni. Dinner warmed my lap all the way out of shopping center territory. The plan was to keep camping all the way to Sandhorn, at any state park more or less along our route, which Lee would trace for me in his dog-eared road atlas.

The pizza was cold by the time we found a place to

stop in the woods, but we devoured it anyway, dangling our legs off the back of the flatbed. I was using my rucksack for a backrest, and he asked, "Why is your pack so big?"

"It's everything I have. Of course it's going to take up a whole bag."

He shrugged. "You can always travel lighter."

"But you need things. A flashlight. Maps. A change of clothes. Something to sleep in, stuff to cook with."

"You got any of that stuff in *your* pack?" He looked at me and waited a moment. "C'mon. Show me what you've got in there."

I loosened the cinch and opened the bag. Lee leaned over to peer inside. Books, mostly, along with a few pieces of clothing. "Those aren't your books," he said.

"Some of them are."

"Which ones?"

I divided the books into two piles on the flatbed—mine and theirs. Mine: *The Annotated Alice*; The Lord of the Rings three-in-one my mother had given me for my birthday; The Chronicles of Narnia, also in one volume; and the Ringling Brothers circus book, which Lee picked up and flipped through.

Then he picked up the first book from the second pile: *The Hitchhiker's Guide to the Galaxy*. "Tell me about him."

I sighed. "It was Kevin's. He brought me up to his room after school to study together for a history test. His parents weren't home yet. Nobody ever knew I'd been there." I paused. "It happened like that a lot. A boy would make an excuse to invite me over after school, and . . ."

"Yeah. I know." Next he picked up *Around the World in Eighty Days*.

"Marcus. He followed me home after the St. Patrick's Day parade in Barron Falls two years ago."

Choose Your Own Adventure: *Escape from Utopia*. "Luke. Summer camp when I was eight. He was the first one. After Penny, I mean."

"Penny was your babysitter?"

"Yeah." I took the book from him and ran my fingers over the cover illustration of the boy and girl racing out of the jungle, the chasm yawning just behind their feet. "Luke was going to be a forest ranger."

"You can't think about that kind of stuff."

I put the book back on the pile. "Easy for you to say." As soon as I said that, a peculiar feeling came over me, as if I didn't care anymore what Luke had wanted for his life.

No, no. *Lee* was the one who didn't care. He didn't have to.

He laid *The Master and Margarita* on top of the pile he was making. "I already know about this one. Andy, right?"

I nodded. We kept on like that until Lee had gone through every book in my bag. He found north with Dmitri's glow-in-the-dark compass, and then he opened the little brown case to find the tortoiseshell eyeglasses. "What was his name?"

"Jamie."

"You couldn't leave his glasses," Lee said softly. "Otherwise they'd have known right away that something had happened to him." He laid the glasses case on top of the book pile. "Is that all of them?"

I shook my head. "I didn't keep anything from the first time."

"Was your babysitter the only girl?"

I nodded.

"Why is that, do you think?"

"I don't know. None of the girls at school ever wanted to be friends with me."

"Lucky for them."

For a minute or two I picked at the scab on my knee. I couldn't let it sting me, what he'd just said. Once again, Lee was right.

He picked up the books and put them back in my pack. "I've never been much of a reader."

"Didn't your mother read you any bedtime stories when you were little?" He shook his head. "She didn't read to you at all?"

"I told you, she wasn't that kind of mom."

"Then you never made friends with novels."

"I guess I just don't see the point of it. All the things they used to tell us in school, how we should read all these books and do all these things to better ourselves. Like learning bigger words makes you a better person."

"It's not about that."

"There's no point. I *can't* better myself."

"But that's not why I read. When I read a book I can be somebody else. For two or three hundred pages I can have the problems of a normal person—even if that person is traveling through time or fighting with aliens." I ran my hand over *The Master and Margarita*. "I need the books. They're all I've got."

He looked at me then like he felt sorry for me.

I wanted to know more about his sister, and his mother, and what he did for money besides taking it from people who no longer needed any, and what had happened that he had to sneak around his own hometown. I mean, I had a pretty good idea, but I wanted the *story*.

I started with the questions he'd be more likely to answer. "What were you doing before we met? How do you get money to live on?"

"Farmwork, mostly. Sometimes I just stay for a day or two, other times I stick around for longer. Depends on the farm and what they need me for."

"And what do you do during the winter?"

"Last year I went down to Florida," he said. "I was driving an old Camaro, that's the car I had before, and I used to park right on the beach and sleep in a tent on the dunes." He laughed. "Guess that makes me a snowbird."

"Were you there by yourself?"

"I'm always by myself." I shot him a look, and he added, "Apart from you."

Better an afterthought than none at all. "Do you think you'll go straight back to Tingley after you leave me in Sandhorn?"

"I guess it depends on what you find there."

That was encouraging. "But I mean, after I get my stuff figured out. After I find my dad. Then what?"

"Yeah," he said. "I'll go back."

"Does she know?"

"Who? My sister, or my mother?"

"Either. Both."

"My mom doesn't know. My sister, well . . . she knows there's something wrong with me, but I hope she never knows the whole of it." He glanced at me. "I'm lucky, I guess. It's easier for me to hide it."

"What happened?"

"I'll tell you sometime. Not today."

"Can I ask you a different question, then?"

"Depends on the question."

"Why did you eat your babysitter?"

He scoffed. "She was a sadistic bitch, that's why. She'd ask me questions, and if I didn't get the answer she'd pinch me hard. *What's the capital of Mississippi? Why does a cow have three stomachs?* Shit like that. I called her the Pinkerwitch. I can't remember her name now, but I guess it must have been Pinker. She lived down the street. I think she was jealous because she couldn't have kids. Good thing too.

"I don't really remember what her face looked like, except that she had really long teeth and I hated it when she pretended to smile. But I remember what she smelled like. It was this stale, sour smell, like she'd been shut up inside a room for years just talking and talking, nothing but evil words, and never brushing her teeth."

I felt a little in awe of him. He'd never spoken so long in one go. "How old were you?"

"Way too young to know the capital of Mississippi. She was always careful to do it in places where it'd look like I'd just fallen on the playground, banged my arm on the monkey bars, something like that. I told you my mom's done a lot of stupid things in her life, but she's not *that* stupid. The last time it happened—the day I ate the Pinkerwitch—I remember my mom kneeling down and whispering in my ear as she was leaving. She said, *This will be the last time you have to stay with her, I promise. I couldn't find anyone else.* Kayla was a baby, and she had to take her to the doctor. I don't know why she didn't take me with her—I wasn't the best kid in the world, but I could be good and quiet if she made me understand it was important.

"Anyway, I didn't really believe it would be the last time—my mom said stuff like that when she didn't mean it—so that day something in me just snapped."

"What was it like? The first time?"

Lee exhaled a long, slow whistle. "I got such a rush. Every time I do it, I get a rush. I knew anyone else would think it was wrong, but I still felt like some weird new kind of superhero."

We drove in silence for a minute or two before I said, "If I have to be like this, I wish I could be like you."

"It's not that different."

I stared at him. "It's *completely* different."

"*They're* different. But *you* like it as much as I do."

I felt a hot surge of anger in the pit of my stomach.

"That's not true," I said in a small voice. "You're just saying that because you don't understand. You only know how it is for *you*." But a part of me was running, away from Lee and into the dark.

He glanced at me. "I told you, Maren. I'm not just gonna tell you what you want to hear."

I pressed my fingers against my eyes. I didn't want to see the words on the walls. "You don't understand."

"I do. You know I do." He waited for me to admit it, then gave up. "Fine," he said. "You win. So are we done talking, or what?"

"No," I said, but only because I wanted to forget all this. "Go on. You were talking about the Pinkerwitch."

"Yeah. Anyway. Even that first time I knew I'd better clean up after myself. When my mom came back she figured the Pinkerwitch had just left me there and gone home. Even when one of the other neighbors came by and told us she was missing, my mom never suspected I had anything to do with it. *I guess that's what happens to bad babysitters*. I remember her saying that."

"Do you miss her?"

"My mom? Hell no. Maybe she's got a good heart, but everything she does drives me crazy. Drank too much with all the wrong guys, never finished school 'cause she dropped out to have me, finally got off welfare and could only get jobs so lousy she never stayed at them long. And her boyfriends, they were the worst part. She went out with some jerk everyone in town knew had gone to prison for beating his wife, and she said I didn't really know him, I should give him a chance. There were others who were just as bad. I never knew my dad, never knew Kayla's." He sighed. "Even without me being the way I am, it just got too hard to be around her. I get so frustrated with her, y'know?"

"Yeah."

"I always wanted her to pick a good guy, a guy who'd stick around. Other kids had dads. Y'know, guys who actually did stuff with them. Did stuff *for* them. It didn't seem like it'd be that hard for my mom to find a guy like that."

"But she never did."

He shook his head. "What's your mom like?" When he glanced away from the road he met my eye, waiting for an answer. This wasn't Lee making conversation. He wanted to know, and he didn't care that I didn't want to talk about it.

"She could type ninety words a minute."

Lee whistled appreciatively. "What else?"

"She didn't really cook. A lot of the time we had grilled cheese and chicken noodle soup out of a can for dinner."

"You could do worse for dinner than grilled cheese and chicken noodle soup out of a can. What else?"

"She used to bend over the rim of the bathtub to color her hair." I thought of those nights we'd curl up on the couch under our comforters watching *You Can't Take It with You,* her wet hair under a towel turned up and twisted around her head. "And she liked to watch old movies. *Singin' in the Rain, White Christmas,* all the Frank Capra ones."

"Who's Frank Capra?"

"He made *It's a Wonderful Life.*"

"Never saw it."

"It's always on TV at Christmas. It's a classic."

"Nobody wanted to watch that kind of stuff at my house." He smiled wryly. "Musicals are corny."

"So what?" I said. "They're the best kind of fantasy. All these beautiful people breaking out into song because talking about what they're feeling wouldn't be good enough."

Lee looked at me like I'd just burped out a goldfish. I reddened, and he smoothed it over. "Go on," he said.

"She read a lot, but she didn't hold on to books once she'd finished them. She could fit everything she owned into one suitcase."

"Did she ever yell at you?"

"No."

"Did she ever tell you that you were a monster?"

"No."

"Did she ever see you do it?"

I shuddered. "God—no."

"But you told her?"

"I had to. She would have found out anyway."

"But that's not why you told her."

"No. I guess not."

"You wanted her to make it right."

"That's how it is when you're small. You think your mother can fix anything."

Lee smiled. "Not my mother."

"Yeah," I said. "Sorry."

I flipped through the road atlas on my lap. The next morning we'd be passing around Chicago.

"Hey," he said. "You want to drive the rest of the way to the park? The traffic's pretty light, and you can just stay in the right lane."

"I can't. I'm not ready."

He shrugged. "You're ready if you say you're ready. Sure you don't want to try?"

If I turned him down, he'd only think less of me. So I spent an hour in a tense perch behind the wheel, reminding myself aloud to press the clutch before I attempted to shift. A few cars sped by in the left lane, honking their horns. "Don't pay any attention," Lee said. "You're doing fine."

We did not get into an accident, nor did we get pulled over by the cops. That counted as a success.

After dinner we lay down in the flatbed, and Lee turned on his transistor radio. At first all we could find on the AM dial were ball games or political blather, and then I tuned in to this:

"*. . . You know, we are all brothers and sisters even though we don't often act like it. Everyone in line at the supermarket checkout, everyone waiting with you at the stoplight, everyone you glimpse in passing on your way to work every morning . . .*"

The man sounded like an old-fashioned preacher, except he was actually making some sense. He had this fierce, trembling, wonderful voice, and I just laid there staring at the radio resting on the plywood between us, listening as if my life depended on it.

"*That colleague of yours who can't seem to say anything nice to or about anybody: she's your sister. The thief who broke into your house and emptied out your jewelry box: he's your brother. We must forgive one another!*" I could picture the speaker so clearly: tall and thin, with a long nose and a knobby Adam's apple, looking very earnest in a gray suit and a crimson bow tie.

I only realized the radio program was live when a chorus of voices called (faintly, but only because they were so far from the mic): "*Amen! Tell it, Reverend!*"

The preacher went on: "*And yet we cannot forgive one another until we have forgiven ourselves.*" He regarded his audience through thick black eyeglasses like men used to wear in the sixties, and he had a little nick of a scar on one brow where his sister's ice skate had sliced him at the age of six.

The audience gave a warm, rumbling reply. "*Hallelujah! Forgive and be forgiven, Brother!*" They'd driven long distances to be there tonight, no matter how many times they'd already seen him. This was one of those churches where people swayed and trembled and called out in praise of the man who died for their sins. (I had never been able to figure out how exactly that worked.)

"*That's why we're here, isn't it? Forgiveness. That's why you're here, isn't it, Brother?*"

"*Sure is, Reverend,*" called a distant voice.

I closed my eyes and saw myself at the front of the crowd. The man in the crimson bow tie turned to me and held out his hand in welcome. *"And you, Sister. Why are you here?"*

I opened my mouth but someone else answered for me, in a tinny voice on the radio: *"To forgive and be forgiven."*

Lee yawned. "Anywhere you go, anywhere in this country, there's nobody but Jesus freaks on the radio."

"This guy isn't some ordinary Jesus freak," I said. "I like what he has to say."

"Sure, sure. They lure you in with all that happy stuff about love and acceptance, then after they've got you they start telling you they need more money and Jesus doesn't want you for a fair-weather friend."

". . . The Lord says, 'There is no peace for the wicked.' Don't we all want to know peace? Yes—yes, I tell you! Even the wickedest man alive yearns for peace. . . ."

Lee reached out a hand for the radio dial, and I batted it away. "Do you *mind?*" I said impatiently.

He rolled his eyes. "Forgive me, Sister Maren."

I turned up the volume to drown out his grumbling. *"Now I want to tell you something. We've been doing these Midnight Missions all across the country for quite a long time now, and I've heard from all sorts of people. They've sinned against themselves, and they've sinned against each other. They stand up and they say, "Reverend, sometimes it's just too hard to be good."*

Lee snorted. "Now *that* I can agree with."

"And I say to them, 'Let the Lord in. Let Him in and He will show you how to be good.'"

The audience erupted in applause and reverent exclamations, and then an announcer came on. *"The Reverend Thomas Figtree of the Nazarene Free Church will hold his Midnight Mission at Harmony Hall in Plumville on Sunday, June seventh, beginning at ten PM. That's tomorrow night, folks."*

"I don't get why you'd want to listen to any of that," Lee said as a commercial for auto insurance came on. "It's not as if any of it applies to us."

"How do you know it doesn't?"

"It just doesn't. There's no place for us in their picture of the world. If they knew what we were, they'd think even hell would be too good a sentence for us." He rolled over on his makeshift bed and plumped up his meager camping pillow. "Besides," he said to the flatbed wall, "Jesus wouldn't want me on my best day, let alone my worst." A moment later he turned back to face me. He'd heard me paging through the road atlas. "What are you doing?"

"I want to see how far we are from Plumville."

"Oh, Maren, don't tell me you actually want to *go* to that thing." He reached for the radio, and this time I let him turn it off. "Let me tell you something. One time last year my sister got dragged to one of those things by this so-called 'friend' of hers. They wanted Kayla to speak, so she got up and said she wasn't sure if she believed in God because of all the horrible things going on in the world, and guess what happened? Can you guess?"

I shrugged.

"They booed her out of the room, that's what. I bet they'd have thrown rotten tomatoes at her, if they'd had any, and Kayla's never killed so much as a spider."

"Reverend Figtree wouldn't throw tomatoes."

Lee sighed. "Tell you what. If you promise to go into that hall tomorrow night and tell your precious Reverend Figtree exactly who you are and what you've done, then I will gladly accompany you." He shot me a hard look. "Are you willing to do that?"

I curled myself up in his sleeping bag and didn't answer. It was stupid even to imagine that somebody could give me absolution without knowing what I'd done.

"You think you're looking for the truth, Maren," Lee said as I tossed and turned, trying to find the least uncomfortable position on the plywood. "But if you'd rather live inside some preacher's little bubble of sunshine and certainty, then you might as well call it what it is."

When I fell asleep and the pictures welled up out of the darkness, of course I was at the Midnight Mission. It was in a church, not a hall. There were stained glass windows rising up, up, up into the gloom of the rafters, and inside the windows the martyrs met their deaths in spectacular ways. Lions, dragons, bonfires of gold and crimson. Out of the corner of my eye I saw there were words painted on the stone walls beneath the windows, but I knew I couldn't read them, so I didn't turn to look. All around me, the congregation was singing a hymn in a language that didn't exist.

I was walking up the aisle. The people touched my arm as I went by, and called me Sister. *Kneel down*, the Reverend said. There was a hard glint in his eyes, and I was afraid of him. *Kneel down for your blessing, Sister Maren.*

I knelt, and he stood over me and laid his palms on the crown of my head. I felt my face getting hot, and all I wanted was to be out of there, gone, back in the flatbed with a friend who would never hurt me. I felt a wave of laughter breaking over the crowd, a thousand strangers smirking behind their hands. *Forgiveness* was a word that belonged to that other language, the one that vanished as soon as I woke up.

7

he next afternoon we passed a sign for Friendship, Wisconsin. "That's where I was born," I said. "Irony of ironies."

"We'll be in Sandhorn this time tomorrow. Do you have a plan?"

I didn't want to think about Sandhorn. I wanted to find my dad, but not yet—not if it meant saying goodbye to Lee. "I guess I'll start with the phone book," I said.

Two miles after the turnoff for Friendship we passed a billboard that said MOTHER OF PEACE CARNIVAL FUNDRAISER. RIDES, GAMES, GOOD FOOD & PRIZES. JUNE 7TH–13TH, OPEN EVERY NIGHT, 5 TO 11 PM. TAKE EXIT 47 FOR GILDER, TEN MILES AHEAD.

We looked at each other and grinned, and I forgot about everything, the bad dreams and all the carnival nights I'd taken away from other people. For that one perfect second I even forgot their names.

We took exit forty-seven through more farm country before we came into Gilder, a one-street town of antiques shops and doctor's offices perched on the crest of a narrow hill. Down again and a mile farther, a makeshift fairground came into view: a Ferris wheel turning and a Galleon going to and fro in a field beside a brick church with a bright white steeple. Lee found a parking space on the edge of a soccer field across the road and left his Stetson on the seat.

As we crossed the road and slipped into the crowd I began to feel like a little kid again. There was a woman in a glass booth turning pink and blue whirls of cotton candy on long wooden sticks, and she handed each stick down to a child as if it were some token of magic. "Like a Prayer" played on the stereo system, and a circle of twelve-year-old girls danced to it as they waited in line for the Galleon. The scents of fried dough and powdered sugar mingled with cigarette smoke and the oily mechanical smell of crunching gears. A clown skipped up to us and asked if we'd like to buy a raffle ticket. "Grand prize is a big-screen TV!" she cried as an accordion of green tickets spilled from the palm of her frilly white glove.

Lee smiled. "No, thanks." He took my hand and pulled me onward through the crowd, and everything around me blurred a little. All I saw was the sunlight twinkling through the trees on the fringes of the fairground, splotches of color and white tennis shoes as the wave swinger whipped its riders toward the sky, and all I could think of was the warmth of his hand in mine.

I heard him say something, and it brought me to. He was pointing out the haunted house and glancing over his shoulder at me with an impish look. It was pretty clear I was going on that one whether I wanted to or not.

Mothers shepherded their children from ride to ride, doling out tickets and fending off demands for more ice cream. Past the bumper cars there was a big blue tent where fathers in their ball caps and jeans gulped from plastic cups of watery beer. My dad wasn't like that. He loved ice cream and carnival rides, but he didn't drink beer and he didn't care about sports.

We got in line at a hamburger stand and Lee pulled out Barry Cook's wallet. I picked up our tray of burgers, fries, and soda, and we found space at a picnic table under a tent near the game booths. As we ate I watched Lee watching people pass, the children either howling because they'd lost a game or fussing because they'd tired themselves out. Men strolled by with their beer cups, and women negotiated their strollers through the crowd, scanning the faces in search of their husbands. The first bars of "My Heart Will Go On" came through the loudspeaker, and when I thought of Mama I found I almost didn't care anymore.

Lee took another bite of his burger and chewed reflectively. "Do you ever get nervous?"

I knew what he meant—pretending to be normal. I nodded. "You don't want to leave, do you?"

"No way. We're not going anywhere 'til we've gone on

that thing." He pointed over my shoulder, and I turned in my seat. A lopsided orange machine came flashing up out of the treetops and dipped again a moment later. It looked like a cross between a Ferris wheel and a roller-coaster.

"That's the Zipper," he said.

"We should've waited to eat."

He grinned as he wiped his hands with his napkin. "Now which'll it be first, that or the Spook House?"

I chose the Spook House. We bought a page of tickets—again, Barry Cook's treat—and got right on. Lee pulled down the lap bar and settled into the seat with a happy sigh. "Will we pretend to be afraid?"

"Maybe I won't be pretending."

"Funny to think of you being afraid of anything," he said as the car jerked forward and we swung around a corner into total darkness. A set of doors swung open, and the next room was lit with blue fluorescent bulbs that buzzed and flickered. A patient lay on an operating table with his guts spilling out onto a filthy linoleum floor, and above him a demonic nurse brandished a bloody surgical instrument in each hand. She leered at us, then winked at Lee.

"Help me!" cried the man on the table. *"For the love of God!"*

"This is good," Lee murmured. "Definitely worth eight tickets."

We passed out of the hospital of horrors back into the dark, and fumbled through a curtain of phony cobwebs as the theme music from *Halloween* started up. A hearse was parked around the next corner. The back door was open, and so was the coffin lid. A man in a moth-eaten suit stood beside the car with his arm extended, inviting us to lie down inside it. His teeth glowed purple in the lurid spotlight. I felt a hand on my shoulder. "Cut it out."

"It wasn't me," Lee said, and a hiss in my ear confirmed it as we lurched ahead into the next room.

The horror movie theme music faded into the sound of crickets and the hooting of an owl. It was a graveyard scene, with a crescent moon in glow-in-the-dark paint above another coffin. This one was closed, but tilted toward us so we could see it was only half buried. There was a pair of shovels stuck in a mound of dirt beside it, like the gravediggers had wandered off before finishing the job. After a moment of silence the coffin lid strained against its hinges as someone pounded on it from inside. A woman screamed and pleaded, and I could tell it wasn't a recording.

We shuttled along a corridor in the dark. Someone laughed in my ear, low and menacing, and Lee put his arm around me. Or did he? It was more across the back-rest than on my shoulders. I inched away from him as we entered the next room.

A wild-haired, wild-eyed man sat at a table with a napkin tucked in the collar of his shirt, sleeves rolled up, a carving fork in one hand and a severed arm in the other. On the table was a head on a platter, so mangled I couldn't tell if it was supposed to be male or female. A second plate was partially shrouded by a red dish towel, but we could see fingers and toes peeking out. There was a glass pitcher full of what was meant to be blood, and two pale eyeballs stared at us from the bottom of an empty drinking glass.

"*Heh heh heh heh heh,*" piped a voice through the loudspeaker. "*You're next.*" There were words scrawled in blood on the wallpaper above his head, but I didn't have the chance to read them before the car swung around the final corner.

We came back out into the sunshine of the early evening. Lee was in fine form. "Now for the Zipper!"

"The Ferris wheel," I said. "*Then* the Zipper." If I couldn't get out of going on the scary one, at least I wanted to have fully digested.

I'd only been to a carnival a couple of times before, but the Ferris wheel was my favorite ride. I loved rising up over the tops of the trees, slowly, so that as you came down again you could look out and watch everyone milling around beneath your feet.

When we got to the top Lee looked down and frowned, and as we began to descend he turned his head so he could keep on looking at whatever it was that had caught his attention. "What is it?" I asked.

"Some guy," he said as he craned his neck. "I think he's waving to us."

I followed the line of Lee's outstretched finger. There he was, just as he'd been the day I first saw him: standing still, smiling and waving, while the rest of the world hurried on its merry way around him. "It's Sully!" I cried, waving back, even as a little voice said, *How did he get here? How did he find me?*

Lee frowned. "What's he doing here?"

I shrugged as we went up for one more turn. "Guess we'll find out in a minute."

He was waiting at the Ferris wheel exit with a whirl of blue cotton candy. "Hey there, Missy!"

"Sully!" I said as he shook my hand and offered me a pinch of sugar. "I can't believe you're here! How did you find us?"

"Knew you were comin' through this way to look for your daddy and thought you might need someone to talk to, case it didn't go too well." Sully nodded to Lee. "But I should've known, a nice girl like you don't have trouble makin' new friends."

"What a coincidence," Lee said as he shook Sully's hand. "Maren told me she met you all the way back in Pennsylvania."

Sully shrugged. "Only so many roads you could take, and I was comin' this way anyhow."

Lee crossed his arms and shifted from foot to foot. "Oh, really?"

"Yes indeed. Got me a cabin up by the lakes. Nice and peaceful up there. Only an hour from here, give or take." Sully glanced over my shoulder at the hot dog stand. "You kids get somethin' to eat?"

"Yeah, we just had some burgers."

Lee turned to me. "Now how about the Zipper?"

I handed him my tickets. "Do you mind going by yourself? I'll just wait here and talk to Sully."

He looked skeptical. "Where will you be?"

I pointed to the nearest bench, where a bunch of boys were just getting up to leave, and Lee cast one more cautious look at Sully. "Just don't go disappearing on me, all right?"

I suppressed a smile. "I won't."

Lee melted into the crowd as Sully and I sat down on the bench. "Cotton candy?"

"Don't mind if I do." I took another pinch.

There was a twinkle in Sully's eyes. "See you got yourself a boyfriend."

I sighed. "He's not my boyfriend."

The old man took another bite of cotton candy. "Maybe he didn't get the telegram."

"Oh," I said, remembering the lady acrobat. "Thanks for the circus book."

He smiled. "You know sometimes you find somethin' nice, and you just don't know yet who it's gonna belong to?"

I smiled. "I wanted to take you up on your offer. I just really need to find my dad."

"You *think* you need to find your daddy," Sully corrected. His tongue was bright blue. "I should've known when I wrote that note that you weren't comin' with me." The Zipper came whipping up out of the trees again, and Sully said, "How'd you meet up with your what's-his-name?"

"Lee," I said. "I was hitchhiking from St. Louis, but this girl left me at a Walmart in Iowa. . . ."

"San Loo! Missy, you've been *all* over since I saw you last!"

I smiled. "Anyway, I got into a bit of trouble at the Walmart, and Lee showed up just in time." I paused. "He's an eater too."

"Yeah," said Sully. "I figured."

"You're only the second one he's met, after me."

"That so? Well, now." There was no more cotton candy on the stick in his hand, so he tossed it in the trash and licked his dirty fingers. "Listen, you kids got a place to stay tonight?"

I shook my head. "I mean, we've been camping."

"Well, I got two nice clean beds for you, if you want 'em."

"At your cabin? Really?"

"Sure. I even got some hobo stew waitin' in the coals."

My stomach rumbled at the thought of another helping of melted-cheesy mashed-up hamburger goodness. A shadow fell across my lap and I looked up. "How was the ride?" I asked.

Lee stood with his arms crossed again. "Pretty awesome. But you were right. You might've lost your burger."

"Sully was just saying we're welcome to stay at his cabin tonight. He's got a late dinner cooking and everything."

Lee opened his mouth, and given how suspicious he'd been acting I was surprised when he took a breath and said, "Okay. Thanks."

"Alrighty then." The old man stood up and scratched his missing ear with his missing finger. "I'll just leave you kids to your rides and games, and meet up with you at the end of the night."

"Look," I said as Sully rounded the corner on the Galleon and vanished from sight, "it's pretty obvious you don't like the guy, but do you have to be *that* obvious about it?"

"Come on. You mean to tell me he came halfway across the country to offer you moral support?"

"I've heard of unlikelier things," I said. "Like, oh, I don't know . . . trolls under railway bridges feasting on babies? Tomato sauce made out of drunken rednecks?"

Lee shoved his fists in his pockets and kicked at a cigarette butt in the grass. "I'm not kidding around, Maren."

"Okay. Seriously, then. If he were up to something, he'd have done it the first time I saw him. Right?"

Lee cocked his head, still eyeing me with that doubtful look. He wasn't going to concede that easily. "This wasn't a coincidence," he said. "There's something about him, Maren. Like he *knows* you."

I shrugged. "Of course he *knows* me. We talked for hours."

"You're not putting this together. How did he know you were going to be here?"

I rolled my eyes. "He didn't, Lee. Come on. I want a home-cooked meal and a nice soft bed, all right?" Until I said it I hadn't known how much I needed it. "We'll lock the bedroom door. It'll be fine, I promise. Now what do you want to do next?"

He let out a defeated sigh. "How about some snow cones?"

"Why did you say yes if you didn't want to go to the cabin?" I asked as we got in line at the snow cone stand.

"Just to buy us the time to talk about it."

I rolled my eyes.

"And here's another thing, Maren. What's with the chewed-up ear and the missing fingers?"

"He's only missing one finger. What, you think you can judge someone for having missing pieces?"

"It depends on how it happened, doesn't it?" He shot me a pointed look. "Did he lose it in a farming accident?"

The little boy in front of us in line turned around and looked up at me with an air of childish curiosity, walleyed behind a pair of Coke-bottle eyeglasses. What boy's ears *don't* perk up at the mention of severed fingers? I tried to smile at him, but I probably wound up looking like I had a toothache. "We'd better talk about something else," I said.

We ate our root-beer snow cones over by the game booths watching kids waste their parents' money on balloon darts or the Wheel of Fortune, which never, ever landed on the number where they'd stacked their chips. A few feet away we found a Lucky Toss booth, where you had to lob a baseball into a grid of milk cans and hope it didn't bounce off the rims. There were shelves all around the booth, and only one sort of toy you could win: an ET softie.

No one was playing. The girl working the booth sat on a stool reading a magazine, looking so bored her expression seemed almost angry. The boy who'd been in front of us in line for snow cones tossed his paper cone into a trashcan and went marching up to the Lucky Toss booth. "How much?" he asked.

"Three tickets, three tries," the girl replied. "You feeling lucky today, goggle-eyes?" She couldn't have been

more than sixteen, but there was too much experience
written on her face. It wasn't the eyeliner. Someone had
been very cruel to her, not just once but over a period of
years, and now she was going to pay it forward.

The boy didn't answer her, just pulled three tickets
out of his jeans pocket and laid them on the counter.
"You're wasting your money," she said as she tossed him
the first ball. It skimmed over his fingertips and he went
scrambling over the pavement after it.

A moment later Lee dipped his toe under the moving
ball so it came up gently into the air and landed in the
boy's hands. He gave Lee a grateful look—which fell on
me instead—and hurried back to the booth.

The first shot went awry, and so did the second. I felt
Lee cringing beside me. We wanted him to win. *Come
on, kid. You can do it.*

He tried a different tack on his final toss, underhand-
ing the ball so it nearly touched the roof of the booth
before it landed with a satisfying *thunk* at the bottom of
a can in the center of the grid. He jumped and whooped
and clapped his hands. "I won! I won!"

The girl folded her arms and glared down at him.
"You couldn't have."

"But it's in that can over there, see?" It was a little bit
heartbreaking to hear him say this, still believing she
would play fair with him. "I made it. I won."

"No, you didn't," sneered the Lucky Toss girl. "Touch
your nose and see if you don't miss."

I could see on the boy's face that he'd been taunted
like this every single day at school, and also that he'd

never get used to it. He reached for an ET doll on a low shelf along the side and clasped it to his chest. "I won it fair and square."

"No." She snatched the toy out of the boy's hands and put it on a shelf high above his head. "You cheated."

"I didn't!" he cried.

She made a face at him, turned and leaned over the grid of milk cans, plucked out the winning baseball, and dropped it in a bucket. "What're you gonna do about it, huh? That's it. Go and cry to your mommy," she said as the boy hurried away from the booth.

Lee threw his paper cone in the trash. "Keep an eye on that kid," he said. "I'm gonna win that toy for him." He went up to the counter and the girl flashed him a smile that turned my stomach. She hadn't noticed us watching her. I wondered how she'd have treated that little boy if she had.

I watched the boy walk up to a woman in line at the funnel cake stand, head hanging, and when she draped an arm across his shoulders I saw him look up into her eyes and tell her what had happened. *Fight for him,* I thought. *Don't let her get away with it.*

"You trying to win something for your girlfriend?" the Lucky Toss girl was saying, lifting her chin in my direction.

"She's just a friend," Lee replied. I knew he didn't mean anything by it one way or the other, but it still made me crumple to hear him say it.

Now the boy was in tears. His mother stepped out of line, led him by the hand to a park bench out of the chaos of the carnival, and let him hide his face in her soft pink blouse. She had no intention of coming over here. Petty disappointments to better prepare him for the big ones—she had a kind face, but she was that sort of mother. Mama would have done the same.

Lee underhanded the ball the way the little boy had done. He missed the first try and made the second. "Can I win twice with the third toss?"

"You're not supposed to," she said, "but no one will know if I let you." (Nor did anyone see me roll my eyes.) She gave him the third ball—letting her fingers linger on his—and it too landed at the bottom of a can.

"Hey," he said as she handed him two ET plushies. "What's there to do for fun around here besides this dumb-ass carnival?"

"I get off at eleven," she said.

I turned away in disgust. For a moment people passed in colorful blurs across my vision, and all the music and chatter of the carnival dwindled to a distant hum. Then I felt something soft at my ear. "ET phone home," Lee was saying. "Nah, he changed his mind—he wants to go with you instead." He pressed the doll into my hands and looked around. "You said you'd watch him for me, Maren. Now where'd he go?"

I pointed to the park bench behind the funnel cake stand. "He's over there with his mother."

Emboldened by Lee's success, a group of boys went up to the Lucky Toss counter, so the girl didn't notice him heading for the boy on the park bench. I followed a few steps behind him, holding the ET toy with cold and sticky root-beer fingers.

"Excuse me," I heard him say. "I believe this belongs to you."

The boy's face lit up, and he held out his hands. In a moment his mother had sized Lee up, and she flushed because a stranger had done the thing it had never occurred to her to do.

Lee reached out and ruffled the boy's hair. "Someday you'll be big enough to give it back, and you won't be taking any crap from anybody, will you?"

The boy shook his head vigorously. "What's your name?" his mother asked.

"Lee."

"Thank you, Lee." She caught sight of me over Lee's shoulder and smiled. "Look, Josh—Lee won an ET for his girlfriend." She cupped his cheeks, brushed the tears away with her thumbs, and nuzzled him close. "You both won tonight, didn't you?"

We waited in the truck until the carnival closed. After Lee gave the ET doll to Josh he'd circled back to the Lucky Toss booth and arranged to meet the girl in the park across the road from the carnival.

Finally it was eleven, and from the truck we watched the bright lights on the rides all blink out at once. "You can go meet up with your ol' pal Sully," Lee said. "I'll see you back here." He took the keys, hopped out of the cab, and strode across the empty soccer field.

Yeah, right. I waited a couple of minutes, and then I got out and followed him. There was a chain-link fence around the playground, and I hid behind a sign by the gate marked GILDER COMMUNITY PARK. The fairground across the street was dark and silent, the steeple turned blue by the moonlight.

The girl was sitting on one of the swings, her back to me. She'd changed out of her red carnival uniform into something two sizes too small and covered in rhinestones. Lee sat down on the swing beside her.

"I never got your name," I heard her say. *Like it matters.*

"Mike. What's yours?"

"Lauren. So, like, who was that girl you were with?"

"I told you, she's just a friend."

"Where is she now?"

"She went home."

"So, like, you're just visiting?"

"Yeah. So where's all this fun you were promising me?"

I saw her point to a deluxe jungle gym at the far corner of the playground. It was made of wood and shaped like a castle, with towers linked by rope-suspension walkways. "There's a tire swing under that tower. No one will see us there." So she led him by the hand to her doom. Part of me wanted to follow them and watch him do it.

I heard soft footsteps in the grass behind me and turned around. Sully stood there with his hands in his pockets. I couldn't see his face in the darkness, but when he spoke his voice was gentle. "Come away from there, Missy." I rose from my heels, and together we walked across the soccer field.

There was another pickup truck parked beside ours, older and red and half rusted over, with a miniature hula girl dancing from the rearview mirror. I peeked in the passenger's-side window and noticed that the seat was covered in navy blue oilcloth printed with lemons and limes. I smiled. "This is your truck?"

"My truck or my castle, dependin' on how you look at it." He chuckled.

For a few minutes Sully showed me around his moving castle, the stash of beef jerky in the glove compartment and the Hawaiian-print curtains and the blue ceramic jar of pipe tobacco hidden under the seat—trying to distract me, I guess—but Lee took much less time than it would have taken me. I watched him emerge from the darkness under the jungle gym, and as he strode across the soccer field I saw he carried a water bottle and a grocery bag stuffed with the shreds of her clothing, the heel of one shoe poking through the plastic. He tossed the bag into a trashcan and paused for a drink of water. I watched him as he gargled and swallowed. Then he pressed the back of his hand to his lips, to wipe away the last trace of her.

Finally he came over to join us. "You ready?" Sully asked. "Cabin's not much more than an hour north of here."

"Sure," Lee replied. "We'll follow you."

Sully hopped up into his cab, turned the key in the ignition, and gave me a wave. "Talk to you in a while, then."

When we pulled back onto the road I half expected Lee to drive in the opposite direction, but he didn't. In the warm summer night we caught the strains of blue-grass coming through Sully's open windows. "How do you do it, when it's a girl who likes you?" I asked.

"What do you mean?"

"Do you kiss her first?"

"What does it matter?"

"It matters to her, doesn't it? For a second or two at least."

He shot me a mocking look. "What, are you jealous?"

I rolled my eyes. "Don't be ridiculous."

For a while we sat in silence, and I tried to pick apart this feeling I was having. How could I be jealous of Loath-some Lauren the Lucky Toss girl?

I wasn't jealous. Not really. I just wanted Lee's atten-tion—if not forever, then at least for the seven and a half minutes it would take him to polish me off.

"You were awfully neat about it," I said. It was easy last time; he'd done it in the bathroom.

"I'm not, really. I took off my shirt and threw it in the grass. Then I used hers to clean off my face." He paused. "I haven't eaten that many girls."

I raised an eyebrow.

"Why is that surprising? Women don't give me so many reasons to hate them. They're more honest. Not always, but most of the time."

I thought of Samantha, who'd left me stranded in the Walmart parking lot, and of Lauren the Lucky Toss girl. I thought of Mama. "I don't know about that."

"All right, so I eat the exceptions." He paused. "Did your mother lie to you?"

I folded my hands over the ET plushie in my lap. "I guess not. Not exactly. But she hid things from me, and isn't that almost the same thing as lying?" Lee shrugged. "What?" I said.

"I'm not gonna agree with you just because you want me to."

"You don't have to disagree just for the sake of it either."

He flicked me a smile as we pulled onto a wooded dirt road, Sully's bluegrass still tickling at the midnight silence. I wanted to talk about something else, so I said, "I've never had a stuffed animal before."

"No? I thought every girl had loads of them."

"Not me. My mother never let me have any, because if I got one then I'd want more, and she said it would be too much to pack." Jetsam. That's what you call the stuff they throw off a ship into the sea.

The cabin was old but sturdy looking, with a well and a cast-iron hand pump just off the back porch. Sully led us through a sitting room with a woodstove, a braided rug, and at least three or four deer heads mounted on the wall. A stag's antlers nearly grazed the ceiling.

"Come on in and drop your things before we eat," Sully said as he flipped the light switch in our bedroom. There were two twin beds, each made up with a red and blue patchwork quilt. "You kids all right sharin' a room? Only two rooms for sleepin' and I get the other one, so if you'd rather you can take the couch, all right, Lee?"

"This'll be fine, thanks." Lee dropped his pack and

edged past us out of the room again. "I'm just going to have a shower, if you don't mind."

Sully and I went outside, and he bent over the campfire pit and poked at our dinner with a long stick. "The longer you leave it, the better it's gonna taste." He reached for a short-handled spade and gently lifted the foil package out of the ash. "If you please, Missy, there's bowls and spoons in the kitchen."

When I returned with the utensils Sully spooned out two heaping bowls of steaming vegetables and tender meat. "Ahhh," he murmured to himself as he brought the first spoonful to his lips. "Now here's what I call a midnight feast."

We sat in old wooden chairs around the smoldering fire, eating in contented silence. Moths gathered and twitched around the porch light. The woods were alive with cicadas, but if I focused on the sound for a moment too long I began to feel uneasy. The forest might go on for miles, and who knew what else was in it?

Lee came out with wet hair in a clean T-shirt. Sully went back to the fire pit to fill another bowl and Lee said, "Only a little for me, thanks."

"You from around here, son?"

Lee applied himself to the stew. "Nope."

"He's from Virginia," I offered.

"You goin' back there, when you see this little lady on her way?"

"We'll see how it all plays out." Lee laid the metal bowl aside and leaned forward with his elbows on his knees. "Why do you ask?"

Sully turned to me. "I know what I told you, that night we met: best not to make friends and all that. But since then I've been thinkin'. It's a long and lonely road, and there ain't no sense makin' it longer and lonelier than it has to be."

Lee stifled a burp. "Well said." I couldn't tell if he was being sarcastic.

"Maybe what I'm trying to say is, folks like us, we gotta make our own family."

I thought of my real grandfather, who drank red wine with dinner and drove a navy blue Cadillac and probably wished I'd never been born. He would never cook a meal for me or offer me a place to stay. "Thanks, Sully," I said as I handed him my bowl for a second helping. "For this delicious dinner—and for looking out for me." The fire flashed in the whites of Lee's eyes as he rolled them.

Sully's hair rope never made an appearance, and I wondered if he didn't want to bring it out only because Lee was there. It was pretty late anyway, so we didn't linger too long at the fire. I washed out the bowls in the kitchen while Sully stoked the fire in the woodstove. Early summer evenings could still get pretty cold up here.

Lee sat on the sofa and looked around. "You said this is your cabin, Sully?"

"Sure, it's mine." The old man shrugged. "Sometimes when things get sticky I come back to one of my usual places, where I know nobody's gonna bother me. Here's a piece of advice from old Sully: Git yourself a place like this, soon as you can manage it."

"When things get sticky," Lee echoed, a little too

pointedly. "Got it." He turned in his seat to regard the wood-paneled wall, studded liberally with deer heads. "Looks like you're quite an avid hunter."

"Those trophies ain't mine, but I do like to go stalkin' a stag every now and again."

"Do you come up here often?"

"Now and then. Good to come right about this time of year. Ain't nobody here in summertime. They're all down by the lakes."

Lee rose and ducked outside, then came back in with the road atlas. "I'd sure appreciate it if you could show me exactly where we are on the map," he said to Sully. "We'd like to get to Sandhorn by tomorrow afternoon, and I don't want to waste any time."

While they conferred at the kitchen table I took out Mrs. Harmon's yarn and needles and curled up on the sofa under a rawhide lampshade. I managed to cast on twenty stitches, but when I tried to knit into them on the next row I got hopelessly mixed up, so I put down the needles and went poking through the end table. In the drawer I saw a deck of playing cards, a book of Mad Libs, *The Midwest Bird-Watching Guide,* and a handful of jacks. When I opened the cabinet underneath I found a basket much like Mrs. Harmon's, with a crochet hook tucked into a skein of bright red acrylic.

Soon afterward Sully wished us goodnight. I took a long-overdue shower and got ready for bed. Lee closed the door and turned the key in the lock.

"Well?" I asked. "How'd you like your hobo stew?"

"Hoboes give me indigestion."

"Har har."

"He cooked enough food for all three of us, and then some. How did he know he was gonna have company tonight?"

I drew up the patchwork quilt over my shoulder, the ET plushie tucked under my chin. "You're getting paranoid," I said.

"I like to think I was pretty darned polite."

"You were awfully . . ."

"Awfully what?"

"Awfully inquisitive."

Lee shot me a look as he turned out the bedside lamp. "I learned that from you," he said. "You don't know if you can trust somebody 'til you've worn them out with questions."

In the morning Sully's truck was gone.

MISSY:

There's eggs and bacon in the fridge, help yourselves. Why don't you come back once you found your daddy and I'll teach you how to fish?

See ya soon,
SULLIVAN

I felt Lee reading over my shoulder. "Why is he always calling you Missy?"

I smiled. "It's short for Maren."

Again he shot me a look. "No, it's not."

We helped ourselves to breakfast, taking our coffee in the rocking chairs on the front porch to soak up the creak and hum of the forest. The bumpy dirt track led away from the cabin, vanishing in the distant trees like a trail of breadcrumbs.

8

he hours it took to get to my dad's hometown were the quietest we'd ever passed together. It felt like Lee didn't want to talk, like
he was nudging me away because we might
be headed in separate directions this time tomorrow. It might take me a while to find my
dad, but when I did I wanted Lee to stay too.

Sandhorn wasn't too far from Lake Superior, and on
the way in we passed lots of roadside shops advertising
summer boating charters and holiday cabins with tranquil
water views. Another small town, a main street, a white
church at the edge of a tidy green lawn. Lee pulled up
to the curb beside a phone booth. "Moment of truth," he
said.

Maybe one of many. I got out with my notebook and
change purse and shut myself in the booth, and with trem-

bling fingers I flipped to the back of the phone directory. There was only one entry. *Yearly, Barbara.*

The address, the phone number. It was so simple.

I found my father's mother as she was mailing a letter. She stood at the bottom of her driveway in a gray shawl cardigan and natty shearling slippers, lifting the flag on the mailbox with a long white hand. As I approached she pulled her cardigan collar snug around her neck and shuddered, as if I carried storm clouds in my wake. It was a gorgeous sunny afternoon, but she was dressed for November.

As I opened my mouth to greet her she turned and walked briskly up the driveway, her slippers scuffing against the asphalt. "Wait," I called. "Mrs. Yearly? My name is Maren. I've come to talk to you."

She paused, her hand on the railing, and turned on the top step to face me as I hurried up the walk. Barbara Yearly looked me over and, satisfied that I was the right age to be the person she suspected me to be, said: "How did you find me?"

I unfolded the birth certificate and held it out to her, and as she peered and read my name her eyebrows went up. "They gave you our name."

What other name would they give me? But I said, as neutrally as I could manage, "My parents were married."

"Yes." The woman handed me back my birth certificate. "Yes, I know. I suppose you have a few questions for me. You'd better come inside."

I followed her through a living room dominated by a fireplace of rough gray stone. The shades were drawn on the windows to either side, so that the only light in the room came from the narrow slivers the blinds cast on the brown shag carpet. In a darkened corner I glimpsed a tiny bar, two leather-cushioned stools, and shelves of over-turned sherry glasses lightly filmed in dust. I wondered if I would meet my grandfather, or if he was still at work.

As Barbara Yearly padded into the kitchen I caught a whiff of something ripe and faintly greasy, as if she hadn't washed her hair in weeks. It was dark but threaded with gray, pulled tightly into a knot at the nape of her long white neck. A few loose strands fell limply into her collar.

"I've never been to Minnesota before. It must get awfully cold here in the winter. Lots of snow?"

"It's cold all the time," she said.

Always winter, never Christmas. I shivered.

With an open palm Barbara Yearly offered me a chair at the table. I sat. "Well," she began. "I certainly wasn't expecting this."

I searched her face, but I couldn't see anything of myself in her. "You never knew my father had a child?"

She shook her head. "The last I heard from your father, he was going to marry Jeanette, I think her name was. She's your mother?"

I nodded. "Janelle."

The woman shrugged. "I didn't think much of it. Figured it wouldn't last. Summer romances seldom do. I know that must sound unfeeling of me, but you might as well learn that now, and spare yourself the trouble."

I cleared my throat. "Well, I'm sorry to surprise you."
I folded my hands on the tabletop, aware that I was try-
ing to make myself look as innocuous as possible. "I guess
I was afraid to call ahead."

"Afraid? Why?"

I shrugged. "Afraid you wouldn't want to see me."

Instead of answering she turned to the faucet, filled
two glasses, and set one at my elbow. I thanked her as she
sat down across the table, took a delicate sip, and waited,
her eyes on the blank Formica between us.

"You're my dad's . . . mom?" I couldn't bring myself
to use the word *grandmother*. I didn't have the nerve.

Mrs. Yearly folded her hands and looked me in the eye.
"We took him in when he was about six years old." She
noted the look on my face and asked, "Your mother never
told you?"

I shook my head.

"Where is your mother? Did she bring you?"

"No."

"Does she know you've come here?"

"Sort of."

The woman gave me a sharp look. "What does that
mean?"

"She's not here," I said. "She's in Pennsylvania."

"Do you mean to tell me you ran away from home?"

I shook my head. "My mother thinks I'm old enough
to live on my own now."

I could almost hear Barbara Yearly's jaw creak as it fell
open, and I saw the muscles in her throat working as she
struggled to come up with an answer. After a moment she

collected herself, took another sip of water, and said, "If you're looking for a home with your father, I'm very sorry to tell you, but that will not be possible. Frank has been institutionalized for some time now."

Just like that, I lost the way to my castle in the sky. For what felt like a long time I sat staring at my hands in my lap, thinking, *Don't cry don't cry whatever you do don't cry.*

Then Barbara Yearly cleared her throat and I thought, *Maybe he's not that sick. Maybe when I come to see him he'll be happy and get better and we can still listen to* Revolver *while he fries the bacon.* I took a deep breath and decided on a new course. "I came for answers," I said. "That's all."

"What did your mother tell you?"

"Nothing, apart from the birth certificate. She . . . I guess she didn't like to talk about him."

I caught a flash of irritation in her eyes. "I never met your mother," said Barbara Yearly. "Frank sent us a picture and invited us down for the wedding, but we couldn't attend. My Dan wasn't well."

Where was her husband? The house felt so cold and empty, I guess I didn't have to ask. "Mr. Yearly—is he . . ."

"He died almost nine years ago. Throat cancer. Your father was already in the home by that point." She took a deep and quavering breath. "Still, it gives me a great deal of comfort to think that Dan and Tom are together now."

"Tom?"

"Tom was our little boy." Barbara pointed to a black-and-white photograph hanging above the light switch.

"You can see him there. We took him to the portrait studio on his third birthday."

The child was perched on a tricycle before a blank background, all rosy cheeks and dimpled wrists. I didn't dare ask her how he'd died. "You must have been devastated when you lost him."

"More than you could ever imagine."

"You adopted my father after Tom . . . ?"

Barbara lifted her chin and nodded. "We knew the boy had been found under mysterious circumstances, but on reflection, I suppose we were too eager to overlook it."

Suddenly it *was* cold in here. I felt the gooseflesh rising on my arms. "What do you mean, 'mysterious circumstances'?"

"There's no use talking about any of that. No one will ever know what really happened."

"I would really appreciate it if you could tell me what you do know," I said. "It matters to me."

"He was found at a rest stop along Route Thirty-five outside Duluth," she sighed. "That's about eighty miles from here. Two witnesses at the gas pump said a man, a strange-looking man, had taken the boy off a Trailways bus and led him around the back of the building. They began to be concerned after a while, and when they unlocked the restroom door they found the child unconscious and covered in blood, and no sign of the man anywhere. The owner of the gas station called the police and they took the boy to the hospital right away, but they never found his parents, nor the man who hurt him.

"The boy remembered nothing before the hospital.

When we got the call from the adoption agency we went and visited him there, and asked him if he would like to come home with us and . . ." Again the woman paused to draw the gray wool collar close around her neck. "And be our little boy from then on. We named him Francis, after Dan's father. Perhaps . . ." She sighed. "Perhaps we adopted him against our better judgment. It was just that he looked so much like Tom. As if they truly could have been brothers." I watched her trace the rim of her water glass, very tenderly, the way she might have fondled the whorl of her baby's ear. "He would have been forty this year." She spoke more to herself than to me.

"I'm very sorry for your loss," I said again, and tried to think of what I could say to get her to tell me more about my dad. "Frank . . . what was he like, when he was a boy?"

"How do you mean?"

What do you mean, "How do you mean"? "What did he like to do, and what did you do together? What were his favorite books? Was he a good student?" *Did he eat people while he lived here? Did you know what he was?*

"No," said Barbara Yearly. "No, he wasn't a very good student."

I waited while she drummed her fingers on the table and looked out the window at a passing ice cream truck. It paused at the far curb as a bunch of kids came tumbling down a lawn, their fists bulging with spare change. Finally I said, "Do you have any pictures of him that I could look at?"

She shook her head. "I'm sorry. I'm afraid I haven't saved anything."

"Nothing? Not even a single photograph?"

The woman folded her arms tight across her chest. "Look, I don't mean to be unkind, so I hope you won't take it to heart. We may have the same name, but you *are* a stranger to me. As much a stranger to me as your father ever was."

"He *wasn't* a stranger." I heard the indignation in my voice but knew that if I let myself get angry it would only drive her to show me the door. "He was your son. You *chose* him." In this universe, however—the universe inside this cold and empty house—there wasn't any such thing as an attachment that had not always been there.

"I *did* have a son. It was my mistake, thinking I could replace him." Barbara Yearly glanced at me, then out the window again, where a black cat sat at the foot of a maple tree, eyeing a little gray bird as it hopped along a low branch. The ice cream truck trundled away and the jingle began anew. "There is no one to blame but myself," she said. "Dan said he would leave it to me, that he'd let me decide for us both. My husband understood that no one feels the loss of a child more than his mother."

I thought of Mama, and again I found I didn't care. She didn't love me, but I didn't need her. "Would you be able to give me the address of the hospital where my dad lives?"

Barbara Yearly rose from the table and drew a faded floral-covered address book out of a desk caddy on the counter. On a matching notepad she copied out the address and handed it to me. "I hope you don't mind my not asking you to stay for dinner," she said. "I haven't cooked since I lost my husband."

She saw me to the door, and this time I noticed more of the living room. Frames of all sizes covered the dark-paneled walls, but there were no seascapes or snowy idylls, no faded Technicolor sunsets, no embroidered proverbs or Raphael Madonna prints. There was only Tom.

The woman shook and released my hand before I could even register that she'd touched me. *I should have known,* I thought. *I should have known I would get much less than I came for.* "Good luck," she said, and I watched her pale face recede into the gloom of the house a moment before the front door swung forward and the lock clicked quietly into place.

Lee and I had agreed we'd meet up at the Sandhorn Public Library that evening, but he wasn't there when I arrived. I asked the librarian where I could find the yearbooks from the local high school. Funny how it took me longer to find my dad's picture than it had Mrs. Yearly's address.

Funny, too, how he didn't look any different from any of the other boys in his class—he wore a necktie and his hair was shaggy, and he had the same surprised eyebrows and slightly embarrassed smile as his classmates. But I saw every point of difference between my mother and me—my eyes pale where hers were dark, my face round though hers was long—resolved in that photograph.

I ran my fingertip over the words beneath the portrait, *Francis Yearly,* as if the name were new to me. This boy would become my dad, and yet he looked like an ordinary eighteen-year-old, ready to go out into the world and make something of himself. *Get real, Maren. What are the odds he'll ever paint your room and cook you breakfast?*

The trouble with questions is that one always leads to another. Where would *I* be in twenty years? Would I always have to live in other people's homes, pretending they were mine? Who would I travel with—or what if I had to travel alone—or what if I *couldn't* travel?

Would I ever be at peace with who I was and what I'd done? How could I be?

It was exhausting just thinking about it—*living* it was unthinkable. I replaced the yearbooks on the shelf, took out my notebook, and began to write.

It was a quarter to eight by the time Lee showed up. "How did it go?" he asked.

I looked at him.

"That bad?"

I nodded.

"Did she give you his address?"

I drew the notepaper out of my pocket and slid it across the table. *Francis Yearly* (as if I could ever forget his name), *Bridewell Hospital, 19046 Co. Hwy F, Tarbridge, WI.*

Lee frowned. "He's in the hospital?"

"It's a *mental* home."

He gave me a look: sad, and not at all surprised. "Oh, Maren. I'm really sorry."

I just looked at him and shrugged a little. I felt old and tired, like I'd lived twenty years inside an hour.

The librarian came on the loudspeaker. Ten minutes 'til closing.

"Do you still want to see him?"

I nodded.

"So it's back to Wisconsin," Lee said. "At least it's not too far." He pointed to the stack of photocopies on the table in front of me. "What's that?"

I handed him one of the pages and he looked it over. *My name is Maren Yearly and I am sixteen years old. I understand that what I am going to tell you sounds like a sick joke, but when you see that the names and dates I have given you below correspond to missing persons reports, you will understand that I am not someone with a poor sense of humor and too much time on my hands.*

"No way," he said. "You're not seriously going to send this to anyone."

"Why not?" *The truth will set you free.*

"Nobody will believe you."

I was going to tell him it didn't matter whether or not anybody believed me, but then I thought maybe he wouldn't understand. Instead I said, "Maybe they will." While I'd been waiting for Lee I'd gone on the computer and looked up the addresses of all the police stations in the towns where I had done the bad thing. I had written out my confession in my notebook and made nine photocopies. I wasn't sure where I should wait for the police, but I could figure that out later and add a postscript.

Part of me felt better for having done all this. The other part was still running in the dark.

"Come on," he said. "You don't have to send it tonight. I want to get to Tarbridge as quick as we can and find a safe place to sleep."

We crossed back into Wisconsin, rolling fields on ei-

ther side. The light was fading when a shape darted down
the hill to our left. I'd seen plenty of deer since I started
traveling with Lee, but only on the cabin walls, or lying
(whole, but just as lifeless) in a heap on the shoulder.
"Wait," I said. Lee braked to a stop. The deer leapt across
the road and ran along the grassy fringe beside a barbed-
wire fence.

There it was, poised in the air above the barbed wire,
cottontail bright in the dusk. It was like the world stopped,
just for a moment. Then its hind legs cleared the wire—
like it took no effort at all—and in a blink it disappeared
over the crest of another hill. I'd never seen anything so
graceful in all my life.

It was well after eleven when we got to Tarbridge, passing
through the town and the turnoff to Bridewell Hospital
on our way to Otsinuwako State Park. With no warning,
Lee made a quick U-turn, and everything in the truck
lurched from one side to the other. "Did you see that sign
back there?"

"What sign?"

"For that new development. 'Designers' Showcase.'
That means the model home is furnished." A real bed for
the second night in a row, if we could figure out a way in.

It was a brand-new street, so they hadn't put any lights
in yet. Lee parked the truck in front of an unfinished
house—it didn't have walls, just the timber framework—
and we walked back up the unpaved road to the house at
the top of the development. It had a perfect green lawn,

precisely trimmed shrubbery, and a wreath with pine-
cones and pink ribbons on the door. Cathedral foyer,
two-car garage.

Lee ducked around the side of the house, and I followed him. There was a broad wooden deck overlooking
another stretch of green lawn, the property line marked
with a picket fence. Lee went up the steps and bent to
examine the lock on the sliding-glass door. He pulled
something out of his back pocket—a little metal rod—and
inserted it into the keyhole.

"Where did you learn how to pick a lock?"

"Shop class." As he wiggled the rod in the keyhole Lee
smiled to himself at the memory. "On days the teacher
was out sick some of the guys gave their own lessons."

I heard a click, and Lee rose and slid the door open.
"After you," he said, and followed me into the kitchen.
There was a round dining table and a red ceramic bowl
piled high with plastic lemons. I saw an island lined with
bar stools on one side, a massive stainless steel refrigerator, and a stove with six burners.

We took off our shoes and began to explore. Inside
the fridge I found a half dozen canisters of ready-bake
cookie dough. "I bet they bake a batch of cookies right
before an open house," Lee said as he peeped over my
shoulder. Then he reached in and took one. "Makes the
place smell homey. You hungry?"

I nodded, and he pulled a cookie sheet out of the
oven, turned the dial to 350 degrees, and popped open
the canister. We washed our hands at the kitchen sink

and spent a contented couple of minutes pulling apart slices of dough and laying them on the baking tray.

Once the cookies were in the oven we went into the dining room. The table was set for a dinner party: china dishes with rosebud sprays along the edges, crimson linens tucked through enameled napkin-holders, heavy silverware, crystal wine goblets, and everything.

The living room beyond was even more formal, with two blue velvet sofas with carved-wood armrests, heavy brocade curtains trimmed with tassels, and a massive curio cabinet taking up most of one wall. Lee moved past me into the room, picking up a vase and putting it down again. "This place is ridiculous," he said. "Somebody's going to buy this house and everything in it, but nobody's ever going to sit in here. It's like a museum."

"Still," I said, "I like it. My mother never decorated like this. We never stayed anyplace long enough to bother."

"We always lived in the same place." Lee bent over a crystal bowl and sniffed the potpourri inside. "What was my mom's excuse?"

I went into the foyer. The mail table by the door was laid out with all sorts of brochures and business cards in little plastic trays. These were the people who made the house look like a family actually lived here. Funny to think that was somebody's job.

The scent of baking sugar cookies drifted through the rooms and up the stairs. First we found a spare room— not a Spare Oom, you can't have a Spare Oom in a spare house—and a children's room with two twin beds. There was a rocking chair in the corner and a blue lava lamp on the nightstand between the two beds, which were made up in matching comforters dotted with tiny rainbows. Down the hall there was a four-poster bed in the master bedroom, piled high with gold-trimmed throw pillows.

"Are you thinkin' what I'm thinkin'?" Lee asked as we stood in the doorway.

"Yup," I said. And we ran across the thick beige carpet and leapt into the air, giggling like little kids as we landed heavily on a comforter made to look like it had been quilted by hand.

The oven timer went off. We went downstairs and had cookies for dinner.

There weren't any electronics in the house. We discovered this when Lee opened the big cabinet on the "entertainment center" in the family room expecting to find a big-screen television. There were bookshelves on either side of the wide brick fireplace; some of the books were real and some were really long pieces of wood, notched and painted in gold and crimson to look leather bound, like you might find on a movie set. A chessboard waited for players on a table by a window looking over the front lawn and the dusty new street, but neither of us knew how to play, so we made up our own rules. The game pieces were heavy, made of some sort of milk-white stone. I hefted my queen in my palm before I put it back on the board, knocking the black king off his square.

After that we decided it was bedtime. I went into the children's room, and Lee followed me. "Don't you want to sleep in the four-poster?" I asked.

"Too much trouble replacing all those pillows just so," he said as he pulled back the rainbow comforter and settled himself in.

I laid a finger on the switch on the lava lamp. "Okay?" He glanced at the curtained windows before nodding, and I switched it on. An eerie blue glow filled the room, and once the lamp got warmed up the rising blobs cast odd upward-moving shadows on the wall. I got under the covers in the bed by the door. The sheets were stiff and smelled of plastic. Of course they'd never been washed.

"Lee?"

"Yeah?"

"Did you ever have a girlfriend?"

"I did, once."

My heart began to thud in my chest, and I was afraid he could hear it. "What was her name?"

"Rachel."

"That's a pretty name."

"Yeah." He paused. "Sometimes you remind me of her."

I propped myself on an elbow so I could see his face. "Really?"

He glanced at me. "Yeah. She liked to read a lot. Jane Austen, stuff like that."

"What . . . ," I began, and almost lost my nerve. "What happened?"

"It's a long story."

I tried to smile. "We've got all night, right?"

"All right." He paused, arranging the memories in the right order. "There was one night—I brought Rachel over to the house because Kayla wanted to meet her, and I thought maybe they could talk about the things you girls talk about, because I could tell Kayla really needed somebody to confide in—my mom could hardly be bothered keeping food in the fridge, let alone telling her anything—and we were having a nice time, just the three of us, drinking root beer and laughing at dumb jokes, before *he* showed up." Lee's hand hardened to a fist atop the rainbow duvet. "Another one of my mom's boyfriends. They were all the same, you know? I'd come home after school and find him slobbing out on the couch, two dozen empty beer cans on the side table and another one open in his fat, hairy fist, the TV tuned to a NASCAR race and the volume up so high it's a wonder the neighbors never filed a noise complaint. He'd tell me to get him another beer out of the fridge, I'd tell him I wasn't the maid, he'd start calling me names that fit himself a whole lot better, saying it was high time my mom turned me out, and I'd say, 'Nah, it's high time we turned *you* out.'" He sighed. "My mother always paid for the beer.

"By this time he'd be up off the couch and in my face, and I could smell every disgusting thing he'd done in the last week. Whizzing in alleys, puking in trashcans. He'd follow me around the room, shouting abuse, and meanwhile I was locking the door and pulling the blinds." He chuckled coldly. "No idea what was coming to him. They were always so drunk, they never had any idea."

"Anyway, the difference this time was that Kayla and Rachel were there. I made them both go into Kayla's room and lock the door, and I . . . and . . . Rachel didn't listen to me. She *saw*." I heard him swallow. "And that's the reason I had to leave."

"What happened?" I sat up in the bed and folded my legs beneath me. "I mean . . . what did she do?"

He stared at the ceiling as he went on. "She didn't scream—not at first. She just stared at me with her mouth wide open for the longest time. I wanted to wash up before I went near her—to *comfort* her, you know— but I was afraid she'd run before I could get to the bathroom, so I just stayed put and tried to talk to her. I told her I'd never hurt her, that I would only hurt someone who hurt other people and that I couldn't help it, but she just stood there in the doorway like a statue." He took a deep breath, and I realized he was crying, or near enough to it. I sat on the floor between the beds and patted his hand.

"Then I heard Kayla open her bedroom door, call my name, and ask if it was okay to come out, and that broke Rachel out of her trance. She ran out of the house, and I couldn't run after her or she'd think I was coming after her, you know? So I cleaned up and waited a few more minutes—it felt like forever—and then I told Kayla I was going out. She kept asking me what had happened, and had Rachel and I had a fight, but I wouldn't tell her." He took hold of my hand, squeezed it, and released, and after that I didn't know where to put my hands.

"I drove over to Rachel's house and her father came to the door. He'd never liked me and I could see it in his face—smug, you know? Like he'd been right about me all along. He locked the screen door so I couldn't come in and he just stood there with his big beefy arms folded across his chest like a bouncer, telling me she'd come home and thrown up and that she was raving about somebody getting eaten. I could see it never occurred to her parents that she meant it literally, they just thought I'd gotten her drunk and tried to . . . to . . ." He sighed and pressed his fingers against his eyes. "Anyway, I told him I hadn't laid a finger on her, that I'd never hurt her, but of course he didn't believe me. I could hear her screaming and crying upstairs, and her mother trying to calm her down." He let his fingers fall from his eyes again. "I loved her more than anybody, but I couldn't put her at ease and make it right. Her dad slammed the door in my face, but before he did . . ." Lee affected a deep, intimidating tone: *"You will stay far away from my daughter, do you understand?"* He paused. "If it hadn't been for Kayla, I would have killed myself."

Until you hear a story like that, you think heartbreak is just a figure of speech. I wanted to comfort him—not just pat his hand and tell him how sorry I was, but actually make things better. If I had to be a monster, why couldn't I have some sort of magical power that might fix this for him? "What happened after that?" I asked. "Did you go to school the next day?"

"How could I go back after that? Things get out. People talk. Everybody knew I'd done something terrible, something unforgivable. They didn't know *what* I'd done, but it was enough."

"What about Rachel?"

He shook his head. "I haven't seen her in two years. Not since that night."

"She didn't ever want to see you again?"

"She couldn't see me even if she wanted to. I ruined her life, Maren. She had to go to the hospital. They took her out of school. There's no way to reach her. I can't talk to her, I can't explain. She's stuck in that place with a bunch of crazy people, drawing with crayons and eating mashed potatoes with a spoon, and no one will ever believe her."

She's stuck in that place with a bunch of crazy people. People like my father.

Lee began to cry, and this time he didn't try to hide it. I sat on the bed beside him, and he sat up and clutched my shoulder and rested his forehead in the hollow of my neck. "All this time, and I've never told anybody about any of this." His voice was eerily calm. I felt his words hum through me. "How could I tell Kayla? She's the only person in the world who still thinks I'm *good*."

"*I* think you're good."

Lee tried to laugh. "I guess you don't know me well enough."

"One of us has to be the good one," I replied. "And it definitely isn't me."

"I never should've brought her home. Why didn't I just take them both out for ice cream or something?" He pulled back from me. His eyes were bloodshot. "Aren't you glad you asked?"

"That's the other reason you keep going back, isn't it? Hoping to see her."

He lay down again and closed his eyes, and I went back to my own bed. The moment was over. "I just sit in the parking lot looking up at the building, wondering which room is hers. Tried to get in a few times, but her parents told them about me. They have a list of people they'll let in to see her, and if you're not on it then you can't get in. I don't think there's any way I can make things right, but if I could just explain things to her, maybe it would help."

"Do you . . . do you still love her?"

"Yeah," he said slowly. "Yeah, of course I do. It's not . . . the same, if that makes sense. I know it's over between us, and I know she deserves better—she always deserved better."

I never thought I'd be jealous of a girl in a mental hospital. And yet . . . if I could have switched places with her, I would have. It would have solved our problems—hers *and* mine. My father and I could have adjoining rooms, play checkers and go for walks up and down the lawn in our white pajamas. We could still listen to *Revolver* together.

Lee opened his eyes. "Are you nervous?" At first I didn't understand.

My father, of course. Frank. "Wouldn't you be?"

"If I were you? Yeah."

In a little while he fell asleep, his face still streaked with tears. I lay on my side, watching the blue blobs take form and bubble upward.

———

The next morning, Lee was frosty. When I woke up he was parting the curtains to let in the pale dawn light. "Who knows how early they come in to show the place?" he said. "And we still have to clean up in the kitchen." I wondered if the real estate agent would notice the missing can of cookie dough. Not that it mattered.

There was a coffeemaker in the kitchen, so we had proper brewed coffee. Only a canister of powdered creamer, though, and no conversation. Every time I came near him—to grab a mug, or borrow the spoon he'd used to stir in the creamer—he moved away from me like it would be a disaster if we brushed hands or elbows.

I didn't say anything at first. I wanted to see if he'd talk to me on his own. Finally I asked, "Why are you being weird? Is it because you wish you hadn't told me about Rachel?"

He sighed as he rinsed out his coffee mug, shook off the drips, and put it back in the cabinet. "Well, when you put it like that . . ."

"It's not my fault."

"I didn't say it was."

"I was just asking about your life. That's what friends do."

He didn't answer. We let ourselves out the way we'd come in, went back to the truck, and pulled out of the unfinished development. It was only another five or so miles to Bridewell, and then what?

Still that stony silence from the driver's seat. I ran through all the possibilities in my head—all that I could say and every possible way he could reply. I knew that if

I asked him, *Do you want to leave me in Tarbridge and drive back to Virginia and never see me again?* and he said yes, I wouldn't be able to pretend anymore that I only cared for him as a passing acquaintance. I would cry, and he would know.

So I had to pretend like it was my idea. "I guess this is it," I said as we took the turnoff for Bridewell.

"What do you mean?"

"You're going to leave me here and go back to Virginia."

"What?" He turned in his seat and stared at me. "What are *you* going to do? Check yourself in?"

The asylum loomed at the lip of a hill, three redbrick stories of barred windows. We pulled up to a guard shack where the parking lot met a tall wrought-iron fence. The man in the booth wore a navy blue uniform with a patch marked BRIDEWELL SECURITY across his bicep. "Visitor?"

Lee nodded.

"All right. We'll just take down your plate number, and you can head on in."

The parking lot was pretty much empty, but Lee pulled into a spot as far from the main entrance as possible. "Answer me, Maren. What are you going to do?"

"Does it matter?"

Lee gave an exasperated sigh and hopped down from the cab.

"I don't know why you're acting like you care all of a sudden," I said as he rounded the truck and opened the passenger's-side door. "*You* were the one who said you didn't make friends."

"I'm not going to leave you here without you having a sensible plan."

"I'll go back to Sully's."

"I said *sensible,* Maren. The man's a creep, and you know it."

"Did he stab you in your sleep? Did he poison your stew?"

"Stop it," he said. "Stop being such an idiot."

"I'm going to see my father now, and anything that happens after that is none of your business."

He actually seemed hurt. "Do you really mean that?"

Of course I couldn't look at him as I replied. "Yes," I said. "I really mean that."

"What if you change your mind?"

"I won't."

"You will. I know you will. But I can't hang around waiting for you, Maren."

I slung my rucksack over my shoulder and slammed the passenger door. "Then don't."

9

he woman at the front desk raised her stenciled eyebrows when I told her I wanted to see Frank Yearly. "Wait a moment while I find Dr. Worth." On the opposite wall there was a larger-than-life portrait of a white-haired man in a tweed jacket. The plate at the bottom of the heavy gold frame read:

GEORGE BRIDEWELL, MD
"Whatever he may diagnose or prescribe,
the physician's finest instrument is compassion."

"Dr. Worth will see you in her office," the receptionist said. "Right this way."

I followed her through a door beside the desk and down a long gray corridor. She opened a door and waved me in, but the office was empty. "Just wait here a moment," she said again, and disappeared.

There was a frog-shaped glass paperweight on the desk not securing any papers, and the bookshelves along the back wall were lined with medical textbooks. The office was very tidy apart from an enormous water stain on the ceiling. It was several shades of brown, as if someone on the second floor had spilled many cups of tea. The windows looked over the parking lot, and my heart swelled when I saw the black truck in the distance.

The doctor came in. She had short red hair and thick wire-rimmed eyeglasses, and she seemed to be a little older than Mama. "Good morning," she said crisply as she seated herself at the desk. "I am Dr. Worth, the director here at Bridewell. I'm told you wish to visit Francis Yearly?"

I nodded. "If you need proof that I'm his daughter, I have my birth certificate right here." I slid the folded blue paper across the desk, but she didn't look at it, just opened the manila folder she'd carried into the room.

"I'm afraid Mr. Yearly is very sick," she began as she looked over the document inside. "My concern is that a visitor after all these years might prove too upsetting for him, and for you."

"You mean he's never *had* a visitor?"

She gave the chart another perfunctory glance. "That's correct."

"Was no one allowed in, or . . . did no one ever come?"

The doctor assembled her features into a mask of professional sympathy.

"I never knew where he was," I said. "If I'd known, I'd have come much sooner."

"Please don't feel any regret on that account. Truth be told, I could not in good conscience have allowed a minor in to visit a patient in his condition." She closed the folder and opened my birth certificate. "You're only sixteen. Where is your mother? Does she know you're here?"

With my eyes I traced the squiggly outline of the ceiling stain, a big brown blotch becoming the map of a lost continent. "She couldn't come, but she . . . she knows I'm here."

"I really shouldn't let you in to see him without your mother present."

I leaned forward and clasped the edge of Dr. Worth's desk. I was literally holding on. "I know my father isn't well, doctor. I just need him to know I'm finally here."

"Do you live with your mother?"

"Not anymore, no."

"Where are you living, then?"

I swallowed. "With a friend?"

Dr. Worth eyed me above her reading glasses. "I see."

"Will you let me see my father?"

She sighed. "It's unlikely he'll understand who you are. I know you're anxious to see him, but no one is ever truly prepared for that."

"Yes," I said. "I understand."

Dr. Worth leaned forward and pressed the intercom button on her phone. "Denise, could you page Travis to my office, please?"

While we were waiting I glanced out the window.

The truck was gone. I closed my eyes and took a deep breath. *I will never see him again.*

A minute later the door opened and a man in gray hospital scrubs came in. He was tall, a bit overweight, and in need of a haircut. There was something very gentle and teddy-bearish about him, and even in that first second I knew he would be kind to me.

"Travis, is Mr. Yearly awake?"

The orderly smiled and greeted me before answering, "Yes, Doctor."

"And how is he today?"

"Fairly good to good. Alert. He ate most of his breakfast."

The doctor nodded and turned back to me. "I will let you in to see your father for ten minutes. For your safety, Travis will remain with you for the duration of the visit."

For my safety?

Maybe you think you know what an insane asylum is like on the inside, but you're probably wrong. There are no raving madmen reaching between the bars to grasp at you, no frantic struggles dissolving into tears and sedation and straitjackets—none that I saw, at least. The radio was tuned to a classical station in the common room, where people of all ages played checkers or solitaire, wrote letters, or painted in watercolors. Some wore pajamas and some were fully dressed. No one was talking to themselves or to each other.

A pale-haired girl in a shapeless gray sweater sat in a chair by a window overlooking the woods behind the hospital, her hands curled in her lap like an old woman's. There was an eager, almost hungry expression on her face, as if she were only biding her time until the fairies came in the night to rescue her. I thought of Rachel.

Some of the older patients were in wheelchairs. If they looked up as we passed I expected to see some spark of curiosity, but a glance satisfied them that I wasn't bringing them food or medication and so, for their purposes, I didn't exist.

A woman in a wheelchair was knitting a scarf with blunt-tipped plastic needles. The scarf seemed to go on for yards and yards, changing colors and folding itself into piles in her lap before disappearing into a large floral-patterned handbag on the floor beside her. She plowed on with competent, listless movements, not even looking at her needles as she knit. A scarf for a giant, or a scarf for nobody.

Travis led me through a series of swinging doors and down a long corridor, and when we reached the door at the end of the hall he took a ring of keys from his belt. My father was locked inside three times over. My heart lodged itself in my throat.

A man was sitting at a small padded table, his back to the door, and he didn't turn as we entered. I caught sight of his bed before I saw his face: white pillow, white sheet, leather restraints hanging from the handlebars on either side, waiting for naptime. I ventured into the room, watching the profile of the man in the chair with each step.

"There's someone here to see you, Frank." Travis spoke with exaggerated tenderness, as if my father were a small child. "Someone you've been waiting for, for a very long time, right?"

The boy in the yearbook photo was long gone. My dad lifted his pale and watery eyes to my face, and I saw his gray-stubbled jaw and neck muscles straining. But he didn't smile, and he didn't speak.

"Hi," I whispered. "Hi, Dad."

Dad: another word in that imaginary language. As I spoke his eyes went wide, tears fell down the sides of his cheeks, and he worked his jaw more strenuously. His lips moved, but I couldn't make out what he was trying to say. My heart clenched. *He'll never sing as he cooks our breakfast.*

"Can't . . ." I began. "Can't he speak?"

"It's the medication," Travis said gently, coming from behind me with a chair. "Here. Why don't you sit down?" I seated myself as the orderly laid a hand on my father's. His other hand, his right, was under the padded table. "It's okay, Frank. Rest easy. It's okay." To me he said, "In the beginning I told him it was too early to expect you, that you'd be much too young to make your way here on your own, but I don't know that he understood." He paused. "I have to say, I wasn't expecting you for a good few years yet."

This man, whom I had only met a minute ago, knew who I was and why I was here. I didn't know how to feel about that, so I just said, "I guess you've been working here a long time, then."

Travis gave me half a smile. "Time goes faster the older you get. Makes sense, I guess. A day becomes a smaller and smaller fraction of your life."

I looked at my father. "Can I touch him?"

The attendant nodded. "Just briefly though. And give him space if he gets upset."

"Is he upset now?"

"Not upset, no. Just overwhelmed."

I reached for his hand—as limp and clammy as I expected it to be—and I watched my father fix his eyes beyond my shoulder, where Travis was opening his bedside drawer. "There's something he wants you to read," the attendant said.

I glanced back at my father, who was still looking anxiously after Travis. "How do you know?"

"It was my very first week on the job, the night your father came to Bridewell. We've always felt like we've been walking this road together, haven't we, Frank?"

Frank nodded, or tried to.

"How long has he lived here?"

"Just about fourteen years." Travis found what he was looking for and laid it on the table in front of me. In that first moment I was convinced the attendant had delivered my own journal. It was older, of course: a marbled black-and-white composition notebook, the cover yellowed with age, the pages inside crinkled from old spills. Horribly, horribly familiar.

I looked to Travis, who now stood by the door like a sentinel. "Should I . . . ?"

The orderly nodded. "He wants you to read it. He wrote it for you."

I opened the notebook and found the first page covered in a masculine scrawl, just this side of legible. This was my father's handwriting? I glanced up at him—his eyes were still wet with unshed tears—before I began to read.

Hello there, little Yearly. I wish I knew your name, but I don't even know if you are a boy or a girl. Man or woman, by the time you read this. If you read this. I want so badly for you to come, but I'm afraid of what you will think of me. I'm afraid you will hate me, and if you do I will understand. Maybe your mother will never tell you about me, and if that's the case I know it is for the best.

Still I will write, in case you come. Otherwise, by the time you get here, I am afraid I will not be able to answer your questions.

I turned the page.

I don't remember my real parents. To this day I cannot even remember the name they gave me. The time I had with your mother is the only time that is still clear to me. Sometimes I wake up in this cold, empty place and feel happy in my heart, like she was in bed beside me all night long. I think I can smell her shampoo on the pillow, and bacon frying in the next room, and I hold on to that moment for as long as I can.

Otherwise my memory is full of blanks, and I know that the longer I am here the less I will remember. But I am safe, little Yearly, and so are you.

I felt a cold trickle down the length of my spine. My father didn't know about me. It had never occurred to him.

I often wondered why the Yearlys kept me. But I guess they couldn't send me back without feeling they had gone back on a promise, and that would have made them bad people. No one, not even me, wants to think they are a bad person.

I had three square meals a day and a warm, clean bed, but I was so unhappy because I could not escape the ghost of Tom. Sometimes they spoke of him as my older brother (on her bad days Mother Yearly set a fourth place at the dinner table), and other times they called me Tom. But most of the time I was what I was, an unsatisfactory replacement. If Tom were here he'd show you how to ride your bike. Tom would have gotten straight As. Tom would have gone to Harvard or Stanford. Tom rescued broken birds. Tom would have been a veterinarian, a doctor, or maybe a lawyer or an engineer, a Somebody, unlike YOU, Frank, who will only amount to a Nobody.

Even when I slept I wasn't free of Tom. Sometimes I dreamed I was awake, and he would ooze down out of the ceiling and perch on the dresser with red glowing eyes and his pointer fingers pulling at the sides of his mouth and his long, thin tongue flicking like a snake's.

Even during the day I could not shake the feeling that someone was watching me. At school sometimes I would look out the window and see a man in a red flannel shirt leaning against the fence, and he was looking right at me. Waiting for me. I never saw him when I was outside, but I was always afraid I might.

I left the Yearlys as soon as I finished high school, and I wanted to go to college but I never got there. When you have no money it is easy to tell yourself you will go to college once you get yourself a job and save up enough for tuition. Then all of a sudden you look in the shaving mirror one morning and know that if you went now the kids in your class would laugh and call you "old-timer." I hope you go to college. I don't know that it would have made a difference in my life, but I feel sure it will make a difference in yours.

In this blank white room of dead bolts and restraining belts, college seemed more impossible than ever. I glanced at Travis. "My ten minutes must be almost up."

He paused to think, then nodded. "I'll be right back."

Now I can tell you about Janelle.

I had many jobs in many places. I didn't have

trouble making new friends, but sometimes they turned out not to be friends after all and when I found out they had lied or cheated me I could never seem to walk away.

When I was 22 I got a job as a forest ranger (I shuddered) at Laskin National Park. My job was mostly to patrol the campsites to make sure no one was dumping trash or cutting their own firewood. Janelle sat at the gate shack window taking entrance fees, and on my first day I came in and we talked and even then, just laughing over the inflatable woman in a red wig sitting in the passenger seat of a single man's car, I knew I would always love her. Your mother is a beautiful woman, but there is so much more to her than looks. The good thing about park jobs is that there is plenty of free time to go swimming or hiking (or if you are working, it is easy to sneak away). I admit that neither of us worked as hard as we could have.

Travis came quietly back into the room. "Dr. Worth is in the north wing with another patient," he said. "It's safe for you to stay a little while longer." He rested a large white hand on Frank's shoulder. "Ready to show her the pictures?" My father dipped his chin, and Travis produced a second object from the bedside drawer, a little leather photo album stamped in gold leaf: OUR PERFECT SUMMER. On the inside cover, in my mother's handwriting, I saw *J.S. + F.Y.* printed inside a neat red heart, and *1980* beneath.

Silently I turned the pages. Mama on a wooded trail

in a crisp green jumpsuit uniform, her long golden legs shod in sturdy hiking boots. Mama, peaches and cream, long before she'd ever had to color her hair in the bathtub. Mama on horseback. Mama laughing over a hot fudge sundae, the camera lens reflected in the diving spoon. Mama, before I ruined her life.

When the summer was over we arranged to stay at one of the caretaker's cabins on Plover Lake, and the rich people paid us to sweep their porches and make sure their pipes didn't freeze. We had friends we had made in the rangers, Sam and Flip and Robby, and on Thursday nights they would come over for drinks and poker and we played in front of the woodstove. One time the lake froze solid and we drove Flip's truck out to the center just for the heck of it. It was dangerous, but we got a thrill. When we came back inside, Janelle had grilled cheese and hot cocoa ready for us. Your mother was never much of a cook, but when she did cook it hit the spot.

In the spring her parents came out for the wedding. They tried their best to be nice to me, but they didn't like that they hadn't been able to get to know me before I asked her. Whenever Janelle's mother smiled at me it seemed like she had pasted it on, and I was afraid she suspected my secret. But they are good people, and I hope you are close to them now.

Your mother didn't know my secret before we got married. She knew there was something I kept from her, but she kept loving me like it didn't matter if I ever told her or not, so I thought maybe I would never have to.

If you ever come here I know what you will ask me. Why did I let myself fall in love with her? What could have made me think that I was good enough for her, that the bad thing wouldn't matter?

Then again, maybe you are old enough now that you have fallen in love yourself. If that is the case then you must already know how I would answer.

For a second I could see myself several years older, frying up bacon and eggs for Lee with a belly as round as the moon. As soon as I saw it, I knew it would never happen.

I wish I could have been a good father for you. A real dad. When Janelle told me she was going to have you I promised myself that I would be, that your childhood would be nothing like mine. Your mama was always a happy person, but while she was pregnant with you she was even happier. She used to sing lullabies all through the day like you were already born.

The breath caught in my throat as I read those lines. Mama had *wanted* me. For a little while at least, I had made her happy.

We hadn't told anybody, but we knew you were on the way and we wanted to save up as much as we could, so Janelle got a job at a hotel up on Whippoorwill Lake. She was at work one night when Robby came over. He had had a lot to drink, and he said things he should not have said, things about your mother's body. He said she wasn't the sweet, innocent girl I thought she was. I knew he was lying, but I also knew I could never think of our perfect summer again without hearing his ugly words.

I told him to leave, but he wouldn't. I told him I would hurt him, but he just laughed. It is so very hard to find out what someone you have called a friend really thinks of you.

I could have written this.

Then the unthinkable happened. Your mother came home early from work.

No matter how many times I told her I would never ever hurt her, not even if we fought, I don't know that she truly believed me. From that night until the night I left, I could feel her love for me but also her fear. I want to believe it was not her fear that kept her with me, but maybe I am lying to myself. It is a relief that I will never know for sure.

One night when your mama was eight months pregnant, we had an argument. Janelle wanted to move back to Pennsylvania, but I told her I wanted our baby to grow up loving those woods and hills and rivers as much as we did. The fight was about more than where to live though. I knew she wanted

*to be near her parents because she was afraid. I told
her this, and she raised her voice as she moved away
from me. I saw the terror in her eyes. I left the cabin
to think things over. Janelle never laughed anymore,
and I knew why.*

I tried to remember Mama's laugh, and I couldn't do
it. But she had loved me. She had.
There were a few blank pages, and then:

*I want to be good for you, little Yearly, but I can't.
I can only be honest. Now I will tell you everything.*

*The first thing I remember is being very small
beside a big long bus at the edge of a gas station. A
man had me by the hand and he was leading me
into a restroom behind the gas pumps. I don't remember his face, but he locked me in with him and
he was trying to get me to do something bad but I
did something much worse. I ate him.*

*I am so very sorry for the pain and shock this will
cause you. I don't know if there is anyone else like
me in the world. I know there are people in the
world who eat other people the way an ordinary
person eats a steak or a hamburger. That is not what
I did. I was only a little boy, but even with my milk
teeth I ground his bones down to nothing, and the
more I ate the hungrier I got.*

*Your mother had a way of making me forget I
was a monster even after she found out what I did.
She made me feel like I could live a good life and be*

an honest man, and that was only one reason why I loved her.

I did not want to leave you. But I had to because even though I knew I would never hurt you or your mother, I also knew that I could never be completely sure of it. The only reason I did not write to her was because I was so afraid she would not write back. I am very sorry for this now, but it is too late.

She was my sunshine. It is the worst pain of my life to know that I will never see her again.

More blank pages, and when the writing appeared again it was much bigger and more childlike.

On the first of each month they celebrate all the birthdays on the ward that happen that month, and there is always a vanilla sheet cake and a game of bingo. I never knew my birthday, so the Yearlys made it January 1st. If I knew your birthday I would ask Travis to remind me when it comes. That way I could picture what you might be doing to celebrate it. Travis says it is April 1, 1991, so I think you are almost nine now. I wish I knew if you were a girl or a boy because it is hard to picture you, not knowing that.

There was a space, and then one more line at the bottom of the page:

Travis is my friend. He is the only one here who knows me.

I looked up at the attendant. "Have you read any of this?"

He cleared his throat, but he didn't look away. "Parts of it."

"He . . . he showed you? He wanted you to see it?"

Travis nodded.

I felt myself hardening toward him. He'd had no right to read this, when my father was clearly not in his right mind. "Why?" I asked. "Why did he let you see it?"

"I'm sorry if you feel I violated your privacy," he replied kindly, and I had to soften. "He was anxious for me to read it. He needed someone to understand, you know?"

I nodded and turned back to the notebook. More blank pages, and then:

I can't keep hold of my thoughts. I have one, and it is gone in the time it takes to pick up the pencil. They won't let me write with a pen, only dull pencils. I think they must pay someone to lick the pencil tips before they let me have them.

There is one good thing about forgetting. Their faces are gone. I can't remember them anymore. When I fall asleep now it is only blackness.

But I take your mother's picture out of the drawer and look at it when I am in bed, as soon as I wake up and right before I go to sleep. This way I will not forget her face. It pains me to look because I know I will never see her again, but I look anyway because if I forget her face then I know there will be nothing left of me.

And on the next page, in waxy blue-violet:

Today they took my pencils away.

There were many more blank pages, and I began to think there was nothing more to read. Then there was a page in bright red crayon, the handwriting so messy I could hardly make it out.

Today I ruined the hand I write with.
HAND IS GONE
GONE
GONE

I glanced up, my heart in my throat. My father's eyes were closed, and I couldn't tell if he'd fallen asleep.

"What did he mean?" I said to Travis. "What did he mean, he ruined his hand?"

Slowly, with eyes still shut, my father withdrew his left hand until it fell into his lap to shield the right. I watched the way his face crumpled, like a sheet of paper spoiled by a single typo. Travis looked at the floor.

I turned the page, and another, and another. The rest of the notebook was filled with one word, over and over in every color in the Crayola box:

Janelle Janelle Janelle Janelle Janelle Janelle Janelle
Janelle Janelle Janelle Janelle Janelle Janelle Janelle
Janelle Janelle Janelle Janelle Janelle Janelle Janelle
Janelle Janelle Janelle Janelle Janelle Janelle Janelle

Janelle Janelle Janelle Janelle Janelle Janelle Janelle
Janelle Janelle Janelle Janelle Janelle Janelle Janelle
Janelle Janelle Janelle Janelle Janelle Janelle Janelle
Janelle Janelle Janelle Janelle Janelle Janelle Janelle
Janelle Janelle Janelle Janelle Janelle Janelle Janelle
Janelle Janelle Janelle Janelle Janelle Janelle Janelle

"Where is your mother?" Travis asked quietly.

"Gone," I said.

"That's what I was afraid of."

I looked at my father. Slowly, very slowly, my sadness turned into anger. "Why won't you answer my question?"

"Please, Maren. I asked you not to upset him." Travis sighed. "Listen to me now. This is important. Dr. Worth is making calls about you."

"Calls? What do you mean?"

Travis's eyes reminded me of a dog's, wet and brown and anxious to please. "Child protective services."

"Why?"

"She said you brought a big rucksack—"

"I left it in her office. Was that wrong?"

"Not wrong, no. But it was pretty clear to her that you were carrying your life on your back."

I sighed. "Is someone coming for me, then?"

"I don't know yet. Listen, Maren, if you don't have anywhere to go . . ."

"I'll be all right," I said quickly.

"My shift is over at six," he went on. "I understand why you feel you ought to say no, and I wouldn't want you to do anything you're not comfortable with. I just know Frank would like me to at least extend you the offer."

My father's eyes were still squeezed shut.

"Thanks. I really can't, but . . . I appreciate that."

"Are you sure? I can help you figure out what to do next. If you don't want to go into foster care, I mean."

"You think there's another option?"

"I don't know. But I'll make you dinner, and maybe we can figure it out together?"

"All right." I turned back to the man in the chair. "I have to go now, Dad." He groped for my hand and tried to squeeze it. I felt like I should tell him I'd be back soon, but I didn't.

Travis stayed behind a moment to offer my father a few last words of comfort.

"Wait." I froze in the doorway and put my fist against the jamb. "I'm not leaving until you tell me what he did to his hand."

Travis gently nudged me aside before he closed the door and turned the key in the first lock. "I think you already know the answer."

At ten minutes past six Travis drove down the Bridewell road in an old black sedan. I got in, and he smiled and said, "I hope the day didn't pass too slowly for you."

"It was all right." It *had* passed slowly—a walk into Tarbridge had yielded very little, not even a public library or a secondhand bookshop. But Travis had stowed my rucksack in his backseat, so at least I hadn't had to lug it around town all day.

He cast me a sidelong look. "How long have you been on your own?"

"Not that long," I said. "Only a couple of weeks."

"A lot can happen in a couple of weeks."

It only really hit me then, how strange it was that a person who wasn't an eater knew there was any such thing. Travis was one of the calmest, pleasantest people I'd ever met. He hadn't shown the slightest flicker of horror or disgust, not even when he told me in not so many words what my father had done to his hand. Maybe it hadn't occurred to Travis that I could be like Frank.

"Did you find safe places to sleep?" he asked. "Were people kind to you?"

I didn't lie—at least not outright. I let him imagine that Mrs. Harmon had seen me off with a wave and a smile, that Sully thrived on farm-stand vegetables and fresh venison, and that Lee had shown up at the Walmart that night in his own black pickup truck. We did not talk about my father.

Travis lived in a little blue bungalow a half-hour drive from the hospital, back in the direction of Sully's cabin. Another cozy, empty house. I didn't like how familiar this was starting to feel.

A small table opposite the stove was already set with a plate, utensils, and a drinking glass on a quilted place mat that reminded me again of Mrs. Harmon. "You'll have to excuse me," he said as he opened a drawer and drew out a second set of cutlery. "I wasn't expecting to have a guest tonight."

"You live alone?"

He nodded. "Since my mother passed."

"Oh," I said. "I'm sorry to hear that."

Travis opened the fridge and bent to retrieve a covered pot with both hands. "I made some stew on my last day off. My mother's recipe. Will that be okay?"

"Sure."

"I hope you like it," he said as he placed the pot on the stove and lit the burner.

"I'm sure it's delicious."

He smiled as he lifted the lid and gave the stew a stir. "I never had to cook for myself before, but I've found I enjoy it. I like making my mother's old recipes because it lets me forget for a little while that she's not here anymore."

"Have you always lived here?"

Travis nodded. "It's a nice little house, don't you think? I never wanted to live anywhere else."

To please him, I cast an appreciative glance around the kitchen and into the living room. There was a brown and yellow afghan on the sofa and a rocking chair in the corner, looking as fragile as if it were made of matchsticks. As Travis went around the room opening the windows he saw me eyeing the chair and said, "That rocking chair has been in my family for over a hundred and fifty years. My mother nursed me in it. My grandmother nursed my father in it. And all the way back to the pioneers." As he spoke he gazed through the patterned rug on the floor, smiling absently. "I guess it was my great-great-great-grandfather who made it."

"Do you have any brothers or sisters?" I asked.

Travis smiled ruefully. "Nope. Just me. I guess you're an only child too."

I nodded.

"My mother was very sick after she gave birth to me. The doctor told her she couldn't have any more."

"Oh," I said.

The house filled with savory smells as the stew bubbled on the stove. My stomach growled loudly, and we both laughed. Travis ladled us each a bowl, and I watched him clasp his hands and bow his head before he picked up his spoon.

The stew was delicious, but I started to feel a little uneasy when Travis kept pausing to watch me eat. "Something wrong?" I asked.

He shook his head and flashed me half a smile as he dipped his spoon. We had seconds and thirds. A cool evening breeze blew through the living room windows, and from a tree in the front yard a night bird sang a song I'd never heard before.

Travis wouldn't let me wash the dishes. "Make yourself at home," he said as he turned to the sink. "I'll bring you some sugar cookies and lemonade for dessert."

I sat down on the couch. "You really don't have to go to so much trouble."

"It's no trouble." He paused, soapy sponge in hand. "I guess it's just nice to have someone to take care of." He shook his head, as if he were arguing with himself. "No, not just anyone—*you*—Frank's daughter. I'll never be able to cook dinner for your dad, but at least I can do it for you."

An uncomfortable silence settled over the room as Travis finished the dishes. When he was done he took out a carton of lemonade and a supermarket-bakery box of sugar cookies, poured two glasses, and arranged the cookies on a plate. He put our dessert on the coffee table and sat down beside me. Travis took a deep breath, and I knew I wasn't going to like what he was about to say. "There's something I need to tell you," he said slowly. "Something I have to confess."

Suddenly he didn't seem so teddy-bearish. "Confess?"

"It's not that I didn't mean it, about helping you to figure things out without going into foster care. I meant it. I really do want to help you."

Weariness trickled over me. "Just tell me, Travis. What is it?"

He drew another long breath before he said, "It's my fault, what your father did to himself."

I stared at him. "What? How . . . ?"

"I thought it would help him if I could show him some proof that he wasn't alone, that he wasn't the only one. I spent months searching out the right people, figuring out how to ask the right questions. I knew it was dangerous, but I didn't care."

"What people?" I asked. "What questions?"

Travis looked at me, sad and grave. "You're a smart girl, Maren. I know why you keep asking questions you already know the answers to."

I stared at the plate of sugar cookies. Suddenly the stew wasn't sitting so well in my stomach. "Why are you telling me this?"

"I knew you would come here," Travis said. "I knew you would be like him."

That feeling settled over me again, the same as when I'd found Mrs. Harmon dead on the couch—like I was hovering someplace miles above my feet.

"Do you see?" he said softly. "It was my fault for telling him what I'd learned. I thought it would comfort him, but I hadn't considered what it meant about *you*. It was a very dark time," he murmured. "In his life, and in mine." Travis looked up, his eyes pale and fearful. "Do you understand what I'm trying to say?"

I shook my head.

"It had never occurred to him that you might be like him. He was devastated, Maren. That's why he . . . he . . ." Travis gulped hard and glanced at me, then back at the floor. "That's why he mutilated himself. Because of me. I was trying to help, and I made things worse." He pressed his palms to his eyes. "But then, that's the way my life has always been. I try to help, but I never do. I ruin everything."

I felt sick. I didn't blame him—I just wished he hadn't told me. "It wasn't your fault, Travis."

He wiped his eyes and made a poor attempt at a smile. "I don't believe that, but it makes me feel better to hear you say it."

"I don't get it," I said after a pause. "You actually went *looking* for people like us?"

He shrugged. "I was fascinated. Anybody would be. I wanted to know how it was possible for some perfectly normal-looking person, a person like you, to gobble someone up just like you were an ogre in a fairy story. I still haven't seen it, but I know it's possible. I know it's real."

"But weren't you afraid you'd be . . ." I left the question dangling, and Travis sighed.

"There was no need to be afraid." For the first time, there was an unpleasant look on his face. "Nobody wanted me." He seemed almost angry as he said it.

"Where did you go? How did you find them?"

"Years ago I had a friend in law enforcement, and one night I had the chance to ask him about it. I told him what I knew—I didn't mention Frank by name, I want you to know that—and he said it was something only a few people in the police force were willing to talk about. People go missing all the time, and when they can't find the body they assume that's what it is. Sometimes the cops know who did it, but they'll never be able to prove it. Eaters can be regular people, *fine upstanding citizens* and all that. My friend even gave me names. That's how I met them. Men just having a drink after work before going home to their wives and kids, you know? I didn't meet any women or girls, but they told me about them. That women did it too." He rested his elbows on his knees, closed his eyes, and rubbed the bridge of his nose, just like Mama used to do. "I wouldn't be surprised if there are cops who do it. My friend had his suspicions."

Again I thought of the needlepoint above the door at the police station, of how wrong it was. I said, "You can't live this life without always running away from it." *Or getting yourself locked up.* Those daydreams I'd had about my father, of living in a house and doing all the things normal families do—they seemed so ludicrous now.

Travis raised his head and looked at me. "Every time you did it, your mother packed your things and you left right away?"

I nodded.

"Ever wonder what would've happened if you'd stayed?"

I shook my head.

"Maybe nothing," he said. "But you thought you had to run, so you ran."

I got up and paced. I couldn't stand to be that close to him, after all he'd said. "Something else I don't get," I said. "Why aren't you afraid of us?" He was still staring at the floor, so I went on. "I mean, the only reason I can think of is if you *are* one of us . . . but I don't think you are. Are you?"

He shook his head. "No," he said softly, and his voice was suddenly hoarse. "No, I'm not one of you."

"Then why? Why are you so . . . so *fixated* on us?"

When he began to cry a new feeling settled over me, a mixture of pity and embarrassment. "I'm so lonely, Maren. It's been like this all my life. I've tried, believe me I've tried. I've tried so hard to make friends. But when my mother died I knew there wasn't anybody left in the world who loved me."

"You just said you had a friend who was a cop!"

Travis shook his head, his eyes on the rug. "He wasn't a friend. Not really." When he lifted his chin and met my eye, I didn't see a man in front of me. I saw an inconsolable little boy. "I know you know how I feel," he said. "Your parents are still alive, but you're just as alone as I am."

"You're not like me, Travis. You're a good person. You can go out into the world and make real friends. I know you can."

"I've already tried. I can't try anymore when it's only going to turn out the same as it always has. I can't put myself through that anymore, I just can't." He drew a Kleenex out of a crocheted tissue-box holder and wiped his eyes. "Can I ask you something?"

I nodded warily.

"What leads you to eat the people you eat? What is it that draws you to them? I know it's different for each of you. . . ."

I shook my head. "I don't want to talk about this."

Travis sighed and patted the sofa cushion beside him. "I wish you'd sit down. It makes me nervous to think of you running out the door. More nervous than I already am."

I took a seat at the far end of the sofa. "Why are you nervous?"

"Because there's something I need to ask you."

He reached for my hand. "No." I stood up again and inched away. "No, no, no."

"Please don't—please don't take me the wrong way. I'm not trying to take advantage of you, honest." He drew a slow, deliberate breath. "I don't even care for women in that way."

"I can't, Travis." I felt myself shuddering, wave after wave after wave. "I'm really sorry, but I can't. I can't."

"I know it's wrong, and I hate myself even more for asking," he whispered. "But ever since I met your father and found out who he was, I *knew*."

"What do you mean, you 'knew'?"

"Please," he said again. "It would mean so much to me."

I was inching my way to the door. "I think I should go now."

"Where are you going to go?" He gazed at me, eerily calm.

I slung my rucksack over my shoulder. "I don't know. I'll figure it out."

"*Please,* Maren. We won't talk about it anymore. I won't say another word, I promise."

I shook my head. "Do you really think we can just eat some cookies and watch a movie and talk like none of this happened? I really need to go."

He leaned forward, elbows on his knees, and rubbed his hands over his face. "All right," he sighed. "But I'd feel a whole lot better about it if you'd let me drive you."

It was a long drive to Sully's cabin, but Travis didn't complain. I nodded off in the car, and when I woke up I felt relieved I hadn't had to pretend. How could we have a normal conversation after what he'd asked of me?

Thankfully, he didn't try. Once I'd roused myself he switched on the radio and we listened to a ballgame. "Are you a Brewers fan?" I asked. It felt weird to say something so ordinary. Travis just shrugged.

Sully's truck wasn't there when we pulled up, though the lights were on and the door was open. "Hello? Sully?" I called, though I knew he couldn't be there. A fire still smoldered in the woodstove. "Maybe he just went out for milk," I said.

"Is he expecting you?" I nodded. Travis sat on the couch and cast an eye over the hunting trophies. "I'd better wait with you until he gets back."

"That's okay," I replied. "You really don't have to." What I meant was *Please go now,* but he either didn't get it or didn't want to.

"You said this guy is a friend of the lady you met at the supermarket?"

"Sort of."

"'Sort of'?" Travis raised his eyebrows.

"I don't mean to be rude, but I don't feel like I owe you any explanations either."

"I'm kind of responsible for you now, Maren. What would I tell your father if something were to happen to you?"

"Listen, Travis. I know you would never hurt me, but that doesn't mean I feel safe with you."

"That's not fair," he said softly. "You *know* you're safe with me, Maren. I know everything about you, and I'm not afraid. Doesn't that count for anything?"

"Of course it does." I felt a stab of irritation, but I

tried not to show it. "And I'm grateful for everything you've done for me today."

We fell into silence. Travis took long breaths between the night sounds coming through the screen door. I felt his hand, cool and moist on my arm. "I can be anything you want. I can say anything you want me to say, if you'll only . . ." He ran his fingers down to my wrist and tried to grab my hand.

Before I even knew what I was doing, I yanked my hand away and slapped him hard across the face. I'd never done that to anyone before, and for a second we just stared at each other in shock. "You promised you wouldn't ask me again," I said at last.

"You don't understand," he whispered. "I don't want to take advantage of you. I'd never, ever hurt you."

"This isn't how it works." Every time I looked at him now I wanted to gag. "You said you understood that."

He reached for me again, and I stood up to get away from him. I felt his desperation clinging to me, sticking to every corner of my body, cold and slimy.

"I know I can make myself into someone you could want," he cried. "I know I can, if you'll only *tell* me!"

I grabbed his hand, pulled him up, led him to the door, and pushed him out. "Thank you for the ride, and for dinner." I couldn't bring myself to look at him as I fumbled with the latch on the screen door. "I really do appreciate it." I watched his hand trembling as he drew his car keys out of his pocket.

For a moment he stood there in front of the door, wiping his other hand over his eyes. I still couldn't look

at his face, but I knew he was crying. Finally he turned
and hurried down the rickety steps, and I came out and
stood on the porch to watch him drive away into the
moonlit forest. I thought I would feel relieved, but I didn't.

An hour passed, and Sully didn't come back. I took
the photocopies of my confession out of my rucksack,
crumpled them up, and fed them to the fire one by one.

> *My name is Maren Yearly, and I am responsible*
> *for the deaths of the following people . . . Penny*
> *Wilson (in her 20s), in or near Edgartown, PA,*
> *1983 . . . Luke Vanderwall (8 years old), Camp*
> *Ameewagan (Catskills), NY, July, 1990 . . . Jamie*
> *Gash (10 years old), Badgerstown, MD, December,*
> *1992 . . . Dmitri Levertov (11 years old), Newfon-*
> *taine, SC, May, 1993 . . . Joe Sharkey (12 years*
> *old), Buckley, FL, October, 1994 . . . Kevin Wheeler*
> *(13 years old), Fairweather, NJ, December, 1995 . . .*
> *Noble Collins (14 years old), Holland, ME, April,*
> *1996 . . . Marcus Hoff (15 years old), Barron Falls,*
> *MA, March, 1997 . . . C. J. Mitchell (16 years old),*
> *Clover Hills, NY, November, 1997 . . . Andy (I don't*
> *know his last name, but he was an employee of the*
> *Walmart near Pittston, Iowa), June, 1998 . . .*

The truth wouldn't set me free. I'd only end up like
my father.

I wandered through the cabin in search of a distrac-
tion. There was a row of ancient paperbacks on a shelf
in the dining area, but they were mostly spy thrillers or

romance novels, nothing I was interested in. I went into the kitchen in search of hot chocolate and grilled cheese fixings—not the right time of year for either, but I guess I needed to feel like this cabin was home, or at least another version of it. There wasn't any bread or cheese or cocoa powder, so I settled for a stick of beef jerky.

Then I opened a cupboard by the back door, expecting to find citronella candles or a stack of board games. Instead it was crammed with an assortment of objects, clothing, and little golden tangles of women's jewelry, Walkmans and collectible coins in clear plastic cases, clunky pewter tableware, and random knickknacks. I thrust a curious hand into the jumble, and a minute later my fingers settled upon an object with contours that felt awfully familiar.

I drew the object out of the cupboard. It was Mr. Harmon's sphinx. I tried to tell myself it was only a memento, but I knew that wasn't true. Sully took things he could sell, not things to remember his victims by.

After that I went into his bedroom, though I didn't dare turn on the light. The bed was made, but all around the room was a mess of things that wouldn't fit into the cupboard: lamps and clocks and porcelain dolls with rolling glass eyes.

I sat on the bed and poked through the stuff on the bedside table. More jewelry. A tarnished silver flask—not the one he kept in his pocket, someone else's. Credit cards with different names on them. Among those credit cards was an ID card labeled NATIONAL PARK STAFF,

FRANCIS YEARLY. In the corner of the card was a small black-and-white photo of him—it was blurry, but I could still make out his smile.

Dad, Dad, Dad. A word with no meaning. What was Sully doing with my father's ID card? This didn't make sense. How had he met my father? What did he want with him?

The sound of a truck engine and headlights passing across the wall drew me out of a daze. I ran into the spare bedroom and hid the trophy and the ID card in the nightstand. I heard Sully's footsteps on the rickety porch steps, followed by the slam of the screen door. "Missy? You here?"

I took a second to gather myself before I came out into the sitting room. "Hi, Sully." *Who are you?*

He stood under the stag's head with a paper bag of groceries. "Well, well. Didn't think you'd be back so soon."

"Is it all right that I'm here?"

"All right? 'Course it's all right!" He set the grocery bag on the kitchen table and put the milk in the fridge. "You hungry?"

"Not really, thanks." I hoped my stomach wouldn't rumble and betray me.

"Where's your boyfriend?"

"He went back to Virginia."

"He leave you off here?"

I nodded, only because I didn't want to explain everything.

"Sorry he's gone?"

I shrugged, and Sully gave me a sly look. "You like to think you ain't." He pried the cap off a bottle of beer, sat down at the table, and tipped it back. I watched his Adam's apple bob up and down as he gulped. He sighed and wiped his mouth. "Give up on finding your daddy?"

"No," I said. "I found him."

His bushy gray eyebrows shot up. "That was some mighty quick detective work."

I shoved my hands in my pockets and toed the edge of the braided rug on the floor. "Yeah, well."

"Well? Don't keep me hangin', girl!"

"He's in a home," I said slowly. "A mental home."

"Aw, Missy. I sure am sorry to hear that." As he said it I wondered how many other lies he'd told me. Sully wasn't sorry, not one bit. He'd known all along who my father was.

"You were right," I said. "I should have forgotten about him and gone with you from the beginning." I didn't know what made me say it. Sully was the last person I wanted to travel with now. *His daddy's pickled tongue, his mama's heart in a stew . . .*

He took another gulp of beer and gave me an odd look. In that moment I felt that there was no more sense of *us against the world*, no mention of that fishing lesson he'd promised me—as if he knew I'd been through his cabinets. "Got any idea what you're gonna do next?" he asked.

I shook my head. I wished I hadn't told Travis to leave. Or Lee. If I hadn't picked a fight with Lee, this horrible night never would've happened.

Sully finished his beer and tossed the bottle in the trash. "Well, you got time to figure it out in the mornin'."

"Will you be here when I wake up this time?"

He nodded. "Sleep tight, Missy."

10

I went into the bedroom and turned the key in the lock as softly as I could manage. I pulled out the sphinx and set it on the night table, and tucked my father's ID card in my rucksack. Then I switched off the light and, without taking off my jeans, climbed into the bed Lee had slept in, burrowing beneath the red and blue patchwork quilt. I could smell him on the sheets, and it comforted me. He was probably halfway to Tingley by now.

When I fell asleep I dreamed of Mrs. Harmon. We were sitting at her kitchen table, and the light streaming through her suncatchers made glimmering pools of green and blue on the linoleum. She was cutting the slice of cake she'd promised me. "It's carrot, with cream cheese frosting," she said proudly as she laid the moist auburn slab on a dish and handed it to me. "This is the last cake I'll ever bake, so I'm glad it turned out well."

Mrs. Harmon poured us each a cup of tea from a china pot as I devoured the slice. She watched me eat, sipping pensively from her teacup. "He's not a very nice man, is he, dear?"

"Who? Sully?"

She nodded.

I raised my hand to my neck to hide her locket. "Because he took your husband's trophy?"

"That's one reason."

"He's given me a lot of good advice."

"You feel grateful to him?"

"Yeah. I guess I do."

"Maren," she began, setting down her cup and resting her hands palms-down on the table, "sometimes it's the worst things in life that have the most to teach us. You take what you can, and as for the ugly parts, well—you 'leave it go and get on with the business of living,' as my Dougie used to say. Do you see what I mean?"

"I think so."

She nodded. "Don't worry about the locket, dear. It makes me glad to know you'll think of me whenever you wear it." She sighed. "I'm just sorry I won't be able to teach you how to knit."

"Mrs. Harmon, there's something I have to tell you."

She smiled at me expectantly. I put down my fork and dropped my hands in my lap. I'd only had one sip of my tea but the cup was empty, and she picked up the pot and refilled it to the brim. I looked at her hands as she poured, and they were the hands of a much younger woman. I thought it would be easier if I said what I had to say while she was still pouring. After all the kindness she'd shown me it would be too hard to look her in the eye. "I'm like him," I whispered.

With a deliberate air she laid down the teapot. "No, dear," she said as she laid her hand on mine. "No, you're not."

The kitchen melted into nothing, and so did Mrs. Harmon. She had her hand on my hand, and I watched it vanish. Then I was back under the pile of coats in Jamie Gash's spare room, a fur collar tickling my cheek, and I heard my mother calling for me. *Get up, Maren. Wake up.*

In my dreamy confusion I was convinced, just for a second, that after all I'd been through she'd finally changed her mind, and she had come and found me using some maternal homing instinct. A second later I was fully awake, my heart in my throat. There was someone in the room, but it wasn't my mother. I should've known there wasn't any point locking the door.

Sully was sitting in a chair in the corner of the bedroom. I couldn't make out his face. "See you found the ID card."

"It was my father's." I inched back on my elbows, pressing myself against the headboard as if I could get away from him. "How did you get it?"

"He left it here." Sully scratched his chin, and it sounded like sandpaper. "He's my son."

"Your *son?*" I cried.

For the second time that night, I felt like I'd been set

adrift somewhere outside myself. It couldn't be. It couldn't.
Aside from my granddad I never did it in the house.

"Damned woman got in the car and took him away
from me," Sully was saying. "By the time I caught up to
her, she'd lost him. Man stole my boy right out from under her nose." He let out a snort of contempt. "She wasn't
the sharpest knife, I can tell ya that."

"My . . . my grandmother?"

"Yeah." He cocked his head, as if this were the first
time he'd considered the connection. "Reckon she was."

"What happened to her?"

Sully laughed, a cold, terrifying laugh. That was my
answer.

"Did you know where my dad was? When he was living with the Yearlys?"

"Couldn't get to him. Not without makin' a scene, and
that was just about the last thing I needed. But I waited
too long. He's hidin', and he knows I'll never get him now.
But then, I guess I don't have to, do I?"

"What do you mean?"

"I knew you was out there. And if I couldn't get to him,
at least I could get to *you*. I was waitin' for ya, Missy. All
that time," he said slowly, "I was waitin' for you to come
back."

A cold sick feeling came flooding out of my gut. "Why
didn't you tell me who you were?"

He chuckled. "Why'd it take *you* so long to figure it
out?"

Neither of us spoke for a long minute. Finally I asked,
"Is that what you were waiting for?"

Sully shifted his weight in the chair, and I heard his bones creak. "Every kid's a mistake," he said. "Every kid who ever was. You see that, don't ya, Missy?"

"I don't know," I said slowly. "What else would you eat?"

Sully laughed. "Now you're usin' your noggin."

His son's pickled tongue, his granddaughter's heart in a stew. He exhaled then, and I smelled it, and it was like a day-old battlefield and a backed-up sewer and a hundred landfills all rolled into a single breath. You can imagine it, can't you? The man feasted on corpses and never brushed his teeth.

I couldn't see the knife, but I knew it was there. He was going to kill me with the blade he'd used to peel his apple.

Get out, Mama said. *Get out, or he'll trap you under the bedclothes.*

I've often wished I were dead, but I didn't want to die like *this.* I kicked off the quilt as he lunged toward the bed. He got on top of me, but not completely—he had my arms, but my legs were still free—and I felt the cold blade of the knife flush against my left forearm.

"You lied to me!" I screamed. "You lied!"

"I never lied," he hissed, and his breath on my face nearly knocked me out. "I only eat 'em once they're dead. I don't always let 'em die on their own time."

Why spend all that time telling me stories? Asking me questions? *Teaching* me things? What did any of it matter if he was only going to eat me?

Entertainment. Or maybe just fattening me up.

Now get your left hand free—make him fumble for the knife—reach back for the trophy.

I drew up my knee and began to kick at his legs with my heel, and while it was a pretty sad effort, it distracted him from his grip on my hands. I pulled my left hand free, batting his knife away by the handle, and I kept kicking as I reached back for the trophy on the night-stand. He fumbled for the knife as I fumbled for the trophy. My heart leapt as my fingers settled on the cold metal contours of the sphinx, and I gripped the trophy by the wing and brought it in an arc over my head. The blow landed on the back of his skull, and he lost his hold on the knife. "Bitch!" he shouted. "You little bitch!" He reared up and lifted his hand to his head, and that's when I clocked him good. He fell on top of me, and I felt the blood, hot and sticky on my fingers. I dropped the trophy on the floor, pushed him over, and rolled out of the bed, groping for my sneakers.

Looking back on it, I know I could have gathered my things into my rucksack. But I had no idea how quickly he would rouse himself, so there wasn't a second to spare. I tore down the creaky wooden steps into the forest with nothing but my journal in my hand and my birth certifi-cate in the back pocket of my jeans.

I didn't have a chance, of course. Even if I could run the two or three miles through the woods back to the main road, I could hardly expect to hitch a ride in the middle of the night. Sully would come after me in his truck. Maybe he would run me over, and I would get what I'd wanted on that Iowa highway after all.

The track was muddy and I slipped more than once, but I got up and kept going, taking great lungfuls of air to push the panic aside. Muddy knees and bloody hands. Even if there *was* someone on the road this late, no one in their right mind would stop for me.

I was almost at the end of the dirt track when I saw a light up ahead. I slowed down as I came closer, and the light resolved itself into a car. An empty car, with the driver's-side door wide open.

I stopped beside the open door, gasping for air, and turned to check behind me before I bent to look inside. It was Travis's car. His Donald Duck keychain was still dangling from the ignition.

I popped my head up and scanned the moonlit forest. I didn't dare call his name, but I had a feeling there was no point. He wasn't out there.

I pulled into Travis's driveway as the sun was coming up, and I quietly let myself back into the house. The lemonade glasses and plate of sugar cookies were still on the coffee table.

I peeled off my T-shirt and jeans and dropped them in the washer. Then I got into the shower, turned on the water as hot as I could stand it, and cried. Nowhere was safe now.

I couldn't even stay here much longer. Travis wouldn't be in to work, and someone would come looking for him. I rubbed his soap between my hands, used his Head & Shoulders shampoo and his white fluffy towel, and looked at myself in the mirror like I was somebody else, somebody with no names written on her heart. I was done pretending to be normal.

When I got out of the shower I rinsed with Travis's Listerine. I put my clothes in the dryer and walked through the house. The second floor was one big room with slanted ceilings and gabled windows, with pictures of his parents on the dresser and night table and a floral duvet on the bed. Maybe he'd inherited the room after his mother died.

I found a new backpack on a hook in the closet and then I opened all the dresser drawers. His clothes were much too big for me, but I needed money and Travis seemed like the kind of guy who would keep some spare cash at the back of his sock drawer.

I was wrong though. The money wasn't in the drawer; it was in the closet, rolled up in the toe of an old leather shoe. I sat on the bed, my hair dripping on the duvet, and counted out seven hundred dollars.

I had to wipe down the steering wheel before I started the car. I wanted to follow Lee to Tingley, but I didn't know what I would say to him. What if *You told me so* didn't make things better? What if he didn't want to be my friend anymore?

I knew I shouldn't go. But doing things I wasn't supposed to do was pretty much my specialty.

After the pickup truck, Travis's car was easy to drive. I figured out how to pump gas when I needed it, and I was careful to keep to the speed limit. I let out a sigh of relief each time a state police car passed me by. That night I did what Lee and I had been doing—found a park, but not too close to a campsite—and I climbed into the back-seat and curled up under a scratchy wool blanket I'd found in the trunk.

When I fell asleep I dreamed about Sully. I was back in Mrs. Harmon's Spare Oom, stifled by the darkness, only this time I didn't throw off the bedclothes in time, and he had me trapped so I couldn't kick. With one hand he pinned my wrists together against the pillow, and with the other hand he reached for the sphinx trophy. He held it above his head and I could see the moonlight glint-ing off the bronze wings. *Ain't no such thing as a clean getaway, Missy,* he said, and I woke up just before the trophy hit my face.

It only occurred to me when I got to Tingley that I didn't know Lee's last name, so I went to the high school. It was summer recess now, but the front office was still open. A nice secretary dialed Kayla's number and handed me the phone.

"Hi," I said. "This is Maren—Lee's friend? At your aunt's house that time?"

"Oh yeah," she said slowly. "I remember."

"I wanted to say hello to you that day, but . . ."

"Yeah," she said. "It's okay. Is my brother with you?"

"You mean he's not there?"

"He hasn't been back since that time you were here."
She paused. "Is he all right?"

"I'm sure he is. We . . . sort of had an argument. I
guess I just wanted to come back here and make it up to
him."

"Did he tell you he was coming home?"

"Yeah. But he probably got tied up somewhere. Maybe
he found some work."

"Yeah," she said. "Maybe."

There was something else I wanted to tell her, but I
didn't know how to begin. Fortunately she saved me the
trouble. "I have to leave for work now, but do you think
you could meet me there later and we could talk? I'm done
at eight." She paused. "If you want, I can probably get you
a free ice cream cone."

I smiled at the receiver. "Thanks," I said. "That would
be great."

True to her word, Kayla met me in the parking lot at Hal-
liday's Ice Cream Parlor with a double scoop of peanut
butter fudge. She got in the passenger's seat. Between
licks I asked, "Did you pass your driver's test?"

She nodded. "I had to borrow my friend's truck, so I
was a little nervous, but I did all right. Remembered to
stop at the stop sign and all that. Lee said if I could learn
to parallel park with a pickup truck then I'd be good to
go, and he was right."

I smiled. "That's great."

She pulled down the sun visor and looked at herself in the mirror. "I see you passed yours too." I shook my head, and her eyes went wide. "You mean you drove all the way here without a license?"

"Never got pulled over or anything. Your brother's a good teacher."

She flashed me a sad smile and watched me slurp down the ice cream. Once I'd swallowed the last bite of waffle cone I was ready to tell her the other reason I'd come back to Tingley.

"Lee said he wanted you to have a car," I said. "So I want you to have this one. Just get Lee to replace the plates for you the next time he's home."

Kayla stared at me, her mouth wide open.

"Just please don't ask me whose car it was. I didn't steal it, and that's all you need to know."

In the morning she poured two bowls of Count Chocula, and we ate on the front steps. "You could stay here awhile," Kayla said. "Wait 'til Lee gets back. My mom wouldn't mind." Their mother hadn't been home since I arrived.

"Thanks," I said. "That's really nice of you. But I don't think Lee would want me to."

She made a face. "I don't think he would either. I just can't figure out why."

"He loves you more than anybody. He wants to protect you."

"Protect me from what?"

I sighed.

"It has to do with Rachel, doesn't it? Did he tell you about Rachel?"

I nodded.

"I liked Rachel," she said sadly.

"Lee said she's still in the hospital."

"I tried to go see her once, after it first happened," Kayla said. "They wouldn't let me in."

"My dad is in one of those places." I stirred the chocolaty milk at the bottom of the cereal bowl. "A place called Bridewell, in Wisconsin."

Kayla set down her bowl and patted me on the shoulder. "I'm sorry."

I showered and changed into a spare set of her clothes. I wanted to ask for a black T-shirt, but I thought better of it.

She drove me back to the interstate, and I got out carrying Travis's backpack filled with food, another change of clothing, and two Madeleine L'Engle novels Kayla had scrounged up for me.

Kayla turned off the engine. "Are you absolutely sure you want to give me your car?"

"I'm sure."

"Where are you going?"

"I guess I'll make my way back to Bridewell."

"To visit your dad? And then what?"

I shrugged. Going back to Wisconsin felt like climbing into Sully's open jaw, but I didn't know where else to go.

"When Lee comes home, I'll tell him to meet you there."

I smiled as she got out and came around the front bumper to embrace me. It was kind of her, but I knew there was no point hoping he'd follow through.

This time, miraculously enough, I had no trouble hitch-hiking. The second day I made it as far as Oberon, Kentucky, where the middle-aged couple I'd been traveling with treated me to a meatloaf special and a hot fudge sundae at an all-night diner. Thanks to Travis, I stayed at a motor inn, took a long hot bath, and fell asleep with the television on.

The next morning I went for a walk in the hills. I crossed a covered wooden bridge over a trickling river, passed laundry on the line outside a ramshackle farm-house here and there. I didn't know where I was going, but for the first time in weeks I felt no anxiety. Being with Kayla had made me feel better about a lot of things. If I never saw Lee again, it was all the better for him. Travis had gotten what he'd asked for, and if Sully wanted to finish me off, then let him come. I would be ready.

I came to a bend in the road and paused to admire the view. An ancient red barn stood at the edge of a meadow—a field, really, but it hadn't been tilled for years—and beyond it, all around, was a dense tract of pine trees rising to a crest in the near distance.

The barn belonged to a farmhouse across the road. The house and yard were enclosed by a white picket fence in a shoddy state of repair, and the house itself was no better off. Some of the windows were broken, and there was a water-stained condemned notice stapled to the front door. No one had lived here for years.

I lifted the latch on the little wooden gate and walked around the building. There was a covered well in the backyard and a small lean-to stocked with rusting tools. I drew out a hatchet and hefted it in my hand. A modest garden plot, encircled by chicken wire, still yielded a spray of basil or rosemary between the weeds and wildflowers.

I went across the road to check out the barn. The latch on the door was still secure, and when I opened it a few nesting birds made their protests from the rafters. Though the stalls were empty, the room still smelled sweetly of hay and cow manure, and the ladder to the loft seemed sturdy enough to support my weight. I climbed up and looked out the window into the trees. I couldn't have asked for a better hiding spot.

I walked back down to the highway and picked up a tent, a sleeping bag, a gallon of water, and a few other necessaries from an army and navy store near the motor inn. This time I remembered the can opener.

For weeks I lived on canned beans and the remnants of the kitchen garden, sleeping in my new tent in the loft with the hatchet at my side. In my dreams my father came to me and smiled as he held out his hand. I opened my mouth and he put his hand inside. I ran down the winding corridors, the walls stained with words, and one by one I found them, each of them, waiting for me in the dark.

Even Sully, slumped on the ground with his back against the wall, taking me in with a weary glance before offering his neck.

I walked down the highway to a drugstore and bought two big bottles of Listerine, and that night I drowned in an ocean of cinnamon-flavored mouthwash. When I woke up I could even feel the burn in my nose.

Some afternoons, as I sat on the barn roof looking out over the road with *Troubling a Star* splayed on my knee, I would spot a rusted red pickup turning the bend in the road, and I'd forget what I'd dreamed and feel my heart suddenly stuck in my throat. Other times I imagined going on living like that forever, doing no harm to anyone or anything as I said hello and goodbye to the sun each day, and made up my own patterns between the stars.

Then, of course, it would rain all day, or I'd find a dead frog in the well, or some neighbors would draw uncomfortably near, and I'd think better of living there indefinitely. There were no secondhand bookshops along that little stretch of highway, and the farmhouse yielded nothing beyond a candle, a stack of decade-old newspapers, and a box of matches.

So the last week of July I packed up my things and climbed down the ladder for the last time, leaving the hatchet on the floor of the hayloft. It had made me feel safe, but I couldn't hitchhike with an ax in my hand.

A woman trucker—a Beatles fan who pretty much lived on Red Bull and those little packages of orange peanut butter crackers—dropped me off in Tarbridge three days later. I walked up the road to Bridewell, hoping the black truck would be there but feeling sick with certainty that it wouldn't be.

It wasn't there.

It wasn't there.

And then it was.

I found him dangling his legs off the edge of the flat-bed, Barry Cook's Stetson shading his eyes from the afternoon sun. He held a can of Pepsi in one hand and a magazine in the other. I came around the back of the truck, dropped my backpack on the gravel, took one look at him, and hid my face in my hands.

"Hey." I felt his hands resting gently on my shoulders. "Hey. It's all right. I knew we would find each other again." I wanted him to put his arms around me, but I had to settle for his fingers on my hair, stroking and smoothing as if I were a downhearted child.

I didn't know what to say, so I said, "What were you doing?"

"Oh, you know. Making myself useful." He flashed that wry smile of his. "Found a mechanic who needed a bit of extra help, so I stayed with him for a couple weeks." Lee looked down at my new bag and frowned. "What happened to your rucksack?"

"Lost it."

"And everything in it?"

I nodded.

"Even ET?"

"Even ET."

He shrugged. "Oh well."

I wiped my eyes with the heels of my hands. "So was this perfect timing, or what?"

"That's what *you* think," he said, but he was smiling. "I've been sitting here every day for a week. Didn't even have my knitting to keep me company."

He sat on the flatbed, and I hopped up beside him. He opened another can of soda and handed it to me. "I'm not knitting anymore," I said.

"Why not?"

I thought of the woman in the wheelchair at Bridewell, and of Mrs. Harmon's yarn and needles stuffed in Sully's cabinet of other people's things. "Long story."

"Thank you for giving that car to Kayla. That really meant a lot to me."

Of course it did. That's why I'd done it. "Sure," I said. "Did you get new plates for it?"

He nodded. "Where'd you get it, anyway?" He looked at me pointedly. "Or maybe you'd rather not say?"

"I didn't eat him," I said.

"Then who did?"

Instead of answering I took a sip of soda. "Did you ever go back to Sully's cabin?"

He shook his head. "You?"

I nodded. "I wish you had." Then I told him everything.

"I *told* you family's overrated," Lee said at last.

I stuck my fists in my jean pockets and kicked at a stone. "I've been really clueless, haven't I?"

Lee shook his head. "I'm just glad you're all right."

"For now, anyway."

"How long has it been—a little over a month? Don't you think he'd've been able to trace you in all that time? He didn't have any trouble finding us at the carnival."

"Are you saying . . . are you saying I might have killed him?"

He shrugged. "You can definitely kill a person if you hit 'em hard enough on the head. It never occurred to you?"

I shook my head and drew an unsteady breath.

"I wouldn't feel too badly about it, if I were you. It was you or him." After a pause Lee asked, "Are you going to visit your father?"

I didn't answer him right away. I looked at the man behind the little window at the security gate, and up beyond the fence at the three endless stories of barred windows. I thought of my father sitting in that chair with the ghost of his right hand hidden under the blanket, getting his face mopped by some other orderly who didn't care about who he was or the kind of life he might have had. I'd come all this way back to Bridewell, and yet I'd never had any intention of going in there again.

Lee looked at me and nodded.

11

e drove to Laskin National Park. It was getting to be prime camping season, and because there were so many people around, sleeping in the flatbed was less appealing than just paying the fee for a campsite like everybody else. At night, alone in my little tent, I closed my eyes and saw the snapshots from my parents' perfect summer flipping by in the darkness. I wished one of us owned a camera.

Then, toward the end of August, we said so long to Barry Cook's pickup truck.

That morning we'd decided on a trip to Door County for some fishing, and we were only a few miles out of the park when the engine made this weird coughing noise, and Lee had to pull to the side of the road. He spent almost an hour bent under the hood, and when he finally told me what was wrong I didn't understand any of it. Whatever it was, he couldn't fix it on his own, and we couldn't call a tow truck for more reasons than one. "It's not your fault," I said as we took our stuff out of the back for the last time. Still, he was prickly, and didn't say much as we walked.

Lee held out his thumb to every passing car, but it was half an hour before someone stopped. The car pulled over ahead of us and a blonde in magenta sunglasses stuck her head out the driver's-side window. "Hey there. You guys break down or something?"

We came up beside her and Lee cast a doubtful glance through the backseat window. There were clear storage boxes stacked to the ceiling.

"I'm driving back to school," she said. "It's all right, I can make room. Where you headed?"

Lee said, "We're headed wherever you're headed."

She got out of the car and flashed her teeth. "Now that's what I call easy to travel with."

He introduced us both to Kerri-Ann Watt, incoming senior at the University of Wisconsin–Madison. She hardly looked at me, and her handshake was as limp as a lasagna noodle. If it had been only me she would've kept driving. Which is why I found myself packed in the backseat while Lee sat in the front. He kept giving me sympathetic looks over his shoulder. Kerri-Ann asked him all sorts of personal questions, and I had to put my hand over my smirk every time he lied.

We got to Madison just after four o'clock, and Lee and I waited in the car while Kerri-Ann checked into her dorm and got her keys. Everywhere there were students in T-shirts and ball caps with badgers on them, everybody laughing and calling to one another across the parking lot, lots of hugs and high-fiving. "You guys don't have a place to stay, do you?" Kerri-Ann asked when she got back. "You can stay with me tonight, if you want. I have a single." She grinned at Lee. "You just have to help me move in."

"Sure thing," he said. "It'll take no time at all between three people."

We carried everything up the stairs and into the room. I'd never been in a dorm before, but I guessed this one was pretty standard: painted cinderblock walls, gray linoleum floors, fiberboard furniture. We waited while Kerri-Ann hung up her posters—Lee rolled his eyes every time she pulled out another one, Tom Cruise in *Risky Business* or Right Said Fred—and then we went to the campus pizzeria for dinner. Kerri-Ann walked ahead of me along the lakeside path, next to Lee, and touched him on the inside of his arm every time she wanted to point something out. This was getting old. Tomorrow morning we'd have to figure out what we were doing next—and whatever it was, it would have nothing at all to do with Kerri-Ann Watt.

"You're so good with your hands, Lee," she said when we got back to her room. "Would you mind setting up my loft bed? It should only take a few minutes. While you're doing that I'm going to unpack all my girly stuff. Maren, you want to help me?"

Kerri-Ann closed the bathroom door behind us and began laying out her toiletries and cosmetics along the counter. "This is my favorite part of a new school year," she said. "Setting up my vanity."

"You have a lot of makeup."

She laughed. "You say that like it's a bad thing."

"I don't know what you need it all for. You're already pretty."

She didn't thank me for the compliment, she just kept arranging all her pots and wands and bottles. I watched her, and in my mind I curled my fingers around her nail scissors.

After a minute or two she was satisfied, and looked me over appraisingly. "You know, you could be attractive if you made an effort."

I folded my arms and met her eyes in the mirror. "And now you're going to tell me I shouldn't wear black all the time, it makes me look pale and sullen and deeply un-happy, and nobody is going to want to be my friend."

"Well, if you've heard it before then don't you think there's something to it?"

"Lee's my friend. He doesn't care what I wear, or what I put on my face."

"Mmm." Kerri-Ann pulled at a wisp of my hair and tucked it behind my ear. "That's what I've been trying to figure out."

"Lee doesn't like me like that."

"So you say. But guys and girls can't be friends."

"Nothing's happened. He thinks I'm a baby, anyway."

"Why, how old are you?"

"Sixteen."

Kerri-Ann laughed. "And how old is he? Twenty?"

"Nineteen."

"That's all right," she said as she drew out a little plastic pot, dipped her finger, and dabbed the pink goo on her lips. "I like them a little bit younger."

Lee was finished setting up the loft bed when we came out of the bathroom. The clock on the nightstand read 11:33. Here we were, hurtling toward bedtime, and I had no idea where I was going to sleep.

Kerri-Ann climbed into her bed and pointed to a box on the floor by her desk. "The air mattress is in there. Lee, why don't you set it up for yourself? It's electric, so you don't have to blow into it. Maren, I think you'll be more comfortable on one of the couches in the common room down the hall. They're comfy—I used to fall asleep on them watching movies all the time last year."

Lee gave me a doubtful look. "Here, why don't I blow the air mattress up for Maren and—"

"The air mattress has a hole in it," Kerri-Ann said flatly. "Don't you want Maren to get a good night's sleep?"

There was no other way to protest without making it into a *thing*. Kerri-Ann tossed me a tatty gray blanket. "We'll see you in the morning," she said.

The light was off in the common room. From the street lamps I could make out a small kitchenette and refrigerator in one corner, a great hulking television set in another, and a bunch of couches scattered around the room. I chose one and settled in. The cushions smelled like beer and dirty socks.

I pictured Kerri-Ann unbuttoning Lee's shirt and casting it on the floor beside the deflated air mattress. I saw him running his fingers along her bare skin. *You're so good with your hands, Lee.* I rolled my eyes at the dark and tried harder to think of nothing at all. When I fell asleep, I was back running in those zigzagging corridors as Kerri-Ann was losing her lead, stumbling over her pink stiletto heels.

The next thing I knew, someone was shining a flashlight in my face. "You should not be here," said a crisp but gentle voice. "The common room is closed. Are you a resident of this dormitory?"

I held my hand up to my eyes, and the figure averted the flashlight a moment before the overhead lamp switched on. A security guard stood in the kitchenette area, tall and stocky, with a buzzed haircut. It took me a second to realize the guard wasn't a man.

"I'm a friend of Kerri-Ann Watt." I almost choked on the word *friend.* "She lives in room two twenty-nine."

"Have you been signed in as an overnight guest?" She spoke with care; English wasn't her first language.

"Um . . . I didn't know we were supposed to sign in."

"Gather your things, please. We will go to your friend's room now."

I followed the guard down the hall, the blanket trailing behind me.

She knocked sharply on Kerri-Ann's door, waited, and knocked again. Finally we heard footsteps approach.

Kerri-Ann opened the door. I glanced over her shoulder

and saw her bed was empty. The air mattress lay in a puddle on the linoleum. "Yes?"

"I found this young woman asleep in the common room. She says she is your friend."

Kerri-Ann looked me up and down with a blank expression. "No. Sorry. I don't know her."

I opened my mouth to protest as the guard made her apologies and Kerri-Ann closed the door, flicking me a tiny glance of triumph behind the woman's back.

"It was not good to lie, miss. Now I must report you. You will receive a citation from the campus police."

"I wasn't lying," I said tiredly. "*She's* lying because she wants my friend all to herself." I should have used those nail scissors when I had the chance.

The guard glanced back at Kerri-Ann's door, then at me, as we went down the hall toward the bright red EXIT light, and I realized it wasn't a matter of her not believing me. She didn't care about any of this. She was just doing her job, and if I disappeared right now she'd just shrug and continue on her rounds like nothing had happened.

"Now we will walk to the campus police station," she said as we went down the stairs. "It is two blocks from here."

I followed her out the door at the bottom of the stairwell, but when she turned the corner on the building I ran the other way. I knew she wouldn't follow me.

I walked a few more blocks to the lake and sat down on a park bench overlooking the water. It wouldn't be light for hours yet. My backpack was in Kerri-Ann's room, I didn't have anything with me but a raggedy old blanket, and I didn't know what to do about it. I'd been homeless for months, but I'd never really felt like it until now.

I must have nodded off, because it was suddenly light out and Lee was sitting next to me. A couple of early morning joggers hurried by, and I felt naked and ridiculous under the old blanket. My throat hurt. "Where were you?" I asked blearily. "You weren't with her."

"I'm so sorry, Maren. I never should have let it go that far. She was a pest from the minute we met her, but I didn't think she'd be like *that*."

"Did she tell you what she did?"

"She didn't have to."

"I left my bag in her room. Do you think you could get it for me?"

"You can get it yourself. But there's no need for us to leave right away." He let out a breath, and I smelled it then—the stench lurking under the mint. He'd probably used her toothbrush. "Now everything in that room belongs to you."

I wore every article of black clothing Kerri-Ann had owned, even her underwear, and every day I used her ID card to get into the university library. No one ever checked to see if my face matched the photo on the card. I just flashed the ID to a bored-looking student behind the front desk and passed through the turnstile, into the biggest library I'd ever seen.

After a couple hours of reading I would wander around in the stacks to stretch my legs, and there were always lots of books on the carts in need of reshelving. There never seemed to be anyone around to do it, so I started doing it myself. It soothed me to put somebody else's books away.

I didn't see much of Lee during the day. Wherever he went and whatever he did, he always ended up at McDonald's or Burger King, and he'd bring me a burger and a strawberry milkshake for dinner.

I didn't know how long we'd be able to go on like this, but I kept thinking the time was almost up just because I *liked* it here. I liked this town. I liked the campus. The cafeteria was all done up like a German hunting lodge or something, lots of dark wood and Gothic script, and when the weather was good you could take your tray out onto a terrace overlooking the lake.

The people were friendly too, even if I couldn't talk to them. A few times I saw three girls knitting together on the terrace, and one day one of them looked up and saw me watching her. She smiled and said, "Do you knit?"

I shook my head. "I tried to learn, but I just couldn't get the hang of it."

"Oh, everybody feels that way in the beginning." The girl leaned over and patted the seat beside her. "Come sit down, and I'll teach you so it sticks."

"Hah," said one of her friends. They'd been knitting all through the conversation. *"Sticks."*

"I don't have time right now," I mumbled.

"Oh, okay." She seemed disappointed. "Well, we knit together a lot, so you can join us anytime."

"We're not much of a circle," said the third girl, "but we talk enough to make up for it."

"People think it's something only grandmas do," the first girl sighed. "So come next week, if you can. Bring your yarn and needles." I nodded and tried to smile as I backed away from the table.

I couldn't believe it. They were so *nice*.

At bedtime Lee started off on the air mattress, but I'd wake up in the middle of the night and find it deflated again. Either he'd found a hiding spot in the common room, or he was sleeping in the backseat of Kerri-Ann's car. Sometimes he was in the shower when I woke up and other times he was already gone. That night I'd offer him the bed again, but he wouldn't take it. He'd pick up one of Kerri-Ann's things, a hairbrush or a tank top, sigh, and say, "Somebody ought to gobble me up one of these days. It'd serve me right."

And I'd say, "Don't say that."

"Why not? Why shouldn't I say it?"

I didn't answer. I could never think of a reason.

The next day, as usual, I set myself up at one of the library desks. I read and wrote for a couple of hours before taking a bathroom break.

When I got back to my desk I found something lying in the gutter of my open textbook, and at first my brain refused to recognize it.

A long white strip.

Fluffy.

Attached to something that looked like a charm bracelet.

I picked it up because I still didn't know what it was. The fur was clumped together with dried blood on one end where someone had severed it.

Tail. Cat's tail. Mrs. Harmon's cat.

Something tinkled faintly as the tail dropped to the floor, and I realized it wasn't a bracelet, it was the collar. I went to one knee and slowly picked up the tag. PUSS, it said. And on the reverse: HARMON—217 SUGARBUSH AVE.—EDGARTOWN, PA. In an instant I was back in the Spare Oom, shutting the door on Mrs. Harmon's beautiful white cat.

I should have let him in.

There were plenty of students in the library, and if they noticed something was wrong I couldn't tell. The silence amplified itself. Everyone had turned into mannequins, but I could feel Sully's eyes on my back. My stomach turned over, and my hands began to ring with the sickening thud of brass on skull.

I could hide the cat's tail and go on sitting there out in the open where he couldn't touch me. But the library wouldn't be open forever.

I closed my books and left them on the table for once, picked up the cat's tail, and quickly found the nearest trashcan. It was a perfect sunny afternoon, and all over the quad there were people playing Frisbee or sunning themselves. I didn't turn to look behind me. I just kept walking back to the dorm.

I went into the stairwell, climbed up to the second-floor landing, and sat on the step. Beyond the double doors the hallways were deserted. I waited for the sound of his boots on the stairs.

The door at the bottom opened and shut, and there they were, slow and steady. I closed my eyes and listened as my hands hummed and my heart hammered. I'd bested him once, but old fear is harder to shake.

When I opened my eyes again he was leering at me, and I couldn't imagine how I had ever trusted him. His pocket-knife glinted in his hand—that horrible hand, crusted blood ringing the fingernails. "Well, well. You know you been a bad girl, and it's my job as your granddad to set you right. Eh, Missy?"

I sighed. "You could have done it a month ago."

"Had to get my strength up. Besides, what's that they say about a dish best served cold? C'mon and get up, now." He jabbed his knife at the door behind me. "I've been through enough trouble without runnin' into any more."

Sully followed me into Kerri-Ann's room and turned the dead bolt. He pushed me toward the bed and I couldn't help glancing over his shoulder, but it was no use. Lee wouldn't be back for hours. The daylight was fading, and the room was thick with shadows.

"Now you listen here. You so much as look at that door again and I'll slit you open right down the middle. Got it?"

I nodded. Why did he even use a knife? Saturn never needed one.

Sully turned the desk chair to face me and sat himself down. With the knife he picked at his fingernails, flicking bits of dirt and dried blood onto the floor. "Second time your boyfriend ain't swooped in to save you." Sully smirked. "Some boyfriend he turned out to be."

"He'll be back any minute," I said.

"Nah. I took care of him."

In that moment, I felt sorry for the man. It was like he hadn't looked in a mirror in forty years. I thought, too, of how Mama had cared for me and protected me. Sully would never know what it felt like to be loved—or near enough to it.

"You mean you killed him?" I asked.

Sully laughed. "Slit his throat and had me an early supper."

He was lying. I didn't have to hope.

"Did you follow me back to Travis's house? Were you watching me while I was cam—"

"Now you just shut it, Missy. You ain't got nothing to say to me besides beggin' for mercy right before I stick you." He winced as he rubbed at the back of his head. There was a nasty bruise, like a rotten spot on a peach, with a jagged line where the corner of the trophy had broken the flesh. He had less hair than he did a month ago. "You hit me hard, and I ain't been right since. I don't just forget things, I forget where I been and what I was doin'. Can't see nothin' sometimes. Can't even go out in the daytime, makes my head hurt more than it already does."

"If you'd left me alone, I wouldn't have had to do it."

He pointed the knife at me. "And if *you'd* just shut up and stopped your kickin', you'd have saved us both a whole lot of trouble."

Well, *that* was true.

Sully went back to picking at the filth under his nails. "Knew a man once," he said, in this weirdly offhand way. "Ate his own mother. 'Course, he might've just said it hopin' for a reaction. But I ain't afraid of nobody or nothin', not even a man that ate his own mama."

"Lee might have eaten his own dad," I said. "He can definitely handle *you*."

My grandfather's eyes glinted in the gloom. "Ain't you been listenin', Missy? Didn't I tell you everybody does it?"

I heard a door slam at the end of the corridor, and another set of heavy, steady footsteps approached. It was Lee. I was sure of it.

"I wonder why you'd say that, when it isn't true," I said carefully. "You know what's going to happen, Sully. You can go on and eat me, but then he's just going to eat *you*. That's what he does. He eats people the world is better off without."

A key turned in the lock. The door strained against the dead bolt. "Maren? Maren, are you in there?"

Sully glared at me. He ran his hand over what was left of his hair.

"Should I tell him you're here?" I asked. It felt strange to be so calm, when I knew he might lunge and stab me. Lee was trying something else with the door. I could hear the rubber treads on his boots squeaking as he worked the lock, metal clicking on metal. "He's going to open it," I said. "He knows how to pick all kinds of locks."

Now or never, then. Sully came at me, and I was ready. I got a firm hold on his right arm, and I watched with that detached feeling as he adjusted his grip on the knife in hopes of sticking me in the hand.

"I'm coming, Maren!"

I let go of Sully's hand at the last minute, and he tumbled forward onto the bed, plunging his knife into the pillow. I scrambled on top of his back and grabbed his knife hand from behind, just as the dead bolt yielded and the door swung open. Sully turned to Lee with a startled, almost frightened look on his face, and in that moment he seemed impossibly frail for someone who'd spent the past month hunting me down.

Lee hardly even glanced at me; he just took Sully by the arm as the door slammed shut. I let go. "Wait in the bathroom," he said.

I ran to the door and turned the bolt again as Sully said, "Now just hold on a minute, there, son. . . ."

And Lee said: "Don't call me *son*."

I climbed into the bathtub, drew the curtain, and pressed my palms against my eyes 'til I saw comets. Seven minutes, give or take. I was safe now. I was very nearly safe.

Finally Lee knocked on the bathroom door. "Can I come in?" I didn't answer, but he came in anyway. He knelt by the tub and pulled back the shower curtain. "Are you okay?" He put his arm around me, breathed on me. I wanted to throw up.

"Sorry," he said. "I'll brush my teeth."

"He said he'd taken care of you."

"If that guy told the truth once in his whole life, I'd be surprised."

I looked up. "Thank you," I said.

"You're welcome." He took my hand and tugged gently. "C'mon. Let's get you out of the bathtub."

Lee washed his face and hands and used Kerri-Ann's toothbrush while I went back into the room. It had never been particularly homey, but now it was even less so, although Lee had already stripped the sheets and laid Kerri-Ann's clean Laura Ashley duvet over the bare mattress. I curled myself up as tight as I could at the foot of the bed. I did see, out of the corner of my eye, a yellow plastic grocery bag on the floor by the door, the handles double knotted over a bulging mass of human scraps. Not that my grandfather had ever been much of a human.

Lee came out, sat down in the desk chair, and rubbed at his eyes. "I can't believe how close I came to losing you," he said.

"Why did you come back early?"

He shrugged. "I just felt like I should."

Something trailed out of the open closet door in the corner. Something ropelike. So Sully had stashed his rucksack in the room before he'd gone to hunt me at the library.

Lee followed my eye and got up to investigate. He opened the closet door wide and picked up the rope of hair. "What the hell . . . ?" As he pulled and the rope came out, and out, and out, Lee had this look on his face—like he'd discovered a severed finger in the salad bar, like he wasn't an eater himself.

The rope formed coil after coil on the linoleum as Lee drew it out of the bag. It was so long it was hard to believe Sully had managed to fit anything else in the rucksack. "Sick," Lee muttered. "Like a Frankenstein zombie Rapunzel." I laughed then, in spite of everything.

When he finally got to the other end he looked up at me, his face bright with that mix of fascination and disgust I'd felt that night at Mrs. Harmon's house. "You saw this before?"

I nodded. "That's her hair there, near the end." Still, the weaving was a few feet longer than the last time I'd seen it. Seeing the whole thing for the first time, it occurred to me that if Sully had only eaten people who were already dead, then there would have been a whole lot more gray, white, and silver along the rope.

Lee kicked it away and sat in the desk chair staring at it. "That is the most repulsive thing I've ever seen."

"Somehow I doubt that," I said. In silence we looked at the rucksack, as if another nasty surprise could come slithering out at any moment.

Then, all at once, I couldn't wait to be rid of it. I jumped up and stuffed the rope of hair back inside the bag, grabbed the strap, and dragged it across the floor.

"What are you doing?"

"Taking it to the Dumpster."

"Wait." He got up and took the strap from my hand. "Don't do that."

"I'm so tired of going through other people's things, Lee. And I especially don't want to go through *his*."

"You don't have to watch."

"There's worse, you know. You should have seen what he left on my desk at the library." I shuddered. "He killed Mrs. Harmon's cat."

For a moment we looked at each other in silence. "Am I still going to feel like this?" I asked. "Even now, when I know he's dead?"

"Takes time for your nerves to settle, that's all," he said. "It'll pass. Why don't you take a shower now, and whatever I find I promise I'll keep it to myself."

Once I was under the hot water I felt a little better. When I came out of the bathroom he held up a thick wad of twenties. "See? This is why I told you not to trash it."

"I don't want it," I said. "It belonged to Mrs. Harmon."

"She wasn't the only one."

He was right. I didn't know what to say, so I picked up Kerri-Ann's copy of *The Strange Case of Dr. Jekyll and Mr. Hyde*. I couldn't read though; I felt his eyes on me. "What?" I said finally.

"I love the look on your face while you're reading. It's like you really are someplace else."

"You watch me while I'm reading?"

He shrugged. "You're so caught up you never notice." He looked like he wanted to say something else, but then he licked his thumb and began to count the money, and I went back to my book.

"Five hundred eighty-nine dollars." He held up a small pouch. "And here's something else." He shook it a little, and it jingled. "I bet it's jewelry."

"Can I see?"

He handed me the pouch, and I loosened the drawstring and tipped the bag so all the pieces came out onto the bed. There were, among a couple dozen things I didn't recognize, the opal and pearl rings I'd laid out on Mrs. Harmon's mantelpiece.

Lee looked up from the rucksack. "Find something that belongs to you?"

"No," I said. "Mrs. Harmon's." I pulled the rings out of the jumble and laid them out in the palm of my hand. I wanted to send them to her niece, but I had no idea how I'd go about finding her. I ran my finger over the locket around my neck and thought of the carrot cake and the bride and groom at the Emerald City.

"This is crazy." Lee laughed as he pulled something else out of the sack. "He was like a demonic Santa Claus." He held up Sully's tarnished silver flask and unscrewed the cap. "Bottoms up!" And he tossed back his head and took a long swig.

"You sure you want to put your lips on that?" I asked.

"Does it matter?" He wiped the rim of the flask with the corner of his shirt and held it out to me. "I shouldn't have brushed my teeth."

"No, thanks."

"You should reconsider. This is good whiskey."

He got up and joined me on the bed. I took the flask and tilted it back, coughing as the alcohol seared my throat. "Yuck," I said. I took another swig. "This is disgusting."

"And yet you keep drinking it." Our fingers touched as I handed it back.

"It tastes awful, but it lights a little fire in your belly." All of a sudden nothing bothered me: not the thought of Sully's knife against my throat, or his bones sitting like a pile of gravel in Lee's stomach. I didn't care that my grandfather would never take me fishing. I didn't care that I had no money that was rightfully mine, or that my father would wake up every morning for the rest of his life hoping I would visit, or that someone might come knocking for Kerri-Ann, see the light on and hear our voices, and turn us over to the campus police. I could see how people fell into drinking.

I pulled the duvet up to my chin. "Here." He held out the flask. "You finish it."

"No, thanks." I had a feeling if I drank any more this warm cozy not-caring would leave me. I felt weak, but in a good way. Tonight I would have happy dreams.

Lee shrugged, tipped it back, and placed the empty flask on the nightstand. "Time to put this day behind us." He got up and turned off the overhead lamp. There were lights on across the courtyard, and it was enough to see by. He took off his shirt and tossed it over the desk chair; then, after raising a hand to his mouth to sniff his breath, he went back into the bathroom for Kerri-Ann's tooth-brush.

He came out again, unbuttoning his fly. "How long

have we known each other, Maren? Has it really only been three months?"

Suddenly all speech, even a simple yes or no, seemed like an incredible effort. The warmth and heaviness had spread down through my limbs, tugging on my eyelids and muffling my tongue.

Still, I kept my eyes open just enough to watch him as he finished undressing. Lee had nice muscles. He bent forward as he took off his jeans, and by the courtyard light I could see the down on his back, glowing as if his shadow were made of gold instead of darkness. I thought back to that first night when I passed out on the waterbed and he went out to sleep on the couch. The useless air mattress lay crumpled in the corner. I wanted to say, *Why are you sleeping here? What's different about tonight?*

He left his jeans in a pile on the floor and climbed over me, carefully, to fit himself between the wall and where I lay. "Is this okay? Are you comfortable?"

How could I be? "Yeah," I whispered.

He cupped a hand on my shoulder. "Maren . . ."

"Mmm?" Through the fog in my head I marveled at how I managed to sound like I didn't care.

He laughed quietly. "You're gonna have a hangover in the morning."

"I only had a few sips!"

"That's a lot, when you've never had any." He rested his chin on my shoulder. He wanted to say something, but I couldn't ask. Finally he said, "As soon as I saw you that night in the candy aisle . . . what I mean is, I felt it.

Something. I don't know. All I know is that I saw you and I felt it."

"Felt what?"

"This," he said. "I knew this would happen."

This? What was *this*? The warmth trickled up again to reclaim me, limb by limb. *Sleep it away*, I thought. *Forget it.* "Did you know what I was? Even in the candy aisle?"

"I didn't know for sure until I saw you in the car." He must have felt me cringe. "Sorry. I know you don't like to be reminded."

Neither of us spoke for a while. He was still propped on an elbow, his free hand resting on my shoulder. Then he began to stroke my head. "Your hair," he murmured. "He would have used your hair."

I'd never really paid any attention to my hair before—it was long and dark and nondescript—but when Lee put his hands on my head it turned to silk. With gentle fingers he brushed my hair away from my neck. He leaned in and kissed me there, just beside the place we always went for first. "Don't," I said.

"Because you don't want me to, or because I shouldn't?"

"Don't . . . because . . . you shouldn't."

"I know I've been cold." He ran his fingers up and down my arm. "I'm sorry. You know I had to be."

And beneath that heavy warmth, the safety I had conjured out of a bottle, I felt my stomach rumble.

12

woke up, and Lee was gone. The bad taste was in my mouth. There was no denying what I'd done.

It was a gloomy gray morning, and in the room there were things that should not have been there. His Stetson hat was on the desk where he'd laid it. His jeans were still in a heap on the floor. There were other things he couldn't leave without, parts of him I should never have seen the inside of.

I shut my eyes and breathed in the smell of him lingering in the sheets. When he held me everything had melted away, everything dark and ugly and rotten inside of me. Lee had made me pure. He'd let me do it. But I lay in bed for a long time, wishing with all my heart that he hadn't. Now his name was written there too.

___

When I came back from the library that night there was a note on pink paper taped to the door: *K-A: Why didn't you show at the Delta welcome breakfast?? Were you hungover or what? Call me ASAP.* —*Melissa*

I didn't know what to do with myself. I couldn't go on like this, could I? Any day now someone would find me in Kerri-Ann's room.

The next morning I was putting books away when I saw a boy at one of the study tables watching me. He was older—he looked like he could have been a sophomore, or even a junior—and although he was as fit as Lee, he wore a crisply tailored button-down shirt that made him look like he belonged at a bank.

When I was finished with my stack I took down a book called *The Legends of Babylon* and I sat down at the table opposite the boy. A lot of it went over my head, but it felt good to *try* to understand. It also felt good to know his eyes were straying off the textbook page, across the table, and up the inside of my arm.

After fifteen minutes or so the boy tore a page out of his notebook and slipped it across the table. *Sorry for intruding, but I couldn't help noticing you're reading about Babylon. Have you read Reginald Toomey's* I Dreamed of the Tigris?

I shook my head and he kept writing. *Look for it in the catalog. Or if it's checked out I can lend you my copy.*

Thanks, I wrote back. *That's very kind of you.*

Are you planning to major in archaeology or anthropology?

I haven't decided yet.

I'm double majoring in both. I'd be happy to answer any questions you might have. Have you read any Claude Lévi-Strauss? Or Margaret Mead?

We went on like that for a few minutes, writing back and forth about books and the classes he was taking. He was cute, and holed up in a library of his own free will. We had just enough in common.

I'm Jason, he wrote finally. *Nice to meet you.*

I wrote my name below his, and his smile was so perfect he could have starred in a Colgate commercial.

Or Listerine, said a little voice.

It was his next question. Of course it was. *Do you have a boyfriend?*

I glanced at him—he was looking at me, painfully earnest—and, because I knew I couldn't make it too easy for him, I wrote, *Yes.* I didn't have to turn the paper around; I felt him cringe as I was still writing it. *Sorry,* I wrote. *Thanks for all the good recommendations.*

I would have given them to you anyway, he wrote back. *I hope you believe me.*

I nodded, smiled, and gathered up my books. I was bound to run into him again. He went to school here; he'd be in the library almost every day.

———

Sometimes, if I sat in on a lecture, I'd do the reading and think about what I would write if I were actually in the class and had to compose an essay about the Jívaro tribe of Ecuador, who used to shrink the heads of their enemies. Maybe they still do. Jason stared at me through the stacks, and I let him.

One day I got tired of reading and started shelving the books like usual, and when I headed back for another armful I saw a man standing at the end of the aisle, his elbow propped on the shelving cart. He wore a white short-sleeved button-down shirt, slightly rumpled and thin enough that I could see the outline of his undershirt. I couldn't help noticing the damp rings under his arms. It wasn't a nice thought, but it escaped before I could censor myself—he was *lumpy*. His nose, his arms, the shape of his face. His black hair hung long and unruly around his ears, and he hadn't shaved in a while. I was taller than he was. I'd seen him nearly every day, answering questions at the reference desk, but I hadn't paid this much attention to him before.

I stood there nervously and thought of pretending to browse the shelves as though I hadn't been planning to replace all the books waiting under his doughy white elbow. He was looking at me, the corner of his mouth twisted into what, for him, probably amounted to a smile. "And all this time I thought those books were putting themselves away."

"It was something to do," I said.

"Don't you have any class reading to do?"

"I finished it."

"Suit yourself." He stepped aside, and I grabbed an armful of books.

He picked up a stray pencil off the cart and tapped it against his nose. "Shelvers get six-fifty an hour. You'll have to register with the library director." With the pencil he pointed to the glass-fronted office at the far side of the room. "It's usually ten hours a week, but we're short right now, so you can pick up a double shift whenever you want." He paused. "You a freshman?"

I nodded.

He held out his hand. "I'm Wayne. I'm working on my Ph.D."

"I'm Maren."

"Charmed," he replied, and suddenly I understood the difference between wryness and sarcasm. I decided I liked him. Wayne and I would never be friends—lucky for him—but he made it clear he respected me, and that meant a lot.

I shuffled from foot to foot. "What are you getting your Ph.D. in?"

"Library science." He shrugged. "Nothing interesting."

We traded a smile. He turned to go, then paused. "Hey—I'll have a word with Henderson. He's the director. I know you've already been working for a week and a half, so I'll just make sure you get paid for it."

"Thanks." Suddenly I felt so grateful I could have cried. "That's really nice of you."

Wayne offered me one last shrug before shuffling back to the reference desk. I returned to the stacks with my arms full of engineering textbooks, smiling to myself like I didn't have a worry in the world.

On my way out of the library that afternoon I picked up a copy of the campus newspaper. I got a sandwich in the cafeteria and spread the paper over the table as I ate, scanning the classified page for rooms for rent. The cheapest option was only a half dozen blocks from campus, which made the two-hundred-dollar rent seem suspiciously low.

Apply to 355 Front Street between the hours of 10 AM and 6 PM. Young ladies only.

The boardinghouse was a rambling, shabby Victorian— lawn furniture stacked on the porch, and garden gnomes with the paint chipping off their jolly faces—dilapidated, but not unpleasant. A woman, as old as Mrs. Harmon and a great deal heavier, answered the door. "Hello," I said. "I'm here about the room?"

She nodded and shuffled aside so I could enter. The front hall smelled of mold and cough drops. Sections of the Oriental carpet runner had worn down in long gray patches. Through an open door on the left I could see a brown sofa studded with needlepoint cushions. "You don't look old enough to be living on your own," the woman remarked.

"I'm a freshman."

"Couldn't get along with your roommate? Well,

nobody'll bother you here. I only take three boarders at a time, ladies only, and the other two are quiet as church mice. Hardly ever see 'em. You won't have use of the kitchen, but you'll be eating on campus, so that won't matter. Do you want to see the room?"

"Yes, please."

She pointed to the staircase. "Second door on the right. Bathroom's at the end of the hall. You'll pardon my not showing you up personally," she said. "I don't get upstairs too much these days."

I nodded and went up. The room was small but very clean, with a desk and a dresser and crisp white sheets on a single bed. I opened the closet door, and a row of metal dry-cleaner's hangers rattled on the rail. The window was closed, but I could hear children laughing in somebody else's backyard. I looked up and found a crucifix over the doorway.

She was still standing in the hall when I came down the stairs. "Well?" Her manner was blunt, but not rude. I could never see her inviting me into the kitchen for tea and cake.

"May I have the room?"

"Rent's two hundred a month. First month's and last month's makes four hundred, and it's yours."

"Will you take cash?"

She raised her eyebrows. "You got that much on you?"

I took what was left of Travis's money roll out of my bag and counted four hundred in twenties.

"Not a wise idea, walking around town with that much money on you."

"I don't, usually." I handed her the money and she licked her forefinger before re-counting it.

"Now, you look like a good girl, but I'd better warn you anyway. It's my rule that I don't allow any men in this house apart from my grandson. He does odd jobs for me now and again, so if you see him don't be alarmed."

"I understand," I said. Then I went back to Kerri-Ann's room, packed my things, and closed the door behind me.

I had a job. I had a home. I should have been thrilled.

It was true, what Mrs. Clipper said about the other girls in the house—except they weren't church mice, they were ghosts. I saw them once or twice a week, disappearing into their bedrooms with dark, dripping hair, their bodies wrapped in white towels. Late one night I could've sworn I heard a man's voice as two sets of footsteps came sneaking up the stairs; I heard noises in the next room, but in the morning only one person—the light-footed one, my ghostly housemate—went down again. I wanted to knock on her door, but I knew she would deny it. I thought of Travis and wondered if there were people out there who did what I couldn't. There had to be.

I had a routine now. I shelved, then I passed my lunch break with a tuna sandwich and an Anne Rice novel in a secluded corner of the library, and then I went back to my spare little room in Mrs. Clipper's house and finished the books I'd begun during the day. I had off two mornings a week, and on those days I'd sit in on a lecture, taking notes like I had a grade depending on it. Other days, if Jason was at the library, I lost all sight of routine—especially if he followed me into the stacks.

"Read any good field studies lately?"

I gasped and glanced up with the latest assortment of textbooks clasped to my chest. Jason smiled slightly, as if he were pleased he'd startled me. "Sorry," he whispered.

"It's all right." I peered at the label on the next spine and moved away from him as I looked for the right shelf.

He said my name, and I tried not to shiver. "Can you put the books down? Just for a second?"

I slid the stack onto a half-empty shelf, and he took a step forward. I felt myself turning to face him—like metal to a magnet, a flower to the sun. He let his hand hover in the air between us. "May I?"

I nodded. He gently lifted my locket and pressed the tiny button, and the lid snapped open. Inside, Douglas Harmon humored a long-dead photographer with a movie-star smile.

"Good-looking guy," Jason remarked. His shirt smelled faintly of laundry detergent, and when he breathed I caught the smoky tang of bacon under a wash of mint Listerine. "Your grandfather?"

I wish. "He wasn't anybody's grandfather, I don't think."

Jason frowned, but I didn't give him the chance to ask if I'd found the necklace in a junk shop. I backed away and the locket fell from his fingers, landing on my skin warmer than it had left. "I'd better get back to shelving." I left him standing in the aisle, his hand outstretched as if Douglas Harmon's picture were still inside.

I never wore the locket after that. It just seemed wrong all of a sudden to be wearing a reminder of the love of somebody else's life, when I could never have one of my own.

Weeks went by, and I began to dress differently. Black cardigans, black skirts, black lace stockings. I thought Jason might like a better look at my legs. I pored over photographs of Babylonian stone carvings in the British Museum, beautiful monsters in polished granite. *The creature lures the foolish adventurer with the ghostly perfumes of the hanging gardens, tempting him to forget that all the flowers were turned to dust a thousand years before. He is a man for only a moment or two longer.*

In the middle of November Jason cornered me with another armful of books and invited me to a Thanksgiving potluck. "I can't," I said.

"It's not a problem if you're a vegetarian or something," he said quickly. "There'll be plenty of other stuff to eat besides the turkey."

I shook my head and tried not to smile. "I'm not a vegetarian," I said. "Thank you for the invitation though, Jason. That was really sweet of you."

The first week of December he followed me into the stacks with a yellow call slip. You had to fill one of those out if there was some really old or obscure book that wasn't on the regular shelves, and a librarian would have to go and get it for you. But you were supposed to ask at the desk.

Jason came very near and let his breath fall hot on my neck. "I need this book," he said quietly. "Do you think you could help me?"

I nodded, took the slip from his hand, and walked through the quietest section of the library. I punched in a code at a door on the back wall, and he followed me into the closed stacks. I led him left and right, zigzagging all the way into the back. The overhead lights flickered and gave out for a minute at a time, and I could smell the dust and mold off the old books—walls of words I would probably never read.

Finally I turned and looked at him. He stood in the aisle, his fingers absently tracing the spines of rare leatherbound volumes as he waited to see what I would do.

I turned away and began to undo the buttons of KerriAnn's frilly black blouse, listening as his breath caught in his throat. I unfastened the last button and pulled off the blouse, and when I turned around his eyes were gleaming, his fingers on his belt buckle. The gooseflesh rose on my arms and across my stomach as I balled up my shirt and tucked it above a row of books.

"Are we safe here?" He was undoing his belt, unzipping his fly. "Are you sure no one will find us?"

"I can't be sure of anything," I said, and shivered. Sometimes you don't know how true something is until you've put the words around it.

"Oh, God." Jason dipped his fingers below the waistband of his boxers. "Oh, God."

I looked at the floor. "I'm not trying to turn you on." That was just the opposite: I'd believed it as I was saying it, but now I couldn't tell if it was true or not.

"Well," he breathed, and took a step closer, "it's not working." With his free hand he reached out and ran a finger along my collarbone and under my right bra strap. I shuddered as he ran his hand along my side and dug his fingertips into the small of my back. Again he breathed on me, the ghost of a wholesome breakfast under mint-flavored chemicals.

"I only took off my blouse to keep it clean," I said.

He grinned. "Then you may as well take off your skirt."

I shook my head and took a step backward, just out of reach. "Do you know what the Dewey decimal number is for cannibalism, Jason?"

He looked at me blankly.

"It's three ninety-one point nine." *Facts. I take such comfort in facts.* "Want me to tell you why I know that?"

He laughed as he came closer, his hand still hidden in his waistband. "Are you going to devour me, little Miss Bookworm?"

I took a step backward. "Demonology, one thirty-three."

"Tell me more," Jason whispered. "Are you a succubus, Maren?"

"If you don't leave—right now—I will eat you. Throat first, then the rest of you." I took a deep breath and waited, but in that space a nasty little thought, a memory, wormed its way through. *There are some things I'm never going to tell you no matter how many times you ask.* All this time, I thought I'd wanted to know.

Jason's eyes shone in the gloom of the stacks. He stepped into me and ran his tongue along the edge of my jaw. "I had no idea you were so *twisted.*"

I sighed as I pressed my lips to his neck. "Nobody ever does."

ACKNOWLEDGMENTS

When people who know I'm vegan hear I've written a novel about cannibals (ghouls, really, but "cannibals" is easier), they think it's bizarre, hilarious, or both. The short version is that I believe the world would be a far safer place if we, as individuals *and* as a society, took a hard, honest look at our practice of flesh eating along with its environmental and spiritual consequences. To that end, I'd like to thank Will Tuttle, whose book *The World Peace Diet* helped me clarify my purpose as I was revising *Bones & All*, and Victoria Moran, mentor, friend, and vegan superstar.

I owe a tremendous debt of gratitude to Mrs. Drue Heinz and everyone at the Hawthornden Castle International Retreat for Writers, who gave me the time and space (not to mention nourishment) to redraft the manuscript in January 2013: Hamish, Ally, Mary, Georgina, and my fellows Helena, Kirsty, Melanie, Colin, and Tendai—thank you so much for your support. Thanks also to Ann Marie DiBlasio and Sally Kim for writing the recommendations to get me there.

I give thanks to Nova Ren Suma and Rachel Cantor for their early excitement (when all I had was "cannibals in love!") over dinner at Dirt Candy, to Seanan McDonnell for being as thorough and as thoughtful as ever, to Kelly Brown and McCormick Templeman for their insight and enthusiasm, and to Elizabeth Duvivier, Amiee Wright, Deirdre Sullivan, Diarmuid O'Brien, Ailbhe Slevin, and Christian O'Reilly for all their kindness and encouragement. Love to Maggie Ginsberg-Schutz and Sarah Paré Miller for hosting me in Wisconsin and to Gail Lowry and Paul Brotchie for showing me how to make "hobo stew." And thank you, as always, to Brian DeFiore, Shaye Areheart, Adrian Frazier, and Mike McCormack.

My agent, Kate Garrick, put a massive amount of work into each draft. It was well beyond her job description and I'm so grateful for her belief in me. Sara Goodman, you are wonderful and I am thrilled to be on your list. Shout-outs to Alicia Clancy, Melissa Hastings, Olga Grlic, Paul Hochman, Lauren Hougen, Melanie Sanders, Courtney Sanks, Steven Seighman, Justin Velella, George Witte, and everyone else who loved this book at St. Martin's, and to Hana Osman and the rest of the team at Penguin UK.

Thank you most of all to my family—blood and *as good as*—who have always taken it for granted that a story of mine is a story worth reading.